When Perfection Fails:

Victory Gospel Series

When Perfection Fails:

Victory Gospel Series

Tyora Moody

www.urbanchristianonline.com

Urban Books, LLC
97 N18th Street
Wyandanch, NY 11798

When Perfection Fails: Victory Gospel Series

ISBN 13: 978-1-60162-715-5
ISBN 10: 1-60162-715-7

First Trade Paperback Printing March 2014
Printed in the United States of America

10 9 8 7 6 5 4 3 2 1

Distributed by Kensington Corp.
Submit Wholesale Orders to:
Kensington Publishing Corp.
C/O Penguin Group (USA) Inc.
Attention: Order Processing
405 Murray Hill Parkway
East Rutherford, NJ 07073-2316
Phone: 1-800-526-0275
Fax: 1-800-227-9604

Dedication

This book is dedicated to the woman who wants to achieve it all. Be reminded as you or someone you know read the pages of this book, there is no such thing as a superwoman.

Acknowledgments

I can't believe this is the final book in this series. I know someone is reading this, thinking, how do you know there won't be more books? I don't, but I sensed as I was writing the first book in the Victory Gospel Series that they were minor characters that had stories to tell. I believe I have told three very different stories of three women bonded by friendship, all with the common goal to move forward from past events and issues.

Now there are a few people I want to acknowledge. Thank you to Celeste Ribbins for explaining to me how city government works. Your briefing was invaluable, and I have gained a new respect for local city officials. Thank you to Robin Caldwell for reading through the manuscript. As always, I value your friendship and advice. Joylynn Ross, thank you for always being available for questions and being a teacher as I continue to grow as an author.

I can't name everyone, but to all my family and friends, book reviewers, bloggers, online radio hosts, social media buddies, and book clubs, thank you for your support of the Victory Gospel Series. It's truly appreciated.

Thank you, readers, for taking the time to read the third book in the Victory Gospel Series. While you don't have to read the series in order, if you haven't already, please check out Candace's story in *When Rain Falls* and Angel's story in *When Memories Fade*. I'm looking forward to bringing you more soul-searching suspense. As a hint, you may see one of the characters from this series again, in the near future. I will let you read to guess who.

Therefore, since we are surrounded by such a great cloud of witnesses, let us throw off everything that hinders and the sin that so easily entangles. And let us run with perseverance the race marked out for us, fixing our eyes on Jesus, the pioneer and perfecter of faith. For the joy set before him he endured the cross, scorning its shame, and sat down at the right hand of the throne of God. Consider him who endured such opposition from sinners, so that you will not grow weary and lose heart.

Hebrews 12:1–3 (NIV)

Prologue

Charlotte, North Carolina, 1989

Lenora clutched the car dashboard and shouted as her friend almost rammed the Honda Civic into the car in front of them. The brakes squealed in protest as the car came to a stop inches away from the back of the Buick LaSabre.

Charmayne smacked the steering wheel. "Whoa, that was a close one." Then, she started to laugh.

Lenora stretched her eyes wide as she watched her friend appear as if she was having a mental breakdown. "That wasn't funny. You need to get yourself together."

The light changed from red to green. The unscathed Buick took off, and the driver behind them was blowing his horn. Charmayne stopped giggling. She grabbed the rearview mirror and made an obscene gesture with her hand. "I know you ain't blowing your horn at me."

Lenora pointed toward the light. "Charmayne, the light is green. Go!"

"Whatever!" Charmayne placed her hands on the steering wheel. The car lurched forward as she pressed the accelerator.

After they had driven halfway down the block, Lenora asked, "*How much* did you drink? Maybe I should drive."

Charmayne shook her head. "Girl, you can't drive. Besides, I'm fine." Her friend held up her fingers and counted. "I had like only two, three beers. I think."

Lenora held her hand to her forehead. "If I had known . . ."

Charmayne held her hand toward Lenora's face. "Girl, would you stop tripping? I can tell your momma don't let you go nowhere. This might have been your first time to a party, not mine. Just sit tight. I will have you home in a second, okay?" She reached over and turned the radio's volume dial up high.

As Charmayne proceeded to sing loudly to Bobby Brown's "My Prerogative," Lenora sucked her teeth and crossed her arms. *Why did I let Charmayne convince me to go to this party?* She felt bad lying to her mother, knowing how hard she worked and expected Lenora to keep up her grades. Tonight was definitely not a study group session at Charmayne's house.

As Lenora glanced out the window, something whizzed by the passenger side. Before Lenora could register what she was seeing, the car slid to the right, crashing into the flying object. The sounds of screeching metal over the loud thumping music terrified her.

"What was that?" Lenora yelled. She turned her body to see what had just scraped the side of the car. "Charmayne, you have to stop the car."

Charmayne slowed the car down and turned the blaring music off. She grabbed the rearview mirror and whined, "Oh no!"

"What?" Lenora spun around to peer out the back window. They had turned down the road leading to her home, and there weren't any other cars behind them. Lenora squinted into the darkness. A streetlight illuminated cars parked along the streets. Her eyes locked in on what appeared to be a body on the road. Panic rose in her gut. She looked at Charmayne. "What did you do? Is that a person?" Lenora spun around and reached for the door handle.

"No!" Charmayne screamed and slapped Lenora's arm. "You can't." Charmayne hit the gas pedal.

The car jerked forward, sending Lenora crashing against the passenger door. Her heart lurched as the door opened slightly. She yelled, "Are you crazy? Char—"

Charmayne made a sharp right turn, sending Lenora scrambling backward to grab the dashboard. Lenora pressed her feet into the car floor as if she could physically stop the car and slammed the passenger door closed. She shouted, "Stop! You can't keep going. We have to call for help."

Charmayne shouted back, "There was nothing there."

Lenora stared at the girl she called a friend. "That could've been a person back there. We should have stopped to check. How could you just leave?"

Charmayne wouldn't look at her. With eyes straight-ahead, she gripped the steering wheel. All that could be heard was the car's engine and both girls breathing heavily.

Charmayne finally spoke so soft, Lenora could barely hear her. "He's going to kill me. I'm probably going to have to explain the car."

Lenora looked at her friend, watching the tears streaming down Charmayne's face.

Explain the car? This girl was suddenly concerned about what her father was going to say about the car? This was the same girl who just dragged her to a party neither one of them had any business being at on a school night, and now she was afraid of her father?

Lenora's mind raced. Her body shook as fear crept up her spine. What if Charmayne just killed a person? *Does this make me responsible too?*

Chapter One

Charlotte, North Carolina, 2013

Lenora Freeman peeked out from under her wide brim black hat and studied her husband's face. Pastor Jonathan Freeman's handsome face was not as strained as it was earlier. Many members of the congregation had come up to her commenting on how eloquently the pastor delivered the eulogy. Jonathan's voice had flowed out over the congregation in a graver tone compared to his usual Sunday banter, but his baritone voice was strong and filled with constrained emotion.

When she heard the skip in his voice, she held her body stiff until Jonathan composed himself. Then she pulled a tissue from her purse to blot the tears that had leaked from her eyes. Lenora had focused on her husband's grief so much these past few days, it hadn't occurred to her how devastating this loss was for her too.

She shifted her eyes to the portrait of the longtime pastor of Victory Gospel Church, Jeremiah Freeman. Usually the portrait hung on the wall outside the pastor's office, but today, it sat on an easel. Members of the church and the nearby community came out in large numbers to the funeral and the cemetery. Now crowds of people gathered in the Victory Gospel Center to fellowship and support the Freeman family.

While Jonathan had served as interim pastor of Victory Gospel for almost two years now, there was still pain in knowing Pastor Jeremiah would no longer preach another sermon or grace their presence. She knew how much Jonathan loved his father, and stepping into the spotlight to take over this massive church had not come without sacrifice.

She would certainly miss "Papa" Jeremiah. He was so much more to her than a father-in-law; more like the father she never had. He loved and accepted her. She almost wished it wasn't him in that casket today.

Lenora quickly asked the Lord for forgiveness. She glanced across the center's fellowship hall to where Eliza Freeman sat surrounded by other mothers of the church. After twenty years of marriage to Jonathan, Lenora had since given up on a relationship with her mother-in-law. No woman would have been good enough for Eliza's only child. When Pastor Jeremiah was alive, his quiet charm would soothe Eliza's sharp tongue. Lenora smiled, remembering that look he would give his wife when he was ready for her to stop talking.

She sighed. Maybe grief would soften the old woman. Lenora peeked over at Eliza again, observing how her black hat fit with a black veil covering her eyes. She knew her mother-in-law was truly grieving, but she couldn't help but think how much Eliza enjoyed the attention. Lenora may have been officially the first lady of Victory Gospel, but she knew Eliza flourished as the center of attention and was not too eager to retire from the role she held almost twenty-five years.

Lenora turned away and found her husband's eyes on her. She smiled at him, but he didn't return the smile. His eyes were slightly glazed over from grief and exhaustion. She had left his side to look for their sons, Keith and Michael, who both seemed to have gone missing in action after they returned from the cemetery. Of course, in the midst of her looking, she was stopped by many church members and funeral attendees.

She never did find either of her sons. The boys, now almost grown men, would be dealt with later. Lenora moved through the crowd to return to Jonathan. As she glided through the crowd, smiling and greeting people, two young children bumped into her. The children's mother touched Lenora's arm. "Mrs. Freeman, I'm so sorry."

Lenora waved her away. "It's okay. Let the children be children."

As Lenora continued walking toward her husband, she stopped and turned as if someone was calling her. No one had called her name, but she felt as if someone was trying to get her attention. She looked around and as if time had stopped, her eyes focused on a man. He was looking in her direction.

Lenora sensed people passing her. She smiled absently at the passersby as a memory clung to the edges of her mind. *Where had she seen this man before?*

Pastor Jeremiah's funeral brought a diverse crowd from all walks of life, but she couldn't figure out if the man was biracial or a tanned white man. He was average height, with a very low buzz cut, and he had no facial hair. Lenora had to be about twenty feet from him, but she was struck by his pale, intense eyes.

Lenora's breathing turned shallow. One thing she hated more than anything in the world was to sweat. She felt beads of sweat above her lip and around the edge of her hat. Lenora pressed her French-manicured fingernails into her hands as a wave of nausea swept over her. She broke her stare and looked away. A memory from long ago flashed in her mind, but she couldn't grasp the image.

Where had she seen him before?

Lenora's mind went to focus on the man, but he was no longer there. She looked to the right, and then to the left to see where he had gone. Her eyes found the strange man as he slipped out of the Victory Gospel Center's side entrance leading into the parking lot.

Forgetting that she was supposed to be returning to Jonathan's side, Lenora stepped around a group of ladies and headed toward the exit where the man had left. She didn't know why she was compelled to follow the stranger, but her gut was churning with nervousness. She just had to know his identity.

Lenora pushed the side entrance door open and stepped out onto the sidewalk. She looked to the left, and then to the right. *Where did he go?* The sun was making its descent for the day. She held her hands above her eyes to squint into the massive parking lot. There were people standing around, but she couldn't tell if any of them were him.

Nobody can just disappear into thin air.

Lenora jumped out of the way as the side door was opened by some teenagers. She noticed one of the teens was her youngest son, Michael. Before she could call out her son's name, something buzzed against her side. Lenora opened the black clutch pocketbook she had strapped around her shoulder and pulled out her phone. Someone was texting her, but she didn't recognize the phone number.

The message that displayed on the phone's screen made her already upset stomach churn again. She clutched the top of her shirt in her fist as she reread the message.

For the wages of sin is death.

A wave of fear swept over Lenora. Who sent this message to her? Is this some kind of joke?

She searched the parking lot again for the man. Why did she think he was responsible for sending the text? He had been staring at her like he could see right through her. While she was trying to figure out the man's identity, she wondered why he chose to make such a hasty exit.

Grief and exhaustion from the past few days were probably influencing her thoughts. She looked down at the phone again. The message was real. She definitely was not losing her mind.

"Mom, are you okay?"

Michael had walked over to her and touched her shoulder. Lenora looked at her son, and then his friends, who were peering at her with curiosity. She looked down and unclenched her fist. Goodness, she didn't realize she had been clutching her shirt over her heart, bringing attention to herself. She felt ashamed of how she must have appeared to her son's friends.

She grabbed Michael's hand and in a quiet voice she responded, "I'm fine, honey. Why don't you check on your father? Tell your friends you will see them tomorrow."

The concern in her usually quiet-mannered son's eyes shook her, but she straightened her shoulders and smiled. "I'm okay. Really."

She watched Michael walk over to his friends. They all shuffled one after the other through the Victory Gospel Center's side door.

Lenora looked out over the parking lot before looking down at the message again. She prayed this was someone's crazy idea of a prank. Why today as she grieved her father-in-law's home going would someone send her a message that more grief was to come?

No weapon that is formed against thee shall prosper.

Chapter Two

Jonathan let out a deep sigh and rubbed his hands across his chiseled beard. His mother seemed to be handling things as she always did with her usual grace. Mother Eliza had shaken every hand and accepted every hug. Now she sat with old friends, smiling and laughing. She didn't appear too heartbroken that they had just buried his father, but then again, his dad had been sick so long, it was inevitable. Still, the experience of seeing his father take his last breath caused Jonathan's heart to sink.

"Dad?"

Lost in his own thoughts, he jumped slightly at the touch on his shoulder. He turned to see his youngest son standing over him.

"Mikey." Jonathan looked around his son. "Where are Keith and your mother?" Jonathan thought he saw Lenora a few minutes before coming toward him, but then she disappeared in the crowd. As much as he loved the church's support, he was really ready to go home. Dad's death the day after Easter had left Jonathan with no time to rest this week.

"She's outside." Michael shrugged his shoulders. "I guess she's coming in."

Jonathan didn't have long to wait as his beautiful wife's face appeared. As Lenora approached them, he thought her face looked especially troubled. *Grief?* He frowned as he watched how Lenora twisted her hands. He hadn't seen her do that in a long time. The girl he met in college was shy and quiet, often looking down and twisting her hands. Lenora had long transformed into a woman who stood steadfast in her faith.

He asked her, "Are you okay? I know this has been a long day."

She reached down and hugged him. "I'm good. Why are you asking me that? I should be asking you how you are doing."

"As best as I can." Jonathan noticed Lenora was smiling, but it wasn't her usual confident grin. Her mouth was slightly curved, indicating she wanted him to know she was okay, but something was on her mind. He inquired, "Where did you disappear to?"

Lenora sat down in the chair next to him. She responded. "There are so many people here today. I wished I could have greeted and talked to as many people as I could." She tilted her hat slightly back and rubbed her forehead. "You know I think I'm going to have to head home and lie down."

"That sounds like a plan. I think we all should probably do that." He looked across over to where his mother still sat with other women in the church. "Why don't you and Michael go ahead? I think Mother needs to be around the church family right now."

Lenora stared at him. "I guess you are bringing Mother Freeman to the house."

Jonathan looked away from his wife's eyes and nodded. "She needs us right now."

"Of course." Lenora rose. She waved her hand at Michael. "Michael, I need you to come with me."

Michael strolled over. "Can I drive?"

Jonathan started to protest, but Lenora cut him off. "You know, that's a good idea. My head is killing me."

Jonathan pointed his finger at his sixteen-year-old son. "Drive carefully, young man."

Michael grinned, "I got this, Dad."

Jonathan watched his wife and youngest son leave the center. He knew there were years of conflict between his mother and wife. He often stood to the side when he should have said something to one or both of them. Hopefully, Lenora understood his mother would move back to her home soon. Mother indicated that she needed some time away from all those memories. She was the main caregiver for his father during his illness, making sure he went to dialysis three times a week.

"Jonathan, where is your wife going? She can't leave now."

He whirled around to see Eliza leaning on her cane. He stood and pulled out the chair. "Why don't you sit down?"

Eliza shooed his hand away from her back. "I've been sitting down all day." She jabbed her finger in the direction Lenora had just left. "She should be by your side."

Jonathan responded. "She's not feeling well. You should probably be heading home to lie down too, don't you think?"

Eliza shooed him. "No need to worry about me. I'm fine." She stretched her arm out. "We are with family."

He agreed. When he was officially installed as the pastor for Victory Gospel Church a month before, Jonathan had many doubts about trying to step into a role his father held for twenty-five years. Jonathan's grandfather had founded the church thirty-five years ago before his father's pastoral time. This was his legacy, and while there had been steady growth in the church, in the back of his mind, Jonathan had doubts he'd never voice to anyone. Was this church truly his calling? Out of all the dreams he had, he'd never pictured himself in this position, legacy or no legacy.

"Did you tell Lenora about your plans?"

His mother had interrupted his thoughts. He looked over at her. "Mother, this isn't the time to discuss it."

"I didn't say you had to announce anything today. If and when you do, Lenora is going to need to know."

"I know that, Mother. I just haven't had time. The funeral arrangements that Dad wanted needed to be carried out."

Eliza patted her son's hand. "Well, now you can move forward. Pastor Jeremiah would be so proud of you. You are going to step into territory that even your father wouldn't."

Jonathan took a deep breath as he thought about the last piece of advice his father left him. A few days before his father had passed away, Jonathan had told him about an opportunity that had been presented to him. Pastor Jeremiah was tired, but lucid. "Son, don't mix politics and the church. You need to think about which road is more important and which one is your true purpose."

Son, don't mix politics and the church.

That wasn't going to be easy for Jonathan. Jonathan had always seen himself being a public servant. After getting his MBA, life took a turn five years ago and he found himself in seminary school. Still, in the back of his mind, he always thought if the opportunity arose, he would consider it.

A few weeks before, his longtime friend, Mayor Alex Carrington, asked to meet with him. The conversation ended with the mayor asking Jonathan to consider running for Charlotte City Council District 2 seat.

Jonathan was intrigued by the possibilities, but he needed to have the support of his wife. Lenora had shown reluctance when Jonathan decided to fill in as interim pastor. She had since grown into her role as first lady and incorporated the facilities on the Victory Gospel Church campus in her wedding planning business.

How would she feel about her husband placing her and the family even more in the spotlight? He wasn't sure if Lenora ever had to worry about it. With his father's death, the church needed him now. Maybe he just needed to let this opportunity pass him by.

Chapter Three

As Lenora sat back on the couch, her body melted into the cushions. She really wanted to go to bed and rest her pounding head on her pillow. Instead, she listened to the phone as it rang in her ear. Finally, she heard a greeting on the other side.

Lenora sat up, "Hello, Candace. I'm so sorry to bother you."

Candace responded, "Hello, Lenora. I'm glad to hear your voice. I wanted to talk to you earlier today after the funeral, but you and Reverend Freeman had so many people around you."

"It's been a crazy day, and I'm happy to get a chance to talk to you now. Not to be rude, but have you seen Keith?" The text on her phone had rattled Lenora. She didn't know if someone was threatening her family or not. The Freemans were well-loved members of their church and community. Still, Lenora was deeply concerned that she had not seen her eldest son in the past few hours, even if he was a college sophomore.

Candace and Lenora had grown as friends the past two years since Candace's oldest daughter, Rachel, had been dating Keith. The young couple both earned basketball scholarships to UNC and were a popular couple on campus as well.

Lenora continued, "I just don't know where he would have disappeared to after the funeral, but I hoped he would be with Rachel."

"Well, no worries. He and Rachel just left awhile ago. I think he probably just needed to be around someone special."

Lenora breathed a sigh of relief. "I can understand. It's just that his father was looking for him. You know this image we have of being a family unit."

Candace said, "I know. We want to hold our children close, especially when there are hard times like a death in the family. When my friend, Pamela, was murdered a few years ago, we were all still struggling with Frank's death. My relationship with Rachel had broken down so much. Believe me, I wasn't prepared, nor did I realize, Rachel was trying to deal with grief in her own way."

"I remember you telling me young adults grieve differently." Lenora also needed to remind herself her son was only nineteen. They had some battles with him as a teenager, but he had grown into a responsible young man. Since getting the basketball scholarship, Keith had been excelling in his grades.

Lenora knew Rachel was partly responsible for keeping Keith on the straight and narrow. She couldn't have asked for a better girlfriend for her oldest son.

Candace interrupted her thoughts. "As soon as he drops Rachel off, I will make sure Keith calls you. Young people don't seem to remember the importance of giving their parents a call."

"I know. They can talk to everyone else, but can't seem to remember to check in. It's okay. I just wanted to know where he was before I lie down."

"I'm happy you reached out. Lenora, I'm here if you want to talk. Speaking of talking, I have been so busy at the salon I need to catch up with you on the wedding plans. I know you are going to kill me for not deciding on the cake yet."

Lenora laughed. Candace would be marrying her fiancé, Darnell Jackson, in approximately one month. "Girl, you know Chef Langston is going to throw a fit. He likes at least two to three months to prepare a wedding cake, but don't worry, he will still work with us. The most important next step is for all the bridesmaids and you to come to the boutique for your final dress fittings."

"All right, get us in order. You know Mondays are my days off from Crown of Beauty Salon. If I can round up all the girls, can you fit us in?"

"Sounds like a plan. Angel Roberts is a part of the wedding party, right?" Lenora inquired.

Candace responded, "Yes, she is, but she has already gotten some great footage of me and Darnell. She contracted another videographer to film the ceremony and reception. I told her she was going to be in this wedding so no standing behind the camera for her."

"Good, maybe she and Wes will actually set a wedding date soon." Lenora and Candace had both been needling their young friend about her yearlong engagement.

The two women said good-bye. Lenora hung up the phone. For a brief moment she had forgotten her headache. Her passion for planning weddings always brightened her day.

The one regret Lenora would never admit to anyone was not having her own large beautiful wedding. Lenora looked over at her wedding photo taken over twenty years ago. Jonathan was dressed in a simple black suit, and she wore a simple off-the-shoulder white dress. Her wedding photo brought Lenora joy, but represented the biggest sin she had ever committed against her mother-in-law, Eliza.

Four weeks before their wedding day at Victory Gospel Church, Lenora was prepared to give her engagement ring back to Jonathan. Jonathan suggested they forget all the wedding plans and go to city hall to get married.

Lenora's mother and Papa Jeremiah were hurt, but both parents eventually forgave them.

Not Eliza. To this day, Eliza felt like it was Lenora's idea to spite her and leave her out of her only son's wedding. For some reason, Eliza couldn't get it through her head that Jonathan had grown tired of his own mother meddling in his love life.

Lenora sighed, and once again, she dialed her son's cell number. This time the phone went straight to voice mail. Lenora left what had to be her third message. "Keith, I know you are with Rachel. Just call when you get a chance. I love you." As she pressed the button to end the call, Lenora heard a voice behind her. The grating voice sent Lenora's temples throbbing again.

"You always let that boy have his way. He should be home grieving his grandfather, not out Lord's knows where."

It was best not to get into it with the older woman right now. *She is supposed to be grieving.* Lenora watched as her mother-in-law shuffled into the living room on her cane. She waited until Eliza sat down in the chair that the boys jokingly called Queen Eliza's chair. It was a French antique chair that Lenora had found a few years before. She had the rest of the set of chairs at Lenora's Bridal Boutique. She still wasn't sure how she got talked into bringing the beautiful, but odd green chair into her living room.

Lenora made an effort to smile through her pain. "How are you feeling, Mother Eliza?"

When Lenora had first met Eliza, she was a bundle of energy. Now, in her midsixties, Eliza was still active, but a weight gain in the past few years hadn't been good for her knees.

Eliza wrinkled her face and smacked her lips. "I could use some water. I'm so thirsty today."

"Sure!" Small talk was not their thing, so Lenora went to the kitchen. She grabbed a glass from the cabinet and opened the fridge. As she poured water from the pitcher in the fridge, she noticed her hands were shaking. She set the pitcher back on the refrigerator shelf and closed the door. What had she eaten today? The headache was an annoyance, but now she was starting to feel discomfort in her stomach. Lenora grabbed the counter and took a few deep, cleansing breaths. When the wave of nausea subsided, she headed back into the living room.

As she handed the glass of water to Eliza, Lenora was grateful to see Jonathan walk into the living room.

Jonathan eyed her and asked, "Are you feeling better, Lenora?"

"No, I haven't had a chance to lie down yet."

Eliza piped up, "She is still looking for that boy."

Lenora closed her eyes and continued to concentrate on her breathing.

Jonathan frowned. "Keith hasn't shown up yet?"

Lenora responded without looking at her husband. "He's with Rachel."

"Good. He probably needed to be around a friend."

The phone rang. Lenora started toward the phone, but since Jonathan was closer, he picked up the cordless receiver first.

He said, "Yes, this is Pastor Freeman."

Lenora concentrated on her husband's face. Her entire body felt as if it wanted to explode with nervousness.

He glanced over at her. "Yes, I'm his father."

Lenora placed her hands to her stomach as she watched an emotion register on her husband's face she'd rarely seen. Fear. She heard Eliza suck in a breath.

Before Jonathan could place the phone down, Lenora went over to him and grabbed his arm. "Who was that?"

Jonathan took in a deep breath, and then hesitated as if he was trying to figure out what to say.

Lenora shook his arm. "Jonathan, what's wrong? Tell me."

He focused on her face. "Keith and Rachel have been in an accident. We need to get to the hospital."

Lenora's body trembled as if someone had opened a window and pushed cold arctic air into the room. Her eyes watered as she thought about the strange text message she had received earlier.

Chapter Four

Serena Manchester sat back in her desk chair and pushed her new pageboy cut bangs out of her eyes. She'd decided to go without a weave for a while and see what the hairstylist could do with her hair. What she really wanted to do was cut her hair down into one of those cute pixie haircuts, but viewers had seen her with long hair for so many years, she decided shoulder length would be enough of a change. She already had more e-mail and social media conversations that she could keep up with each week.

The bangs were definitely not working for her though. She couldn't wait until her hair grew in more and she could easily brush it to the side.

It had been a long day, and despite it being Friday, Serena was looking forward to spending time at home. As she closed her eyes, she blocked out the noise of the newsroom around her. She almost laughed out loud. *Me alone on a Friday night?* This job had become her man. Maybe it was a good thing since she always chose losers or went after the good men that were already taken.

Serena opened her eyes to see Wes Cade heading to his desk. She couldn't help but grin. Wes and his bow ties were just too cute. She sighed. Too bad Wes would be officially off the market when he married his girlfriend, Angel Roberts. He was too young for her anyway, but Serena did admire his ambition. She moved from behind her desk and walked toward Wes's office.

"What's up, kiddo? What you got on your plate to-night?"

Wes jumped at her voice. "Hello, Serena."

Serena sat on his desk. Wes rolled his chair back and looked at her. His discomfort amused her. "What are you working on?" She frowned. "Weren't you at your church most of the day yesterday for the funeral?"

Wes rubbed his head. "Yes, Victory Gospel Church. Pastor Jeremiah Freeman was laid to rest yesterday. Unfortunately, the family got hit with some heavy news last night."

Serena asked, "Really? What happened?" Serena typically stayed away from stories with any type of religious slant on it. She rarely attended church.

Wes grabbed his phone out of his pocket. "The Freemans' oldest son, Keith, and his girlfriend, Rachel, were in a serious car accident last night."

"That was them. I saw the vehicle on the morning report. Did they survive?"

Wes nodded. "Yes, they are both pretty banged up, but they are alive. God's grace was definitely on them. It's just really sad to see things like this happen to really good people."

"You sound like you know them very well."

"Well, yeah, I have talked to Pastor Freeman and First Lady a few times. They are just like this perfect couple."

Serena wrinkled her nose. "The perfect couple? There is no such thing."

Wes shook his head, "Okay, not perfect, but—"

Serena interrupted, "I mean, I know you are getting married, but life changes after the honeymoon."

"I know—"

Serena slid off Wes's desk and stood. "I mean, believe me, I should know. I've been married twice. Been there done that! Did I tell you twice?"

"Yeah!" Wes held up his arms. "You know it's been great talking to you, Serena, but I have to get this story ready for tonight. A lot of folks want an update on the accident last night."

Serena felt warmth gravitate across her embarrassed face. "Sure, kiddo. I need to wrap up what I'm working on too. Tell Angel I said hello." She turned and walked away.

Great going, Serena!

Wes must really have thought her to be a basket case now.

Not that she cared. Okay, well . . . that wasn't exactly true. She cared about what Wes thought and considered him more than just a coworker, but a friend. She really liked his fiancée, Angel, and thought they were a great couple.

Serena sat back at her desk. *But* there really was no such thing as perfect couples. She knew Wes and Angel were both Christians, but they would have problems too. Serena spoke under her breath. "Just you wait and see, kiddo."

She clicked her keyboard to wake up her monitor screen. Then she pulled up the Victory Gospel Church Web site. She'd seen the Freemans before. Serena clicked to the About page. Just as she thought, the typical photo of a handsome pastor and his regal, beautiful first lady beaming at the camera.

No one had the perfect life even if they went to church. Serena's mamma dragged her to church when she was younger. All that shouting sure didn't stop what happened to Serena. Seemed like her life had become one big heartache after another. She concentrated on what she was good at—getting the story.

"The truth shall set you free." Serena spoke as she closed out the church Web site. "Serena will certainly bring you the truth, honey."

An e-mail notification popped up in the right-hand corner of Serena's computer. She glanced at the notification as it faded away. A name caught her attention. She clicked over to see her full mailbox and opened the e-mail. The From line was from somebody named Lance Ryan.

"Two first names? Really?" Serena sat up straight in her chair. "Let's see what Lance Ryan has to say."

Ms. Manchester,

I thought you might want to know there is trouble brewing in your city. You may be the best person to help bring justice. Would you be interested in meeting for more information? I promise you won't be disappointed. You will thank me later.

Thank you later. The boldness of this man with his two first names.

Serena smiled and hit Reply. She typed, "Mr. Lance Ryan, I look forward to meeting you. Name the time and the place."

She hit Send. Who knows? Lance Ryan might be the man she was looking for in her life. With that, she laughed and grabbed her bag. *Desperation does not suit you, girl.*

Chapter Five

Lenora wiped her eyes as she looked at her son. She didn't want Keith to see her so upset, but she was beyond grateful to see him alive.

"Mom, I'm okay. I will be out of here soon." Keith Freeman had caramel skin like his father that was now a blend of blue and purple from the left temple down to his cheek.

She squeezed his hand. "I'm just grateful. It could have been worse." With no clear reports from the authorities, Lenora had prayed feverishly during the ride over to the hospital. She folded her arms as she questioned Keith. "You still can't remember what happened?"

Jonathan spoke up from the other side of Keith's bed. "Lenora, let's give the boy time to rest. The police will get down to the bottom of who ran into his car last night. Like the police officers said, the other vehicle had considerable damages too."

Keith shook his head. "Yeah, I can't believe they just took off. It all happened so fast. Rachel and I . . ." Keith's eyes grew wide, and he sat up in the hospital bed. He grimaced in pain. "Where is Rachel? Is she all right?"

Jonathan rose from his seat and touched Keith's shoulder. "Son, Rachel is fine. Both of you were under God's favor last night."

Keith tried to move against his father's strong arms. "Dad, I have to see her."

Lenora stood. "Your father is right. Keith, you need to rest your body with those broken ribs. I will go check on Rachel and come back with a report for you, okay?"

Her son lay back down on the bed. Lenora's heart dropped to see the tears brimming in her man-child's eyes. She knew Keith really loved his girlfriend and was even more grateful that the young couple escaped last night's crash with their lives.

Lenora walked down the hospital hallway and turned to the right. She knocked on the closed door. On the other side of the door, a female voice said, "Come in." Lenora opened the door and poked her head in to see Candace and Rachel holding hands.

"Lenora." Candace walked over to embrace her. She stepped back so Lenora could see Rachel. Rachel's right arm was in a sling. Similar to Keith, the young woman had bruising around her face. Lenora moved toward the bed. "How are you, Rachel? Keith was asking about you."

Rachel nodded. "I'm okay. Just have to deal with this broken arm, but I'm glad we walked away. It was pretty scary. How is Keith?"

"He is going to be out of commission for a while too. He has broken ribs."

Rachel winced. "Ouch! I guess basketball season is officially over."

"You both will be as good as new." Lenora addressed Candace, "You mind if I talk to you outside?"

Candace nodded her head. "Sure. Rachel, I will be right outside."

Both women walked out of the room. Lenora grabbed Candace's hand. "I'm so sorry about all this."

Candace shook her head. "Lenora, you can't do anything about a crazy person causing an accident and leaving the scene."

Lenora opened her mouth, but then stopped as the words wouldn't come. What could she say to Candace? That some crazy person sent her a threatening text yesterday? Suppose it was just some prank. Lenora never believed in coincidences.

Candace took a tissue out of her pocket and wiped her eyes. Her voice trembled as she spoke. "I don't know what I would have done if I lost her."

Lenora wrapped her arms around Candace. "I know. I'm so sorry."

Candace asked, "Does Keith know what happened?"

Lenora clasped her hands together. "He said it happened so fast. They were talking, and the music was going. He never saw the car, just felt something ram into the back of the car."

Candace held her hand to heart. "You know God was watching over our babies. Did you see Keith's Jeep?"

Lenora nodded. She leaned against the wall. She wished the media hadn't showed the wreck on television. With Victory Gospel Church as their extended family, she understood that many would have been interested in an update on the young people involved.

She prayed they would find whoever did this soon. Lenora had taken great precaution with her boys when they were younger, and as a parent, she knew she couldn't protect them from everything. At this moment, her mother radar was in full alert that danger lurked nearby. She just didn't know why.

Chapter Six

Lenora couldn't help but smile and admire the brides-maid dresses that had arrived for Candace's wedding party. The final selection came after hours of each bridesmaid trying on several designers. Candace was so determined that everyone feel good about the selected dress.

Sarah Hines walked in with the remaining dresses. Lenora was five foot nine and with heels on, which she wore most of the time, she easily stood six feet. She towered over her petite consultant, who wore a pale pink coatdress today. The light brown-skinned woman always wore her hair short. Today, she wore pearl stud earrings and a very minimum amount of makeup.

Ever since the young woman walked into Lenora's Bridal Boutique three years ago to interview for the consultant job, she had impressed Lenora. It made Lenora feel a sense of confidence knowing she had a capable woman to help her with the brides. She had since hired two more women, but no one kept a tight ship like Sarah.

She commented to Sarah, "Candace did a great job picking out these dresses."

"Yes, she did. Do you think everyone will be able to make it in for the final fitting? We are cutting it close on this one. Usually we would have had this fitting months ago."

Lenora grabbed one of the dresses to help Sarah hang them. "Yes, I know. I called Candace and confirmed Thursday instead of Monday as the appointed day for the wedding party final fittings. We both agreed it was best to stay close to our injured children during this first week after the accident."

Sarah shut the wardrobe and spun around. "Oh my! I'm so sorry about the accident. It's good that your children were able to walk away."

"Yes, it's a blessing." Lenora was grateful to be back in her boutique on a Saturday, if only for a few hours. Keith was doing better and could come home. Candace had let her know that Rachel was a bit depressed about her arm, but in pretty good spirits about being home. Maybe Lenora could finally shake the dark cloud that seemed to be hanging over her.

"Hey, Lenora. Did the dresses arrive yet?"

Lenora whipped around to see Angel Roberts walk into the back of the boutique. She grinned at the young woman. "Yes, ma'am, but you will have to wait until everyone else comes for the fitting on Thursday. Sarah, we'll be up front. Thanks for getting the dresses unpacked for me."

Sarah smiled. "Not a problem. Hey, Angel, I love your hair."

Lenora took a closer look at Angel as they walked up toward the front. "Look at you, Ms. Thang. I am loving your hair too."

Angel's usual mass of curls had been flat-ironed into a silky mane. She twirled and flipped her hair over her shoulders. "I think Wes is going to like it too."

Lenora laughed. "Girl, you are going to set that man back. You two need to get hitched fast. When are you going to set the wedding date? You've been engaged for almost a year."

Angel let out a deep sigh. "We are getting close to setting a date. Grams is walking around with her walker really good and you know she wants to be at her best for the wedding."

"I know she does." Lenora observed the way Angel held her head down, choosing not to look directly at her. "I do have to ask, are you really waiting for your grandmother to fully recover from the stroke, or is this another excuse not to set a date?"

Angel opened her mouth to protest, and then turned away. "I'm not making excuses. I do want to marry Wes. I just want the timing to be right."

Lenora touched her shoulders. "No pressure! I want you two to have a long, happy marriage. I'm just glad to see you bounce back after last year. Follow me." Lenora walked into the bridal dress showroom with Angel behind her.

Angel folded her arms and leaned against the wall. "You know last year after finding out about the way my mother died and all she went through, it tore me up more inside than I thought. But now I feel like I'm a stronger woman for knowing the truth."

"I can tell. You have come a long way in your confidence."

Angel stepped away from the wall and walked over to the rack. She pulled out a dress and held the midlength taffeta dress in front of her. Then she twirled with the dress a few times, and stopped to wink at Lenora. "I might even try on a wedding dress soon. Grams would love me to do that. She keeps asking, 'When are we going to Lenora's Bridal Boutique to find a dress?'"

"Well, I agree with your grandmother. It's time for you to start planning your day, and you know I can help you find the perfect dress. Speaking of dresses, Candace did tell you to be here on Thursday for the final bridesmaid fitting, right?"

Angel rubbed her hands together. "Yes, I can't wait. I've never been a bridesmaid either. It's going to be so exciting to see her and Darnell finally get married."

Lenora responded, "I believe a lot of people have been waiting for those two to walk down the aisle. I hate that Rachel is going to have to wear her arm in a sling when she walks down the aisle though."

Angel yelped. "Oh no! That's right. You know, I stopped by here to check on you and ask you about Keith. How's he doing?"

"Thank you, Angel. Keith is doing well. I think both Keith and Rachel are thankful basketball season was over. Neither one of them could've tolerated being on the bench."

Angel asked, "Do they have any clues about the accident?"

"They have some pieces from the car. They know for sure it's an American model truck. Girl, how they know all that I don't know. My youngest son is absolutely fascinated by it all."

"Well, they can do some amazing things with forensics. Being a reporter, Wes always has some great stories to share."

"I bet." Lenora put her arm around Angel. "You do know I was joking before about setting a wedding date. You need to do this when your heart says it's the right time."

Angel nodded. "I know. You care about us, and I appreciate you. Believe me, I also know Wes and I haven't set a date because of me, but I'm going to be ready soon."

"I know you will. In the meantime, you are going to knock Wes out when he sees you in that bridesmaid dress."

Angel laughed as they both walked toward the boutique entrance. "You are too much. I can't wait to get back here on Thursday. It's going to be so much fun."

Before opening the door, Angel turned. "Lenora, if you need anything, please let me know. I know this has been a rough few days for you and your family."

"Just keep us in your prayers, honey. Prayers are always appreciated."

The two women hugged, and Lenora watched as Angel walked out to her car. She locked the door. Usually she would have taken appointments on a Saturday, but decided to take it easy today despite the approaching wedding season. She wouldn't be any good to her brides in the frazzled state she'd been in ever since Pastor Jeremiah's funeral and her son's accident on Thursday.

Lenora walked to her office in the back. Her desk was neat with all her files in stacks. She sat down in the chair. Really, she had accomplished what she wanted to do today. Spend some time in her boutique preparing for the week and finding some normalcy, if at all possible.

A chirp from her cell phone startled her. She had purposely left the phone in her office as she worked out on the boutique floor. She picked up the phone and focused on the text message.

For the wages of sin is death. Someone will pay the price.

The calmness that she had been enjoying instantly left her body as she stared at her phone. "Who is doing this?" Lenora said out loud. "This has to stop."

She scrolled to see the phone number associated with the text. Lenora didn't recognize the number or even the area code. She hit the Call button and lifted the phone to her ear. The office seemed even quieter than usual. The only sound was the steady hum of the computer under her desk.

Lenora gripped the edge of her desk as she listened to the phone ring.

Finally, she heard a click and waited for a person's voice.

Lenora frowned and pulled her phone from her ear. It was no longer ringing. No dial tone. She held the phone back to her ear and said, "Hello."

A cackle ripped through the phone, and then a male's voice asked, "How's Keith doing?"

Lenora jumped up from her chair, dropping the phone on her desk. She didn't recognize the man's voice, but he seemed to know her and her family. Her hands shook as she grabbed the phone and yelled, "Who are you?"

Her ears were met with a dial tone.

The feeling of dread returned. She had to get to the hospital now.

Chapter Seven

Before Lenora rushed out of the boutique, she tried calling Jonathan. Frustrated that he wasn't picking up, she held the steering wheel tightly. As she stayed in the left lane, she gunned the gas pedal, glancing down at the speedometer. She took a breath, looked to her right, and passed back to the right until she crossed over to the lane leading to her exit.

"Please protect my family, protect my child. Lord, please send your angels," she prayed over and over again.

It took her longer than she cared to find a parking space. By the time she found a space in the hospital parking garage, Lenora's heart was beating so fast she feared they would be giving her a hospital bed. She smashed the elevator button as if she could make one of the elevators doors open magically. Then, she nervously twisted her hands and watched the elevators make a slow descent. Her mind was overloaded with thoughts.

Who was the man, and how did he know her family? Whoever he was, did he purposely target her son? He was certainly tormenting her.

As soon as the elevator doors opened, Lenora pressed the floor number and leaned back against the elevator walls. Her family had been featured on the news and several Charlotte magazines in the past year as the church and her business had grown. Not to include the social media connections everyone in the family had. Anybody could have found simple information like her sons' names.

The media had been keeping the story of the hit-and-run accident in the news as well. Many people she didn't know probably knew about her family. It didn't explain the text messages which, she had to admit, were downright threatening.

Lenora stepped off the elevator and walked briskly down the hall toward her son's room. She opened the door and stopped.

Her heart did another slight drop. Keith was not in the bed. *Where is he?* Lenora spun around and went toward the nurses' station in the center.

"Hello, have you seen my son?"

The short nurse looked at her. "Your son? Oh, Mrs. Freeman. I believe he is scheduled to be discharged today."

"Today?" Jonathan didn't tell her.

"Lenora?"

She turned around at the sound of her name. "Jonathan." She walked away from the nurse. "Where's Keith? I don't understand."

Jonathan reached his arm out and placed it around her shoulders. "He's fine, Lenora. The other nurse came and took him for a walk down the hall. They should be back soon. In fact, the doctor said we can take him home. I was going to call you after I signed the discharge papers."

Lenora shook her husband's arms off and looked at him. "Well, why is he up walking? I thought he should be resting."

Jonathan stared at her, and then looked behind him. He leaned into her. "Quiet your voice down, Lenora. Look let's go in Keith's room. I will explain what they told me. okay?"

She took a breath and walked ahead of Jonathan into the room. Lenora could feel her husband's stare.

After a few seconds of silence, he asked. "Are you okay?"

Lenora held her hand to her forehead. "Yes, I just want to know why Keith isn't lying down resting. Why is he being discharged now?"

Jonathan sat down in the chair. "The doctor gave orders for him to get up and move around some. With broken ribs, a person is more susceptible to blood clots and things going on with the lungs. There isn't really anything else they can do. The ribs will heal naturally with time and rest. This is a good thing, Lenora. There's no need to worry."

That made sense to her. Lenora bit her lip and sat down in the other seat. There was a slow ache at her temples now. She closed her eyes and rubbed the sides of her head.

"You didn't answer my question."

Lenora opened her eyes and looked over at her husband. "I just panicked when I didn't see Keith. That's all."

"If anything was wrong, don't you think I would have called you?"

"Of course, you would. Look, don't sit over there and look at me like I'm crazy. I'm a mother, and my child could have died. The person responsible is still out there."

Jonathan frowned. "It was a hit-and-run accident." He folded his arms. "You sound like someone is out for our son."

Lenora looked away, blinking to keep a sudden appearance of tears from flowing down her face. A memory from long ago floated in her mind.

Her mother had been gone a decade. Joan Houghton was strict, but loving. She couldn't make up for Lenora's dad not being there, but she did what she could to keep her children happy. Thoughts of her mother always brought memories of her older brother who she lost when she was twelve. Her brother was sixteen, the same sensitive age that Michael was, when a classmate took his life.

She could never articulate to Jonathan or her boys how deeply losing her brother had affected both her and her mother. Her mother made up for her brother's loss by being extraprotective of Lenora. Lenora, in turn, tried to protect her own sons who, in height and features, so often reminded her of her deceased brother.

Lenora would not let harm come to her sons.

Keith and his nurse showed up at the door. She rushed to Keith's side. "Honey, how are you? I can't believe you are up and walking. I'm so glad we can bring you home."

Keith cringed as they slowly sat him on the bed. "Yeah, but everything hurts. I need some more pain medicine."

Lenora asked the nurse, "What kind of medicine can we give him for the pain?"

The nurse responded, "Ibuprofen or Tylenol used as directed will work for the pain. In about two to three weeks, the pain should completely go away."

"Good." Lenora gently rubbed her hand across Keith's forehead.

"Mom, really?"

"What? You are never too old for your mama to rub your head." For added measure, Lenora did it again.

Keith grinned and lay his head back on the pillow.

She loved her sons, and yes, she had been overprotective of both of them. Lenora sensed Jonathan was watching her, but she wouldn't look at him, knowing he still had questions about her behavior.

Being married to someone for twenty years, it was hard to keep things from the other person. Lenora was rarely rattled by anything, which was why she was the most-sought-after wedding planner. She could put a bride's mind at ease, tell a family to back off, and make sure the caterer and all other participants stayed on time.

She probably should have shared the text messages with Jonathan, but she knew he was still adjusting to his father's death. He wouldn't admit it, but his growing role at the church had become his sole focus. He was the third generation in a legacy established by his grandfather and carried on with his father's grace.

With Keith's accident, the last thing Jonathan needed was to have the weight of someone's nasty prank on his shoulders. The problem was, Lenora really wasn't sure the text messages and *that voice* were a prank. She was determined to find out.

Chapter Eight

Jonathan shook the hands of each of the passing members. Most Sundays, Lenora would be by his side at the end of the service.

An older woman who stood almost as tall as he, with the exception of the slight bow in her back, gripped his hand. "Pastor, we are praying for you."

"Thank you, Mrs. German. My family appreciates all of the kindness from the Pastor's Aid Club. We especially appreciate you." Martha German was a legend here in Charlotte. The former teacher marched and had participated in the civil rights movement.

Jonathan noticed the silver-haired woman continued to hold his hand despite the long line behind her. "Pastor, that's why we are here. I'm just so glad to hear the boy is doing better. Life is not promised to any of us."

Jonathan agreed. "Yes, ma'am. We're grateful." He gently pulled his hand from the older woman's grip.

Still not ready to move on, Mrs. German proceeded to ask, "How's Mrs. Freeman? I noticed she wasn't in church this morning."

"She's fine and by our son's side." Jonathan looked at his watch, and then smiled at Mrs. German. "Keith is resting from his injuries at home today."

After Mrs. German moved along, Jonathan greeted as many members as he could before heading to his office. As he pushed the door open, he started to unzip the robe with his other hand. He stopped halfway in the office when he realized there were people in his office. He looked back and forth. "Mother, what's going on?"

Eliza was sitting behind the desk. She pointed to the man sitting in the chair across from the desk. "Honey, Mayor Carrington came to visit us. He just snuck in Victory Gospel Church today."

"Alex, nice of you to visit Victory Gospel this morning." Jonathan completed unzipping his robe, and then reached for the hanger on his closet door. He'd known Alex since their days as Alpha Phi Alpha line brothers. While both men were the same age, Alex seemed to be fitter in his forties compared to Jonathan, who had gained a bit of extra weight around the middle.

Alex stood. "I'm so sorry to make a surprise visit, but after hearing about Keith's accident, I just felt like I should attend Victory Gospel Church this morning."

Jonathan wrapped the robe around the hanger and zipped it up. "I saw you were here for Dad's funeral too. We appreciate your support."

Eliza interjected. "My son's sermon was brilliant, wasn't it?"

Alex grinned. "Which one? Today or the eulogy? Mrs. Freeman, you have an amazing son."

Jonathan glanced at the clock on the wall. "Mother, why don't you let me talk to Alex? I'll be ready to head to home in a few minutes."

"But, son—"

"Mother, this won't be long."

Eliza narrowed her eyes. "Okay." She stood and grabbed her cane from behind the desk. "Mayor Carrington, it was nice to talk to you."

Alex stood and reached for Eliza's hand. "You too, Lady Freeman. I enjoyed our talk too."

What exactly did they talk about? Jonathan was not too happy about his mother going behind his back. With the level of upheaval in his life, this conversation with Alex could have waited until another time.

When the door closed behind his mother's slow exit, Jonathan sat down behind the desk and eyed his long-time friend. "You know this isn't a good time to come by to check on my answer."

"Oh, Jonathan, of course, I wouldn't try to force you into some decision right now." Alex sat up in his seat. "I'm your friend, and I want to encourage you. Man, I don't think you realize how well-admired you are in this community, even more so than Pastor Jeremiah, and the people loved your father. I just want you to really consider the opportunity that awaits you."

Jonathan looked down at his watch and clasped his hands together. "As I told you a few weeks ago, I will definitely consider running for the district seat, but I haven't even run this opportunity by my wife yet. Time and circumstances have not allowed the opportunity yet."

"Surely Lenora would support you. People look up to her as well, ever since she had the feature article in *Charlotte Weddings*. Her business must be booming with wedding season approaching."

Jonathan nodded. "Yes, the article drew a lot of attention for Lenora. I do want you to not forget . . ." Jonathan spread his arm out, "this massive church is my legacy and responsibility."

"I know, I know, but that's even more reason to consider this role. You will be an advocate for many of the very members that attend Victory Gospel Church. That's a win-win."

"What's in it for you?"

Alex held out his hands. "Why are you questioning my intentions, brother?"

"Come on, Alex. It's well-known you have some city council members that haven't been willing to play nice. Why are you approaching me?"

Alex stood and buttoned his suit jacket. "You're right. I need some people who are true leaders and willing to do what it takes to make the city of Charlotte a phenomenal place to live for its residents." Alex pointed to him. "You are the man I need on my team and what Charlotte needs."

Spoken like a true politician. Alex's pitch did sound appealing, but something about the timing nagged Jonathan's mind. He stood and held out his hand toward Alex. "I need to pray more. This may not be the right time."

"I respect a praying man, and especially an honorable man of the God." Alex shook Jonathan's hand. "Give my love to Lenora and a speedy recovery to Keith and his girlfriend."

He turned toward the door, and then stopped. "By the way, I put in a word with the police chief to make sure they do everything they can to look for this person. How dare someone leave the scene of an accident like that!"

"Thank you, Alex. I appreciate you putting in a word with the police. Lenora and I will sleep much better once we know the person has been caught and brought to justice."

After Alex left, Jonathan looked over at the 8 x 10 framed portrait of his family on the corner of his desk. He didn't want to display how upset he was over the accident in front of Lenora and Keith, but it truly angered him that someone almost caused the death of his child. They'd just buried his father.

Jonathan knew bad things happened, and God was ever faithful and to be trusted. It was just too bad he was a pastor, Jonathan thought, because his inner man really wanted to hurt the person who caused harm to his oldest son.

Chapter Nine

After she took a sip from her vanilla latte, Serena eyed the man in front of her. She felt the sweetness hit her tongue, and then roll down her throat. It was midmorning on a Monday, and the crowd had long since dispersed from the popular coffee shop. She'd been intrigued with Lance Ryan ever since he found her in the corner booth. Her mind was racing with questions, but she needed to slow herself down. Serena placed the coffee cup down on the table. "These are some serious allegations, Mr.—"

"Lance. You can call me Lance."

Is that even his real name?

The man took a sip from his cup of espresso; his pale green eyes conveyed a hint of amusement as he observed her.

Serena had been sitting across from Lance for about fifteen minutes in Starbucks. She was often mistaken for just being another pretty reporter, but her quick wit and intelligence allowed her to get a lot further in her career on more than beauty alone. Her ability to read people and pick up on a story were a part of her trademark style of reporting.

Right now, she couldn't read Lance Ryan.

Serena noted the jacket that fit snugly across Lance's broad shoulders was expensive. He wasn't wearing a tie, and he had the first two buttons of his shirt open, displaying a hint of a muscular physique underneath. There wasn't a glimpse of hair, and it appeared Lance either recently spent time at a beach or a tanning salon.

She glanced at his hands. The man took better care of his hands than she did, which is where the oddness began to bother Serena. Or maybe it was the skinhead buzz cut that revealed a tiny scar from the top of Lance's left eyebrow into his bare hairline. The ruggedness just didn't seem to match the expensive clothes and manicured appearance.

Still, he reminded her of an older version of Channing Tatum, but without the boyish charm. She sensed an underlying uptightness when he spoke.

Okay, Serena, you are here for the story. Focus.

Lance leaned forward and clasped his fingers together in front of him on the table. "If you have doubts, Ms. Manchester, I can vouch for everything."

Serena continued to be drawn to the man's eyes, which she now realized were more hazel. They were green and now appeared to be turning blue. She moved her coffee cup to the side and sat up in the chair. "I need solid facts before I try to investigate anything going on at city hall. Mayor Carrington and I, well, we have our differences."

That was an understatement. Mayor Carrington was still none too pleased about the way Serena reported on his past indiscretions during the last election. She was doing her job, making sure the public knew they were dealing with a man who was an obvious womanizer. Of course, the incumbent mayor won the election, despite the tight race.

How in the world did his wife stay with him was beyond Serena. Her second husband had cheated on her one time, and that was his last. Serena was never good with sharing.

She inquired, "Why is this important to you? What do you get out of this, Lance?"

He smiled, displaying a set of perfect white teeth that had to have been set with braces at one time. He countered her questions. "Why is it important for you to have this story? Don't you want justice served? Isn't it your mission to serve the public too?"

Wasn't she supposed to be asking the questions here? Serena grabbed her coffee cup. This time she swallowed the remaining coffee before placing the cup back on the table. "What are you, a Good Samaritan?"

The man grinned. "In due time, you and this city will appreciate me."

Serena raised her eyebrow as she eyed him. She sensed Lance meant what he said, and that made her more nervous.

No one made her nervous.

Serena smiled. "Okay, you give me what you have and I will be the one to decide if it's worth my time to investigate."

Lance reached down and placed a briefcase on the table. Serena could tell it was made of expensive leather. He clicked it open and passed her a thick folder. Then Lance stood slowly, his eyes never leaving her face. "I will be in touch very soon. You will see what I have is going to bring the truth to light about some very important people." With that, the man moved through the forming early lunch crowd and left the coffee shop.

Serena followed him with her eyes. Lance walked with his back superstraight, almost like he was a soldier. He stopped and turned toward the window and smiled.

She gulped. *No way!* She knew he shouldn't be able to see her, but it felt like he was looking directly at her. It could have been because she was near one of the coffee shop exits, but she was pretty sure the chill that crept up her back had nothing to do with the brisk weather outside.

Serena was so caught up in watching Lance move out of her line of sight she didn't realize she was clutching the folder he had left her. That man was on a mission and from experience, she needed to get her story but tread carefully.

She relaxed her shoulders and flipped open the folder. Did Lance really have evidence to bring down a city council member? There was nothing worse than finding corruption in city government, especially among local leaders who people trusted and had voted into office.

Serena frowned when she saw the spreadsheets, but then she started to see familiar project names. One in particular had been in the news a lot lately. The Hudson Housing Development. As she continued to browse the contents of the folder, the chill Serena had experienced before transitioned to warm excitement. Now *this* was the kind of story she loved to come her way.

Chapter Ten

Lenora had tried in vain to convince herself the texts were meant for someone else. Maybe the lines had crossed and the person asking about Keith was a well-meaning soul who knew her family. When she compared the number from the text on Thursday to the number from the text on Saturday, they were two very different numbers. When she called both numbers, they seemed to be dead ends.

That's when her mind went back to the pale-eyed man she saw and went looking for on Thursday. The way he'd disappeared still puzzled Lenora. She had been exhausted from the funeral, but could a person dream someone into existence? Why was his face so familiar to her?

Lenora's thoughts were interrupted by Michael walking into the kitchen. Her youngest son dropped his bag on the floor and headed straight to the refrigerator.

She frowned. "Hello to you too." Both of her sons were tall. Having two tall parents helped.

Michael grabbed the carton of orange juice and sat down at the table.

Lenora raised her eyebrow. "You *are* planning to get a glass from the cabinet, right?"

He grinned and got up to get a glass.

As Lenora watched her son pour the juice, she casually asked, "Do you ever get strange numbers on your cell phone?"

Michael shrugged. "Yeah, all the time. Sometimes it's just a telemarketer."

"I know you watch a lot of crime shows. How can someone get away with making a call or text without letting you know their identity?"

Michael grinned. "Wow, Mom. What are you up to?"

She swatted at him and returned the smile. "Nothing, I'm just getting these strange calls, and I would like to know who is calling or texting me."

"Well, people can get burner phones."

"What's a burner phone? Sounds pretty high tech."

"Naw. Go to the store, buy a prepaid phone, use your minutes, and text. Then throw it in the trash."

"Oh, okay." Lenora frowned. So this person took the time to use a burner phone to contact her. As she pondered the thought, the phone rang in her hand. Lenora jumped and almost dropped the phone. She peered down at the phone, and then let out a deep sigh.

Lenora looked at her son, "Well, I know who this is." It wasn't someone she looked forward to talking to at the moment, but she answered the call dutifully.

About an hour later, Lenora rang the doorbell to a familiar house from her teenage years. She wasn't sure why she was summoned here, but the urgency in an old friend's voice motivated Lenora to get in her car and drive over. She figured it didn't hurt to reach out and be a friend. Lord knows, how many times she'd been disappointed by her willingness to be available.

The door opened, and the woman leaned up against the door frame and folded her arms. "It's been awhile, Lenora. I was starting to think we had stopped being friends again."

Lenora raised her eyebrow as she eyed Charmayne Hudson. "Hello, Charmayne. It's good to see you too. You seem to only want to be in touch when something's wrong." This time Lenora folded her arms. "What's the problem?"

"Girl, get in here. I can't believe you would say such a thing."

Before crossing the doorway, Lenora smirked. "There's been a pattern that's not easy to ignore."

Lenora stepped into the house Charmayne grew up in, but had since remodeled. She noted that Charmayne didn't waste any time in putting her imprint on the home since the death of her last living parent late last year.

While she kept in touch with Charmayne, Lenora had kept her distance as an adult. She hadn't talked to Charmayne since high school graduation until ten years ago. When she had opened Lenora's Bridal Boutique, she had no idea one of the first customers would be Charmayne.

Unfortunately, after months of planning the wedding, Charmayne never walked down the aisle. To this day, Lenora was not provided reasons why Charmayne chose to break off a wedding with a man who loved her, and to Lenora's knowledge, had captured Charmayne's heart.

Lenora followed Charmayne into the living room. Charmayne reached for a wineglass off of the coffee table. When Charmayne turned around, Lenora almost ran into the wineglass.

"Oh!" Lenora stepped back to flick some of the wine that had sloshed on her coat.

"I'm so sorry. At least you are wearing a black coat." Charmayne drained the wineglass. "Speaking of black, I know your family is in mourning. How's Jonathan? And Mrs. Eliza? When I saw Pastor Jeremiah had passed, it brought back so many memories of Daddy for me."

Lenora cleared her throat. "Jonathan is fine. You know Eliza bounces back from anything. I figured that's why we didn't see you at the funeral last Thursday."

Charmayne shifted her eyes away. "I'm sorry. I couldn't. I feel like I let you both down because you have been so supportive of me. I do remember you both being at Bishop

Hudson's world famous home going." Charmayne lifted her empty wineglass in the air as if she was toasting her late father. "I certainly do miss you, Daddy."

Lenora remembered very well the turnout for the bishop's funeral. While there was a large turnout for Pastor Jeremiah, there were several well-known celebrities and legislators who showed up to wish final good-byes to the man who had been a force to reckon with since his days in the civil rights arena.

She also knew Charmayne really didn't miss the late great Bishop Hudson. Their father-daughter relationship might have appeared perfect to the public, but Lenora had witnessed a long history of intimidation and resentment between Charmayne and her father.

"I hope this doesn't make me look bad to you. I really couldn't deal with another funeral. I mean, are you and Jonathan going to support my run for District 2 again?" Charmayne added, "I hope you will."

"I'm sure Jonathan wouldn't mind letting you speak before the congregation. You seem to be doing well, and obviously, you enjoy the public service work." Lenora frowned. "Is this why you called me over? You seemed really upset on the phone . . ." Lenora pointed to the wineglass, "and stressed."

Charmayne snapped. "Well, I am stressed. You know having Victory Gospel Church behind me would mean a lot. The bishop's former congregation, Greater Heights, is ecstatic that I'm running again. Which is why I'm confused by the rumors."

"Rumors? What rumors?" Lenora couldn't resist adding. "Who would start rumors about Bishop William Hudson's daughter?"

Charmayne stared coolly at Lenora. "Really? Not funny. You, of all people, know how desperately I would like to not live in my daddy's shadow." Charmayne walked over to the bar in the corner of her living room. Lenora was pretty sure the bar was a part of the add-ons to the house. It wasn't there when they were younger.

She followed Charmayne over to the bar and set her purse down. "Seriously, Charmayne, people respect that you stand on your own merit."

Charmayne picked up an expensive-looking bottle of wine from behind the counter. As she poured, most of the liquid spilled over the side of the glass. "Oh my!" She placed the bottle down and reached down again. This time she had a roll of paper towels in her hand. She snatched several towels from the roll and began wiping the counter.

"My stuffy, religious, fire-breathing daddy wanted to make sure his agenda or whoever he had in his pocket had their agenda satisfied. Not everyone liked him." She stopped wiping the counter and added under her breath, "Including me."

Charmayne picked up the dripping red-soaked towels and slammed them into the nearby trash can. She pointed to Lenora, and then back at herself. "Now me and you, I know we don't stay in touch like we could, but I never thought you would become my enemy. How can you come up here and lie in my face anyway?"

An old angry feeling shot through Lenora's body. She grabbed her bag off the counter and stared at Charmayne. She kept her voice low. "Excuse me. What are you accusing me of this time? I don't have time for whatever paranoid thoughts you have going on in your head. I need to be with my family."

Charmayne marched around the bar and jabbed her finger toward Lenora. "Your husband is going to ruin my career goals. This council seat is mine. It's a stepping-stone to me being mayor of Charlotte. I've worked too hard for this opportunity for someone to just stand in my way, especially with no political experience."

Lenora blinked. "You have always been ambitious, but why would you accuse Jonathan of standing in your way?"

Charmayne huffed and placed her hands on her hips and stared at Lenora. "Don't pretend to me like you don't know."

Lenora gripped her bag tighter. She had a vision of swinging it to knock some sense into Charmayne's rant.

Charmayne stepped back, and then she threw her head back and laughed. She shook her head, and then cupped her hands over her mouth. "You don't know?"

Lenora hated Charmayne's laugh. She sounded like a witch cackling.

"I'm leaving. I can't believe I came over for this nonsense. You need to stop drinking. You want someone to support you? It won't be me anymore. This is the last time you reach out to me. I'm through with you." Lenora turned to walk away.

Charmayne traipsed behind her as she headed to the door. Like a little child, she sang. *"There must be trouble in paradise. The darling couple of Victory Gospel Church has secrets. Who knew?"*

Lenora whirled and shouted, "What are you babbling about?"

No one made her crazier than Charmayne. Why did she continuously get sucked into this relationship? She didn't owe this woman a thing, but in the strangest way, Lenora had always felt sorry for Charmayne.

Right now, Charmayne stood a tad bit too close for Lenora's taste. Lenora wasn't wearing heels, but she still had two inches of height over her friend. "Back up, Charmayne."

Charmayne took a step back. "I'm sorry to be the one to break this to you, but your husband is in cahoots with the mayor. He's thinking about running against me for the

District 2 seat. Apparently he doesn't share everything with you, or maybe he was waiting for the right time. I don't really care, but I would like you to advise your husband that he needs to tend to the business of his church and leave the politics to me."

Lenora's mother had gone to glory ten years ago, but she held fast to her mother's rule to not say a word if you can't say something nice.

She stared at Charmayne. "I'm leaving now, let me out."

Charmayne unlatched the locks on the door.

Lenora moved past her and quietly said, "Good-bye, Charmayne."

As she walked down the driveway, she ignored Charmayne calling out her name. For some odd reason, Charmayne lost her mind and forgot they both were grown women. When they were younger, Charmayne had to control the friendship and being the sheltered girl she was, Lenora followed.

Not anymore. This time, Lenora meant it. She didn't need to be disrespected by a woman who, time and time again, she'd been there for—both good and bad. Where was the reciprocity in their relationship?

As Lenora opened the door to her Lexus, her mind switched to the man she had married. She knew her husband. Next to Charmayne, Jonathan was the most ambitious person she knew. Long before Jonathan took over the church for his father, he had dreams.

She slammed the car door shut and hit the steering wheel. Lenora couldn't understand why she seemed to be the last person to know about a possible decision that could be the final straw of their marriage.

Chapter Eleven

Serena threw her hands up and shot out her question, "What about the Hudson Housing Development? You, Mayor Carrington, were really looking forward to that funding being approved before, but you don't approve now when you did a few months ago. Why not? What changed?"

Mayor Carrington eyed Serena. "That funding would be better suited to other projects here in Charlotte, in particular, transportation."

Despite the other reporters around her, Serena glared at Mayor Carrington. Knowing she had his full attention, she continued her badgering. "But the Hudson Housing Development has been on the city council's agenda for many years now. Bishop William Hudson was an important civil rights leader, not just in that district, but in the city and state. Are you planning not to honor the wishes of this great man and for all that he fought for during his life?"

The mayor looked like he wanted to walk from behind the podium and strangle her. The room grew quiet as he shuffled his papers. He reached for the microphone and started to speak, but then shut his mouth. Mayor Carrington finally responded with a strained voice.

"Ms. Manchester, we all loved Bishop Hudson and what he did for Charlotte. We have had much funding appropriated to several housing developments the past few years and now it's time to invest in transportation. It's vital to this rapidly growing city."

"But—"

Mayor Carrington glared at her. "Ms. Manchester, I believe you have asked enough questions. Please let someone else have a turn."

Not to be put in her place, Serena pounced back. "Well, I'm sure everyone here has the same questions that I have. I mean, it's known that there is a split on the council right now and with it being an election year, the people need to know where you and other council members stand on this issue."

The mayor gripped the sides of the podium. "There are some disagreements, but we are dedicated to making the right decisions for the city that we serve."

A host of reporters suddenly held up their hands and began to shout questions.

Mayor Carrington said, "This press conference has come to close. Thank you for attending." He walked away from the podium, leaving the unanswered questions lingering in the air.

Serena smirked. "Just like a politician, never giving all the facts . . . or the truth, for that matter." She placed her notepad and phone in her bag. Inside her bag was the folder Lance Ryan gave her.

Now that man was a complete mystery. She looked up information about Lance, but the man was nowhere to be found. This disturbed her a bit, but she couldn't deny the spreadsheet numbers were suspicious. There was a great deal of financial support thrown toward the Hudson Housing Development. It seemed strange that it remained on hold. Serena looked up to see a woman walking fast down the hall.

Serena smiled. "Well, maybe I might be seeking out the wrong person for answers." She grabbed her bag and quickly headed down the hall behind the woman. The woman wore black pumps and was dressed businesslike in a blue suit fit with a white shirt. Her black trench coat was thrown over her arm. The woman leaned over and pressed the button on the elevator. The doors instantly opened.

Serena caught up to her and sprinted in the elevator. As she turned around, Serena caught her breath. Right outside the elevator on the other side of the hallway was Lance Ryan. For a half second, Serena tried to figure if she should get off or stay on the elevator.

She had a lot of questions for her elusive source. Who was he and what was his true interest?

The doors closed, sealing Serena's decision. She looked over at the woman who was grooming her short hair in the elevator's mirror.

Serena said, "I love that new cut on you. I was thinking about cutting my hair shorter."

The woman turned and frowned. Then she smiled and said, "Thank you."

Serena smiled. "You know you are just the person I wanted to talk to, that is, if you have time, Ms. Hudson."

Charmayne Hudson continued to smile, but her eyes narrowed slightly as she observed Serena. "What did you want to talk to me about? It's Ms. Manchester, correct?"

Serena held out her hand. "Yes, Serena Manchester from WYNN."

Charmayne returned the handshake.

Serena plowed forward. "I would really like to know what's happened with the Hudson Housing Development. Your father, bless his heart, wasn't it his dream?"

Charmayne looked away. "Yes, it was. Why don't we talk in my office?"

Serena smiled. "Sounds good!"

The two women waited in silence until the elevator stopped and the doors opened. Serena followed behind Charmayne to her office. Once inside, Charmayne closed the door. "Please have a seat, Ms. Manchester."

"You can call me Serena. No need to be formal." Serena sat down in the cushy seat across from the old oak desk as she watched Charmayne place her bag beside her desk, and then sit. Charmayne sat forward in her chair and clasped her hands together. "So what exactly do you want to know, Serena?"

"Your father, the late great Bishop Hudson, fought for this housing development for years. By the way, I want to pass on my condolences about his passing. It was right before the holidays, correct?"

"Yes, it was."

"Such a shame, and with the passing of Pastor Jeremiah Freeman just last week . . . We are losing some really solid leaders in the African American community. I'm just delighted to see you making your place here in Charlotte."

"Well, thank you. That's not always recognized. It's hard to be the daughter of a bishop, but I do want to make sure the funding goes forward on this housing development. Many people who attend Greater Heights Church as well as Victory Gospel Church would benefit."

Serena had pulled out her notepad and recorder. "That's what I thought. I mean, with this growing population, I can understand the mayor and other members of the council wanting to focus on transportation."

Charmayne looked at the recorder. "I don't disagree with the mayor, but people need a place to make home. Are you recording this?"

"Do you mind?" Serena asked.

"I'm not sure why we need to. You just wanted a statement from me, I presume. I want to seek funding for housing, but transportation seems to be more important. That's all."

Serena continued to hold the recorder. "But there was a considerable amount of money raised by Bishop Hudson. How does that money play a role in this project?"

Charmayne sat back in her seat. "Yes, there was money raised, but we are talking about a massive construction project here. That money wouldn't cover the budget."

"Do you have figures on how much money was raised over the years?"

Charmayne frowned. "Why?"

"Well, I think Mayor Carrington is holding the position that you don't need taxpayers' dollars. I just wondered why he was taking that position now." Serena moved up in her chair. "I could be wrong on this, but Mayor Carrington seemed to support the Hudson Housing Development until your father's death."

Serena observed Charmayne clench her hand into a fist. For a brief instance, Serena recognized the real woman behind the couture suit, makeup, and sculptured cut was not a woman you wanted to cross.

Serena waited as Charmayne composed herself.

"I don't know why Mayor Carrington is taking the position he has and why he has turned his back on my father's dream. He and I just don't see eye to eye on many things."

Serena nodded. "You wouldn't mind allowing me to see the donation records? I mean, so we can come down to a reason why the Hudson Housing Development is on hold. The people will want to know."

Charmayne tapped her fingers on the desk. "Sure, this office has nothing to hide. I can ask my assistant to pull those records."

"Thank you, Ms. Hudson." Serena stood and extended her hand. "It was a pleasure talking to you. I do admire you. When you were elected for your first term, I recall you were the youngest African American woman ever elected to the city council. Do you plan to seek a fourth term this coming November, or are you ready to throw your hat in the mayor's race?"

Charmayne stood. "The people seem to think I've been doing a good job in District 2."

"So you are going to stay where you are? You don't know of anyone who plans to throw their hat into the race, do you? Being the incumbent, you received over 60 percent of the votes the last two terms."

Charmayne took a bit too long to smile, almost like she was thinking as she was trying to figure out what to say. "I'm not aware of anyone, and like I said, the people are satisfied with my public service."

"I will be looking for those records. Thank you so much for your time."

Serena walked out and headed to the elevator. Something was going on here. Mayor Carrington didn't want to move the Hudson Housing Development forward for a reason. She had photos from the last mayor's race to prove that the mayor and Bishop Hudson were good friends. What changed after Bishop Hudson's death? Why did the bishop's daughter seem to be insecure about her future?

The elevator doors opened, and Serena entered. Before the doors closed, a hand grabbed the inside of the doors. Startled, Serena watched as Lance entered the elevator.

The doors closed behind him as he focused his intense eyes on her. He stepped up beside her. "Did Ms. Hudson give you what you wanted?"

Serena swallowed. She was a tough chick, but this man was standing way too close even for her comfort. She answered, "She said she would get the records to me."

Lance scoffed. "What she gives you, I'm pretty sure, those numbers will be altered from the records I gave you."

Serena cocked her head. "How do I know whose numbers to believe? You never told me what providing this information does for you."

"I have nothing to lose, Ms. Manchester. There are some people here who have an image of being perfect, holy, and righteous."

Lance stepped even closer to her now, brushing his arm up against her arm. Serena had smelled a hint of his cologne and it almost suffocated her.

"There are those who seek to establish their own righteousness."

Serena stared into Lance's eyes, almost forgetting to breathe. The one thing she could not stand was religious mumbo jumbo. Lance really believed whatever he was talking about, which made him crazier than he looked.

The elevator doors opened. As quickly as he entered, Lance exited and moved through the crowd outside the doors. A man entered and asked, "Are you getting off?"

Serena shook her head, "No, not yet." This was her second meeting with Lance Ryan, and the man always left her feeling the need to catch her bearings. This story spelled of city corruption, but her gut sensed there was more, and if she didn't tread carefully, she would burn bridges she could never mend.

Chapter Twelve

Jonathan turned over to the other side of the bed and reached out his arm toward his wife. He moved his arm across the sheets, and then opened his eyes. He sat up in the bed and looked around the master bedroom. Jonathan had a feeling his wife never made it to bed. He let out a deep sigh. He didn't like when Lenora was moody. It was like she was there in another place.

He wasn't sure if she was disturbed by the hit-and-run accident or something else. His wife had always been overprotective of their sons. How often did he preach boys would be boys to her? They were really blessed. While Keith was not happy about his injuries, their son was in good spirits that he would be healed in time for the next basketball season. In the meantime, they would work out how to get his work from the professors.

In the back of his mind, Jonathan knew he was the blame for some of the distance between him and his wife. When they dated, he told Lenora he would never follow in his dad's footsteps. The church was not for him. He had his own career ahead of him.

Unfortunately, when his father started to suffer kidney failure, his mother begged him to take over Victory Gospel for his father. She would not stand to have someone from the outside to serve as shepherd for the church. It seemed like the right thing to do, but he and Lenora had been slowly drifting apart since then. It didn't help that Lenora stayed so busy at the boutique. With wedding season getting ready to kick off, they would rarely see each other except when an event demanded their appearance as a couple.

He grunted and swung his legs off the bed. Jonathan pushed his feet into his slippers and reached for the robe at the end of the bed. It was still chilly at night, even though spring had come. The first week of April was still being held hostage by winter.

Jonathan moved through the hallway. He stopped briefly at each of his son's rooms. Keith was snoring softly. Thankfully, the boy was comfortable, despite being in pain. Jonathan peeked in Michael's room and heard the boy's steady breathing. This was good to hear as Michael had been prone to asthma since he was a little boy.

Jonathan walked away from Michael's bedroom door and leaned over the stair railing. There was a faint glow coming from downstairs. When he reached the bottom of the stairs, just as he had seen many nights, he could see Lenora's body curled up on the couch with the glow of the big flat-screen television shining across from her.

He walked around the couch and sat down next to his wife. Whatever sleep his wife was getting it certainly couldn't be restful. She twitched in her sleep and let out a tiny yelp. He gently shook her. "Lenora."

Lenora woke up with a start, clutching her nightgown to her. Her face was shiny with sweat. She focused on him, and then relaxed her arms and shoulders.

"What wrong? Is it a bad dream?" he asked.

She nodded. "Sorry, I was watching a movie on television, and I guess sleep finally came."

"What were you dreaming about?"

Lenora looked away and shivered. "I don't remember now."

Jonathan pulled the blanket that was wrapped around his wife's legs closer to her shoulders. "Why don't you come upstairs?"

Lenora pulled the blanket closer up to her chin. "When were you going to tell me?"

Jonathan frowned. "Tell you what?"

"Isn't running Victory Gospel Church enough for you? Or are you having second thoughts now?"

"Why are you asking?"

Lenora shook her head. "It's the only reason I can think of why you would want to consider running for city council."

Jonathan rubbed his hands across his head. "How did you find out?"

Lenora sat up, the blanket sliding to the floor. "It's true?"

"I haven't told you because I haven't decided."

"You haven't decided? How about letting me know you are even considering before you make a decision?"

Jonathan turned away. "I needed to personally think this through. Of course, I would consult with you."

Lenora shook her head. "When we were younger, we discussed everything together." She turned away from him and bowed her head. "There are people who seem to know that you are considering placing your name on a ballot, and they are pretty threatened."

Jonathan moved closer to his wife. "Who might these people be? Did someone threaten you?"

He watched her hesitation. Finally she spoke, "No threats. But you do realize the position you are placing us in. Charmayne Hudson has had this position for three terms. She is the daughter of the great Bishop William Hudson. Your dad and the bishop were good friends."

Jonathan leaned back against the couch. "Which is why I'm praying about this opportunity. I was approached by

Mayor Carrington a few weeks ago. There is a conflict between the mayor and Charmayne for some reason. He seems to think she has her own agendas that are not what the people want."

"Charmayne says differently. She does feel threatened by the possibility that you would run against her. Both Greater Heights and Victory Gospel are in the same district."

"So this is coming from Charmayne? I never understood how you and she manage to retain a friendship. You are so different. She's like a walking spokesperson for negativity." While he grew up in the same circles with Charmayne, they never were friends. Jonathan heard rumors that Charmayne was a spoiled, mean girl and that was the kind of person he avoided. It surprised him when he realized that Lenora had been friends with Charmayne since they were young girls.

They sat in silence for a while. Lenora spoke up softly. "You are doing it again?"

"Again?" Jonathan spoke sharply. "What am I doing, Lenora? I was presented with an opportunity. You, of all people, know that I was heading in this direction before Dad—"

"I know. That's why this is bothering me. You don't need to take on too much."

Jonathan quieted his voice. "You know things happened fast with Dad. No one in the church wanted to look for another pastor while Dad was sick. It was appropriate at the time to fill in for him. I never imagined being here, but I don't regret it. Please don't tell me being at Victory Gospel Church hasn't been rewarding for you in some ways."

Lenora closed her eyes. "I love Victory Gospel. I love the people . . . but I miss us."

Jonathan looked at his wife. He had just thought the same thing a few minutes earlier. He grabbed her hand. "You are the most important person in the world to me. I would not make any decisions without you."

The overhead lights above them suddenly came on. "What's going on in here? How is a person supposed to sleep with all this noise?"

Jonathan spun around to see his mother standing in her nightgown, leaning on her cane. He let go of Lenora's hand and jumped from the couch. "Mother, we didn't mean to wake you."

Jonathan looked over at Lenora. She held her head down, not looking at him and started folding the blanket. She carefully laid it on the couch. Then she grabbed the remote and shut the television off. Without a word, she passed by him, his mother, and headed upstairs. A moment later, Jonathan heard the bedroom door close.

Eliza questioned him with her eyes. "Did I interrupt something? I'm an old woman, and I need my sleep."

Jonathan walked over to his mother and grabbed her by her shoulders. "Why don't we all head back to bed?" He turned her gently toward her room.

"I surely hope I can go back to sleep now that I'm awake." Eliza shuffled back to her room.

Jonathan waited until his mother closed the door, and then climbed the staircase. He reached for the bedroom door handle, almost expecting it to be locked, but it wasn't. Lenora was already in the bed, but her back was turned away from him.

As he slid under the covers, his conversation with Lenora invaded his mind. Jonathan lay his head against the pillow and stared up at the ceiling. In the midst of all that has happened, he had this sinking feeling his marriage was on the shakiest ground it had ever been. If he did pursue his dreams, what would the cost be?

Lenora stirred next to him. He wanted to reach for her, but clasped his hands across his chest and closed his eyes instead.

Lord, help me to do your will.

Chapter Thirteen

Lenora watched the coffee drip into the carafe. She tried to go back to sleep last night, but she had slept fitfully. Jonathan had returned to their room and slid into their king-size bed. She stayed so far near the edge she probably could have fallen off had she strayed an inch. Jonathan had tossed and turned in the bed beside her until she finally heard the rhythmic breathing of him sound asleep.

She hated the distance between them, and she supported him serving as interim pastor for his father and now as the official pastor. Like he said last night, twenty years ago they would have never imagined being called as leaders of a megachurch. Victory Gospel Church was a small tight-knit church back during the early days of their marriage.

Jonathan supported her when she opened Lenora's Bridal Boutique and her hours were crazy too. She had waited until both of her sons were teenagers before she branched off into what she had loved to do so many years. She had planned what seemed like hundreds of weddings before she decided she wanted to have dresses to supply her clients with. She had a great staff of consultants and seamstresses.

That's what nagged her last night. She was living her dream. Was Jonathan?

Michael strolled into the kitchen. Lenora looked at the clock. "Honey, aren't you running a bit late? You're not dressed yet for school."

"I'm not feeling well."

Lenora arched her eyebrow. She knew that Keith had been receiving more attention since the accident and sensed her youngest son was feeling left out. Still, he was a good boy and did well in school. She went over and touched his head. "You do feel warm. Let's take your temperature. We don't want to send you to school if you have a fever."

As Lenora reached into a cabinet for the first aid supply kit, she heard behind her, "Oh, good, you have coffee ready."

Lenora closed her eyes, took a deep breath, and placed the first aid kit on the counter. She turned around. "Mother Eliza. Good morning. I'm going to take Michael's temperature."

The older woman pulled out a chair and slowly sat down. "Oh, son, you're not feeling well?"

Michael shook his head. Lenora placed the thermometer under his tongue. "Sit still for a minute," she told him. She then said to her mother-in-law. "Eliza, you want me to pour you some coffee?"

"Yes, cream and sugar, please."

Lenora grabbed two ceramic white mugs from the dishwasher. As she poured the coffee, her mother-in-law turned the television on and flipped channels.

Lenora brought the steaming mugs over to the table. Then she went over to Michael. "Okay, let's check your temperature." Lenora read the thermometer. "Mmm, looks like it's normal." She peered at her son. "What's hurting on you?"

Michael grabbed his stomach. "My stomach hurts bad."

"Okay, I tell you what, you lie down for a while. Let's see how you feel in a bit. I need to get to the boutique because I have appointments. I will call you to see how you are doing. You've already missed school for your grandfather's funeral and were out with Keith."

"That's right, you do what your mother said. Give your grandmother a hug."

Michael hugged Eliza, and then left the kitchen. Lenora knew Eliza loved her grandsons just as fiercely as she loved her own son.

Eliza asked, "Did the police say anything else about finding the culprit who ran off from the accident?"

Lenora sat down in the chair opposite Eliza and shook her head. She still hadn't told anyone about the strange messages and voice on her phone. Keith and Rachel were both doing well. Surely, the accident was random and the coward would be found soon.

She looked over at Eliza who was rubbing her knee. "How's your knee doing?"

"It's not too bad today. The doctor wants me to replace it, but I just can't—"

"But won't the surgery make you more comfortable getting around?"

Eliza waved her hand. "Those doctors just want to cut on me to get my money. I'm fine. They sure didn't help Pastor Jeremiah."

Lenora swallowed her coffee. Eliza was stubborn, but she felt bad watching the woman lose her husband. She had been wondering why her mother-in-law was so against getting medical assistance for her bad knees. It was almost as if she wanted to suffer.

"Where's Jonathan so early this morning?" Eliza asked.

Eliza's question brought back memories of last night's argument with Jonathan. Lenora tried to remember where her husband was today. Usually, she was more in tune with his schedule. "I'm not sure."

"Mayor Carrington came to see him on Sunday."

She stared at Eliza. "About the city council seat?"

"Oh, so that's what you two were talking about last night. I was wondering when he would tell you."

So, Jonathan can discuss his consideration of running for office with his mother, but not his wife? "So, I guess you think it's a good idea."

"The community loves Jonathan. It will be good for him and Victory Gospel."

"But the congregation has grown and is still growing. Don't you think Jonathan should be more focused on the church's needs?"

"Never doubt what God can do, Lenora."

Lenora protested, "I'm not, I . . ." She stopped. Getting into an argument with her husband's mother was not what she needed to be doing. In fact, Lenora was pretty sure Eliza did what she could to encourage her only son's ambitions for her own personal need to be the center of attention.

She swallowed the rest of her coffee and placed the mug in the sink. "I really need to get to the boutique. I have a wedding party fitting today."

"You *are* going to support Jonathan's run for office."

This old woman really needed to stay out of her marriage. "He hasn't decided yet, Eliza."

"It's just that you sounded like you were against him."

This time Lenora didn't bother to hide the expression of disgust on her face. "You were listening to our conversation?"

Eliza held her hand to her chest. "Of course not. You were talking loudly, and the bedroom is right down the hall from the living room. I got up to remind you I was still here."

And when are you going to return to your own home, Lenora wanted to ask. Instead, she took a deep breath. "I have been married to your son for twenty years. I do believe I have shown and proven my support for whatever he decides to pursue."

"I just want to be sure you wouldn't stand in his way."

Lenora narrowed her eyes. "Stand in his way of what, Eliza?" She crossed her arms. "I want him to make a decision that is best for the family. The boys have had to adjust to becoming a preacher's kids overnight."

"Those boys are almost grown men. They are not children anymore, Lenora. The community loves Jonathan, even more than they did Pastor Jeremiah." Eliza grabbed the remote and increased the volume. Then she exclaimed. "Plus, someone needs to get that woman out of the way so real progress can be made."

Lenora looked at the television to see Charmayne's face on the news. She had to admit Charmayne was an unstable chick behind closed doors, but quite frankly, being in a public office suited Charmayne.

"Why? You were good friends with Bishop Hudson and First Lady Valerie Hudson. You watched Charmayne grow up."

Eliza smirked. "The Hudsons were no friends of mine. Bishop was a big bully behind his fancy robes. That girl walks over people like her daddy did." She reached for her cane and pointed at the television. "You support your husband. Moving that woman out of office is going to be for the greater good."

Lenora watched her mother-in-law leave the room. She never knew Eliza was that interested in politics. Maybe because politics didn't interest Lenora. One of the reasons she wasn't sure about Jonathan branching into this area was because that world was unknown to her. She only dealt with an occasional bridezilla or controlling mother of the bride.

Was Jonathan seriously considering stepping into this arena? She knew when Charmayne didn't get her way, she could be ugly. What were the ramifications for the church, the boys, and her if Jonathan was attacked publicly in a campaign?

She couldn't do this now. It was time to head to the boutique for Candace's wedding party fitting. Lenora left the kitchen.

As she grabbed her coat and her keys, she glanced down at the *Charlotte* magazine on the table. Last summer, Jonathan, Keith, Michael, and she posed for that magazine cover which was accompanied by a glowing article. She picked up the magazine. Jonathan and her sons looked so handsome. The title next to them read, "THE FACE OF CHARLOTTE'S FAITH-CENTERED FAMILIES."

She placed the magazine back on the table. There was a sentence in the article that described her as a woman who took care of her family and business. Right now, she was feeling like that toy that spun around and around, with no clear sign of where it would stop.

Lenora whispered, "Lord, I need you. I'm so troubled in my spirit, and I don't know how to shake this off."

Chapter Fourteen

Lenora stepped back and smiled. "You are all beautiful. Candace, I do believe you picked a bridesmaid dress that works for everyone."

Candace beamed. "I believe so myself. Angel, turn around again."

The young woman was radiant as she twirled in the lavender cocktail-length dress. "Candace, this is nice. I like how it fits right above the knee."

Beulah Samuels, a stylist in Candace's salon and her maid-of-honor, sashayed. "Girl, even an old woman like me with these hips don't look half bad."

All the women laughed. Lenora noticed tears in Candace's eyes as she watched the last bridesmaid arrive from the dressing room. While her right arm was in a cast, Candace's daughter, Rachel, looked beautiful. The dress showed off Rachel's long legs. Candace walked over and hugged her not-so-little girl.

Lenora noticed there was still a bruise on Rachel's face from the accident last Thursday. She took a deep breath and tried to enjoy the special moment. It was with relief that both Keith and Rachel were on the mend, but Lenora was still angry. This beautiful girl should not have to have her arm in a cast on her mother's wedding day.

She turned away to compose her face. Lenora felt a hand on her shoulder.

"Ms. Fredricka, how are you doing?"

"I'm good. I'm so happy to see these women getting ready for Candace's big day." Fredricka Roberts winked.

"We have to make sure my granddaughter, Angel, will have her day soon."

Lenora looked over at Angel. "She and I have talked. I think after participating in Candace and Darnell's wedding, she will be ready to set a date. How are you getting along?"

Fredricka had a stroke last year, but seemed to be getting around more with her walker. "Good days and bad days, but I'm glad to be here. How are you? I know you must still be upset about the children's accident. Have they found anyone yet?"

Lenora must have not done a very good job of hiding her emotions. Of course, Ms. Fredricka was a pretty sharp woman. Lenora shook her head. "No, ma'am. It does make me angry that this coward walked away from an accident he or she caused."

"How's your son?"

"Keith is getting better, still in a lot of pain, though." Lenora swallowed, surprised by the tears that flooded her eyes. This was not like her to feel so out of control with her emotions. "It could have been worse, and that's the scary part."

Fredricka touched Lenora's arm. "I know. Sometimes it's those scary moments that remind us we need to draw closer to God, although we shouldn't wait for the bad things to happen."

Lenora leaned over and wrapped her arms around Fredricka's petite, frail shoulders. She pulled back and smiled. "You are a very wise woman."

"Honey, I'm old enough to have earned some wisdom." Fredricka winked.

Lenora laughed.

"Lenora!"

Lenora turned to look at who had shouted her name. She widened her eyes, and then glared at her visitor. *What in the world is she doing here?*

She walked over and strained to keep her voice quiet and civil. "Charmayne, I'm with clients. What are you doing here?"

Charmayne's short hair was sticking up on her head like the woman had decided she wanted to rip her hair out. "We need to talk. *Now*."

Lenora turned around and caught Candace's attention. "I'm sorry for the interruption. Candace, I will have Sarah take notes of any adjustments needed for the bridesmaid dresses. Everyone looked pretty good to me though."

Candace was watching Charmayne. She glanced at Lenora and said, "Sure, we will touch base when you're finished."

Lenora mouthed a "thank you" to her.

She turned toward Charmayne, who appeared to be swaying. Lenora grabbed her arm. "Let's go to my office before you embarrass yourself and me."

Getting Charmayne to the office was no easy feat as her troubled friend leaned into her and proceeded to cry softly. Lenora guided her to the chair in front of her desk. Charmayne collapsed in the chair. Lenora closed the door and sat in the chair next to her. She swung the chair around to face her friend. "What is going on with you?"

"Someone is trying to destroy me," Charmayne whined.

Lenora sat back. "Really? Who's out to get Charmayne now?" She got up from her seat. "I can't believe you came in here like this. I'm like your last friend, but I don't need you to come with your pity party."

"Listen to me, Lenora."

Lenora shook her head. "I told you the other day I'm through with you. You get mean and ugly when you are like this. I don't know why I bother with you."

Charmayne brushed her short hair off her face. "Will you listen to me? I'm sorry, but I need your help."

Lenora paced the floor. She didn't want to be close to Charmayne because she had visions of smacking some sense into her. For the life of her, she didn't know how Charmayne kept this destructive side of herself from the public. Maybe this was what Eliza was referring to the other day. Now Lenora was starting to see the bigger picture here. The people in Charmayne's district did deserve better.

She took a deep breath and spoke slowly. "Charmayne, I spoke to Jonathan. He has not decided anything yet. You said yourself that the people support you. Really, you are acting like it's the end of the world."

"No, no. You don't understand." Charmayne picked up her bag. She pulled an envelope out of her bag, and with trembling fingers, she unclasped the envelope. "Somebody is threatening me." She pulled paper-clipped papers out of the envelope and slapped them on Lenora's desk. "Look at this."

Lenora looked down at what appeared to be a newspaper article. There was a note held by a paper clip on top of the article. She reached for the document. Then she grabbed her stomach as a wave of nausea washed over her body. She read the note again . . . and again.

For the wages of sin is death. Death is knocking at your door.

She lifted her eyes to look at Charmayne.

Charmayne was visibly crying. "It's not fair. I'm sorry for that night. I've made up for it."

Fear shook Lenora's body as she thought about the words she had just spoken to Fredricka a few minutes before. *It does make me angry that this coward walked away from an accident he or she caused.* The hypocrisy of those words rocked Lenora as she stared at the note.

Somebody knew. Lenora couldn't even claim innocence. She was just as much a coward as Charmayne was that night.

Chapter Fifteen

Jonathan shook hands with Wes Cade. "It's good to see you, Wes. What can I do for my favorite WYNN reporter?"

Wes chuckled. "Thanks, Pastor Freeman. I appreciate the support."

"Well, come in. Let's catch up." Jonathan opened his office, and Wes followed. It was still hard to get used to, but he was slowly making it his own. The big desk in the middle was a favorite and had been around for a long time. Jonathan walked around it and sat down.

Wes sat. "Well, I came to talk to you about a personal matter, but I wondered if you wouldn't have a word to share about your son's accident."

Jonathan sighed. "I just want to continue to say what I have been saying. I hope the person who left the scene of the accident will come forward and turn themselves into the police. This could have been more serious."

Wes questioned, "What if no one comes forward to admit responsibility, Pastor? How will that affect your family?"

Jonathan thought for a moment. "I won't sit here and pretend that it won't be difficult, but our family will forgive and move on so we can all heal."

Wes nodded. "I do hope we can draw out the person responsible for the accident."

"Thank you, Wes. I appreciate your thoughtfulness. You know I was hoping you would come see me soon. If I'm not mistaken from talking to your buddy, Darnell

Jackson, didn't you two get engaged around the same time last year?"

Wes sank down in the seat. "You're right. One of the reasons why I wanted to come talk to you was to discuss some issues."

"Issues, son?"

Wes rubbed the arms of the chair. "Yes, sir. You know Angel and I are members of Darnell and Candace's wedding party next month."

"That's right. I think I did see you on the list that my wife shared with me. It will be good for both of you to watch a Christian couple walk down the aisle. Those two have been through a lot, and I'm sure you and Angel can relate."

"Yes, Darnell and Candace have both been great mentors to us. In fact, Angel and I admire you and the First Lady Freeman too."

Jonathan's smile faltered a bit. If only this young man knew the troubles on the home front. "Thank you, Wes. All marriages have good times and bad times. It's how the husband and wife both respond to those difficulties. You have to include God in the mix."

Wes said, "I know marriage won't be a honeymoon for long. I just . . ."

Jonathan leaned back in his seat. "Speak, son. Are you having doubts?"

"No, I'm not. I wonder if Angel is having doubts. She said yes, but it seems that trying to get a wedding date is impossible."

Wes got up from the seat and twisted his hands. He turned to Jonathan. "I have tried to be patient. She had to work out finally being able to mourn her mother. Her family had to get through the trial of the man responsible for her mother's death. Ms. Fredricka has had a long road, but she has bounced back from the stroke."

Jonathan interrupted, "But Angel is the one who still doesn't want to set a date yet?"

Wes sat down. "She's excited about Candace's wedding, and I asked her the other day out of frustration, 'When will it be our time?' She just looked at me and walked away. I think I pushed too far. Pastor, I have to know. I'm a man. I have needs."

It was Jonathan's turn to chuckle. Then he started to reflect on his own marriage. The intimate part of his relationship with Lenora had been lacking for some time. It was easy to overlook with all that has happened, but last night he did want to be close to her. And his wife was the most emotionally distant she had ever been from him at that time.

"Wes, all I can say is if you really want to marry Angel, don't push her. You don't want to pressure her into the marriage. She obviously loves you. I know that from just seeing her interacting and talking with my wife. She needs to know she can trust you and you will be there for her through the ups and downs."

Wes sighed. "I love her so much. I know I have been guilty of pushing her forward before she was ready. I even think maybe I should have waited longer to propose."

"I tell you what, why don't you two come in together for counseling."

"Counseling? Is that necessary?"

"It is if you want to know if this is the right decision for both of you. Yes, I think we need to ask the hard questions. Maybe get to the root of some issues. It is either going to drive you closer together or reveal some problems that may need to be addressed before you walk down the aisle."

Wes hung his head. "Wow, I don't know if I want to know, but I guess you are right. I'll talk to Angel. I believe she is at your wife's boutique getting fitted for a bridesmaid's dress."

Jonathan nodded. "Good, let's make plans to talk next week. Knowing my wife the way I know her, I imagine Angel is hearing similar advice right now."

Wes grinned. "I would love to be a fly on the wall." He grimaced. "Or not."

Both men laughed.

"Hey, I need to go, but I was wondering if I could ask you something else. It's more about you and your plans."

Jonathan frowned. "My plans?"

Wes inquired, "Are you thinking about running for office?"

Jonathan stared at him, and then sighed. "You know, it's hard to keep conversations confidential in this day and age."

Wes widened his eyes. "So, it's true?"

"I'm just considering. I don't have to make a decision to file for candidacy until July. I'm not quite sure how this is getting around or why my consideration seems to be stirring up controversy."

Wes responded. "Probably because of your competition, Pastor. Charmayne Hudson is expected to run for a fourth term. I hear she has intentions of running for mayor in the future."

Jonathan leaned forward. "Wes, I hope you won't quote me on this as we were here talking about other matters."

"No, sir. I wouldn't do that."

"Good, because I want you to know that I don't consider this some competitive sport. After much prayer, I will pursue this race if I feel it's the best action to take. I really don't need the media or anyone blowing this out of proportion."

"Oh, I know that, Pastor. It's just that you got to be prepared. How will the campaign affect you, your family, or Victory Gospel?"

"I'm giving all of the above some thought."

"Good!" Wes leaned over and held out his hand. "I appreciate your time."

Jonathan stood and shook hands. "Not a problem. You and your future wife come see me and let's talk. See if we can get a date for my wife to start planning your wedding."

"Will do." Wes turned to go, but hesitated before walking through the door. He turned around. "Just to let you know, I had a chance to really cover the last campaign with Charmayne Hudson. I don't know if you remember those attack ads. She created some real enemies."

"Thanks for the warning, Wes."

Wes nodded and left.

Jonathan leaned back in his chair and placed his hands behind his head. Deep in his heart he knew where his decision was turning toward. He didn't want to shake up the community or his own family, but he was well aware of Charmayne's ways. She learned them from the best.

Her father.

Jonathan heard on many occasions some choice words from his own father about the bishop. Pastor Jeremiah felt Bishop Hudson chose tactics at the expense of other people, in particular the very people who attended the church Bishop Hudson founded, Greater Heights Church.

Knowing Charmayne was cut from the same cloth, Jonathan had no doubt she would scheme to get her way. The fact that she purposely upset Lenora this week, telling his wife information before he had a chance, didn't sit well with him. Jonathan was aware on past occasions how Charmayne manipulated Lenora.

He'd seen many people come and go out of their lives. Jonathan couldn't figure out why Lenora insisted keeping Charmayne in her inner circle. Why did his wife feel obligated to *that* woman?

Chapter Sixteen

Lenora picked up the article with the note attached to it. She eased slowly into the chair as past memories stirred in her mind. She shook her head in disbelief and asked "Who sent this?"

Charmayne stared at her wild-eyed. "I don't know. I need you to help me find out." She leaned over the desk and jabbed her finger toward Lenora. "We are the only two people who knew about this."

Lenora glared at Charmayne. "Really, Charmayne, that's not exactly true, and you know it." God certainly knew what happened that night. Lenora had been filled with guilt and shame about her own lack of actions. Like Charmayne, she moved on with her life, but the article she held in her hand was a visible reminder of her sins. She continued, "Everything happened so fast. We don't know if someone saw us in the car that night or not."

She averted her eyes away from the neatly typed note and read the attached copy of a newspaper article. It was dated May 3, 1989.

Pedestrian Struck in Hit-and-Run Accident.

A pedestrian was found severely injured late Wednesday night after a hit-and-run accident in the Benson neighborhood. A few minutes after 10:30 p.m. a male pedestrian was riding his bicycle

*down the 2100 block of Benson Drive, police said.
He was struck by a small-sized dark car, which
fled the scene. Police said the car should have
passenger-side damage. If you have any information, please contact the Charlotte-Mecklenburg
Police Department.*

Lenora closed her eyes. This was over twenty-five years
ago, but the incident clung to her like a vague, unwanted
memory. Charmayne's black Honda Civic was in the
vicinity of this accident and not too far from Lenora's
home. After Charmayne had dropped her off, she walked
in her home too stunned to even care about her mother's
anger for missing her curfew. She wouldn't look into her
mother's eyes, not out of shame for attending a party
instead of a study group, but because only a few blocks
away, she was sure someone had been injured due to
Charmayne's recklessness.

That night she could've blamed her mother's tirade for
not choosing to go back to where Charmayne's car made
contact with something or someone. Instead, she closed
the door of her bedroom and remained awake all night,
wondering why she didn't tell her mother, a nurse, who
could've provided medical attention. Sleep didn't come
that night, nor did she sleep the next several nights as she
monitored what happened to the man on the news.

Most of the time the news was no help with providing
information, because they reported on what was new and
hot. She did eventually catch a news article that stated
the man had been released from the hospital. *Is this him
doing this now? After all this time? Why?*

Lenora reached for her bag underneath the desk.

Charmayne yelped, "What are you doing? We need to
figure this out."

"Didn't I tell you to keep your voice down?" Lenora glared, and then turned to pull her phone out of her bag. "Last week at Pastor Jeremiah's funeral, I received this text message." She scrolled through her phone and showed the message to Charmayne.

Charmayne looked at her, and then read the message. She clutched her shirt and stared back at Lenora. "What? Did you tell anybody about this yet?"

"No. I'm still trying to process these messages. A few hours later, my son and his girlfriend were involved in a hit-and-run accident."

Charmayne tilted her head to the side. "You said messages. Have there been more?"

Lenora responded, "I received a similar text message a few days later right before Keith was being approved to be discharged from the hospital. I tried to call the person back. A man picked up and asked me. 'How's Keith?'"

Charmayne opened her mouth, and then snapped it closed again. She began to rub her arms like she was freezing. "Lenora, that's crazy! It's a coincidence. I mean, you certainly don't think someone purposely tried to harm your son."

Her face felt warm. Lenora placed her hands under her chin. "I don't know what to think. I thought this was a prank . . . until I heard the man's voice."

"You didn't recognize the voice either?"

Lenora eyed Charmayne. "Either?" Her brows furrowed as she observed the way Charmayne had wrapped her arms around her body. Her friend, in all her bravado, was visibly trembling. Lenora picked up the article on her desk and stretched out her arm toward Charmayne. "This wasn't the first time you received something like this. You've had someone contact you on the phone."

Charmayne twisted her hands. "That's how it started. The phone. I picked up the phone, and I knew someone was there. For several days, they wouldn't say a word. I was almost ready to change the number, and then one day I heard a man's voice ask, 'How do you think it will feel to lose everything?' This all started a few days after Daddy died."

The silence that swarmed down on them was almost deafening. Lenora sat back in her seat and clutched the arms of the chair. "Are you seriously telling me you've been getting threats like this for almost three months? Why haven't *you* said anything? Surely, you went to the police by now."

"No."

Lenora stood, forgetting to keep her own voice down so no one would hear her outside the office. "Why?"

Charmayne snapped, "Because I was trying to figure out the identity of this person. It wasn't until today when I got this envelope I realized this is someone from the past. Someone who is holding this accident over my head. Our heads, I guess."

Charmayne gulped as tears flowed down her face. She sputtered out her words as her shoulders heaved with emotion. "I've been driving myself crazy because it's like the whole world is against me since Daddy died. The mayor, the council, the other day I thought you and your husband had turned on me too."

Lenora walked from behind the desk. "Okay, calm down. We'll figure this out. You've been getting threats for almost three months, and it started after Bishop Hudson's funeral. I started to get strange text messages after Pastor Jeremiah's funeral."

Charmayne took deep breaths. "Why would someone do this now? What's so significant about sending threats after these funerals?"

Lenora shook her head. In her mind, she knew Bishop Hudson had made several enemies. There was no way there was any connection to Pastor Jeremiah. After all, the message came to her, not Jonathan.

Something else was still bothering Lenora. *Why am I being targeted?* That means someone knew she was a passenger in the car that night too. Lenora paced. This made no sense. She stopped pacing and turned to Charmayne. "You never told me what you told Bishop Hudson about the damages to the car."

Charmayne frowned. "What does that matter?"

"It matters a lot. Someone might have connected the damage to your car to the accident. That's basically what they are trying to do with Keith's accident last Thursday. Parts of the other car were left on the road and also left damages on Keith's car. Technology today is way more advanced than twenty years ago, but the damages on your car back then still had to be suspicious."

Charmayne rubbed her hands through her hair, making it stand up like a punk rocker. "So, why wouldn't someone come forward back then if they suspected my car was in this accident?"

Lenora narrowed her eyes. "Don't you think it's odd that someone would threaten you after your father's death?"

"What are you saying?" Charmayne looked at her.

Lenora walked toward her friend. "I'm going to ask you again. What did you tell your dad about the car? I know you had it fixed by the time graduation came because you were driving the car."

Charmayne's voice trailed off. "I don't remember. I said I hit something, but it was too dark to see."

"Did you tell him where? You know these things have to be reported to insurance. What other details did you give?"

"Will you stop? I'm telling you the only two people who knew exactly what happened were you and me. When my dad took the car to get it fixed, I'm sure there was nothing to report other than his daughter was reckless with the car."

"No. You're trying to make this some big secret between us, but it's not. Somebody has targeted me and possibly my family. How does this person, whoever they are, know that I was in the car with you? How do they have these details?" Lenora sighed deeply. "If you only had had the decency to stop and let us check out what happened that night."

Charmayne snapped. "Me? You were always the Goody Two-shoes. Why didn't you go back if you felt so guilty? For crying out loud, the man didn't die. He spent a few days in the hospital, and as far as I know, he recovered. It was so long ago."

Lenora dropped her hands to her side. "Because I felt this insane need to protect you. You were scared of your father, which I still don't get. We were out obviously doing something he wouldn't have approved of. Now someone thinks it is past due time we pay for our sins."

Charmayne grabbed her bag. "I'm sorry for what happened. You may not believe that, but I am. I realized I acted as a child, and . . ." Charmayne's voice trailed off, and she held her head down.

In all the years she had known Charmayne, Lenora rarely saw this side of her. The mean, spoiled girl she called friend genuinely looked apologetic. But what struck Lenora even more to her core was the fear on Charmayne's face.

Charmayne lifted her head. "I'm sorry, Lenora. I will take care of it for both of us." She opened the office door and closed it behind her.

The world tilted around Lenora. She leaned against her desk, conscious of her fingernails being pressed into the palm of her hand. The ten years after graduation when she had no contact with Charmayne had its trials, but not the kind of drama that came from being around Charmayne. Lenora's mother never liked Charmayne, even if she was a preacher's daughter.

Something ain't right about that girl. Lenora could hear her mother's voice as if she was standing in the office. Her mother would've been so disappointed in her. Sure, the injured man had recovered, but that didn't make it any better because Lenora had gone on with her life, never stepping forward to let someone know what happened that night. She was just as bad as Charmayne.

Their whole friendship always seemed to be based on protecting Charmayne. The patterns were always there even after they befriended each other years ago to plan Charmayne's wedding that never happened. Lenora was pretty sure Bishop Hudson had something to do with why Charmayne cancelled her wedding plans. As a teenager, Lenora was afraid of him. When the man walked into a room, he could command attention from anyone with his six foot three stature and booming Barry White voice.

Charmayne feared her father, but her fear wasn't enough to quench the rebellious spirit. Even now as an adult, Charmayne was fighting to control the situation. What exactly was Charmayne planning to do? *Do we have a clue about who's doing this to us?*

What puzzled Lenora was the length of time that had passed. Why after all this time did someone want them to pay? Lenora knew where she should start, but before she researched what happened to the injured man, she would need to decide how to confess her past transgressions. Confession was good for the soul, but should she tell Jonathan and her sons now or wait?

Someone knocked at her office door. "Yes?" Lenora called out.

Candace opened the door. "Hey, everything okay? The girls and I are set with the dresses."

Lenora smiled and stuttered. "Good. I will be right there to confirm dates for everyone to pick up their dresses." As her client and dear friend stood at the office doorway, Lenora realized she prided herself on making a couple's dreams come true. What if an event from years ago now turned her life and those around her into a nightmare?

Chapter Seventeen

Jonathan pulled his Mercedes into the garage. It was good to be home. He promised himself that tomorrow would be an even better day. He was grateful to be home with his family. He looked over at Lenora's Lexus. At least she was home. Jonathan knew as they got further into the wedding season and when Keith returned to UNC, it would become rare when the entire family was together.

Jonathan exited the car and popped his trunk to get his briefcase. He sprinted up the steps toward the side door that led into the kitchen. When he opened the door, his mother, Keith, and Michael were at the kitchen table. He caught sight of pizza boxes on the counter. "Is this dinner tonight?"

Michael was munching on a pepperoni slice. "Mom said order what we wanted for dinner."

Keith had a slice in one hand and held up the other hand. "No complaints here."

Jonathan looked over at his mother, knowing this was not her type of meal. "Mother, is this going to work for you, or do you need something else to eat?"

Eliza shook her head. "I'm fine, Jonathan. I'm just so happy to be with the boys. Now you need to check on your wife to see if she's all right. She came in here and threw her bag down. Seemed upset about something. She's upstairs." Eliza looked over her reading glasses. "Did you do something?"

Keith and Michael stopped eating. Neither son looked at him directly, but Jonathan could tell both of his sons were quietly listening to the conversation.

He responded, "Be sure to save me a piece of pizza, guys. I'll check on your mother. She probably is just frustrated and tired."

Jonathan wondered what could have set Lenora off. He knew she seemed overly upset about him considering a run for city council. Keith's accident had encouraged the paranoia that Lenora often displayed about her boys, especially when they were young.

Before heading upstairs, he opened his office. He considered his home office his sanctuary, where he prayed and prepared his sermons. Jonathan placed his briefcase on the desk and took a deep breath. He wanted to close the door and sink into his leather chair, or better yet, the leather couch he splurged on years ago, but instead, he decided it was wise not to delay the conversation with Lenora.

He sprinted upstairs and headed down the hallway to their master bedroom. Jonathan quietly opened the door and peeked inside. Lenora was curled up on her side of the bed under her favorite blanket. "Lenora, are you okay?"

She turned her face to him. Her eyes were visibly red, and her face was tearstained.

He rushed to her side and sat on the bed next to her. "What's wrong? Please tell me I'm not the culprit responsible for those tears. What do you need me to do?"

Lenora wrapped the blanket she had around her tighter. "This isn't about you."

"Tell me what I can do. Are you not feeling well?"

She responded, "You can't fix everything, Jonathan."

"Lenora—"

Lenora let out a long sigh and closed her eyes.

"Weren't you upset the other night about me keeping things from you? What's this?" He wanted to keep the anger out of his voice, but Lenora was guilty of shutting him out too.

Lenora wiped her face. "I'm sorry, and I feel like a hypocrite now, but I need to process some things alone."

Jonathan frowned. "Alone?"

"Yes, I'm sure you understand."

What can I say to that? He didn't like that Lenora was choosing to deal with whatever was ailing her alone.

Something had been off with Lenora for some time, and Jonathan couldn't put his finger on when the communication in his marriage had started to go awry. There was no need to start an argument. He was too tired. "You know I'm here when you're ready to talk."

She nodded and turned back over on her side.

Jonathan looked at her for a few minutes; then he left and closed the bedroom door behind him. When he reached the bottom of the stairs, he almost collided with his mother. "Mother, what are you doing here in the dark?"

"I just wanted to check to see if Lenora was okay."

Jonathan peered up the stairs. "She needs to rest."

"Are you sure everything is all right between you?" Eliza questioned.

Jonathan went into the living room and sat down on the couch. He stretched his arms across the back of it. "All couples have struggles. I don't need to tell you that, Mother. Besides, how are you doing? It's been one week since we buried Dad."

Eliza looked away from him. "I know. I miss Pastor Jeremiah."

Jonathan observed his mother. Why did she always refer to her husband, his father, as Pastor Jeremiah? They'd been married for forty-four years, but he'd often felt the distance between his own parents. They were the perfect couple, but at home sometimes, he never saw either one of them speak to each other for what seemed like days.

Was that where his marriage was heading? Would he and Lenora last the next twenty years at this rate?

He focused on Eliza as she sat down on the love seat. She held on to her cane and looked at him. "I've been thinking maybe I should return home tomorrow. I don't want to be in anyone's way."

"Mother, you are not in the way. Besides, the boys won't admit it, but they love having their grandmother around to dote on them."

"I appreciate my grandsons. And you're a good son, Jonathan."

It was always nice to be appreciated, even if it was just his mother. Right now, Jonathan wasn't feeling very confident about what was happening in his marriage. He got up and walked to his office. He closed the door behind him and plopped down on his office couch.

Whatever Lenora was going through, he would have to be patient. What was it he told Wes earlier today about his fiancée? Don't push.

He should have advised Wes a bit differently. There was a push they could do. Pray until something happens.

Jonathan slid down from the couch to his knees and began to pray about his marriage and his family.

Chapter Eighteen

Visions of the man with the pale eyes from the funeral disturbed her as she slept. Lenora shot up in the bed, trying to grasp the man's identity and at the same time shake away the dream. Jonathan stirred next to her. She tried to control her breathing by gulping in air. Her husband turned on to his back without waking up. Lenora focused on Jonathan's broad chest rising up and down until she felt her own body calm down from the dream.

She had fallen asleep easily, not hearing when Jonathan slipped into bed. Lenora hated to push him away last night. Everything in her wanted to talk to him, but how could she explain that she was involved in a hit-and-run accident? No, she wasn't the driver, but she certainly didn't insist on finding help or a way to come forward either.

After Charmayne left yesterday, it was hard for Lenora to concentrate on her brides as her guilt rose back to the surface. She was always the one who kept order, but her life was slowly unraveling from a past transgression.

It occurred to her last night as she lay wrapped in the blanket how visible both she and Charmayne were to the public. When Jonathan took over as interim pastor, the role shot their family into the spotlight. Over the past few years, local, state, and even national media had featured stories about the growing church.

It dawned on Lenora that Charmayne was right. They needed to figure out who was behind this. She wouldn't let something she did or didn't do affect her family and the church.

Lenora looked at the clock which read six o'clock. She quietly peeled herself from the bedsheets so she could get herself together. By the time Lenora had taken a shower, she decided she would assign her afternoon appointments to her other consultants. After yesterday, she needed to touch base with Charmayne as soon as possible.

She went downstairs and grabbed her phone from her purse and started to dial Charmayne's phone number, but then she thought it was best to wait. There was no way Charmayne would be up this time of morning. Really, Lenora wasn't ready to be emotionally charged by her friend. She was still trying to process.

About an hour later, Lenora sat at the table with her cup of coffee when Jonathan entered the kitchen. Their eyes met. She said, "Good morning."

Jonathan grabbed a cup. "Is it a good morning, Lenora?"

"Yes, it's a good morning. It will be a good day. Today, I'm taking Candace cake tasting."

"Sounds like fun." Jonathan poured some coffee.

Lenora smiled slightly. "I'm looking forward to something fun." Her husband had no idea how much she needed to distract herself from the thoughts running through her mind.

Jonathan drank from his cup and observed her as if something was on his mind. He finally revealed his thoughts. "Mother thought it might be time for her to go home. I thought you might need some help around the house, especially with Keith getting rest for his rib cage. That boy certainly doesn't know how to stay still."

"He never did. Keith was always into something," Lenora replied. "Even I know the boys are old enough to take care of themselves, but I know it does Eliza some good to be around them." Lenora couldn't believe those words had come out of her mouth.

"Good. I told her she could stay as long as she needed to, and that we were all here for her." Jonathan took a swallow of his coffee.

"Of course." Lenora didn't have the energy to argue with Jonathan's statement. It sounded like he'd already made up his mind about his mother's extended stay. "I'm going to check on Keith and get Michael off to school."

Jonathan drained his coffee and placed it in the sink. Then he grabbed his keys. "All right, well, I hope we can talk later." He turned and went out the door leading to the garage.

Lenora stood still and listened to Jonathan start the car. When did they stop doing their morning ritual of kissing each other good-bye before leaving the house? They barely touched each other, and both were guilty of sleeping someplace else in the house other than their shared bed. And when they were lying next to each other, there was a gap of space between them.

Lenora shook herself into motion and began preparing breakfast for the boys. She whipped up some oatmeal, adding cinnamon, walnuts, and cranberries to the lumping mixture. Lenora poured orange juice and placed it next to the bowl of steaming oatmeal. She had grabbed the tray and headed upstairs when she heard her cell phone ring. Trying to figure out if she should take the plate to Keith or answer the phone, she opted to leave the phone.

She balanced the tray and knocked on her oldest son's bedroom door. After she heard him call out, she entered. "Here you go, young man."

"Breakfast in bed. Thanks, Mom. I appreciate this."

"Enjoy! You know the wedding season is about to pounce on me. I wanted to be able to make sure you were set before I left."

Keith winced as he sat up in bed. "I'm good. Yeah, I talked to Rachel. She said her mom and the other women were trying on dresses yesterday. It's cool her mom is getting married again."

"Yes, it is nice to be able to find love again. Rachel and her family have been through a lot, and she really likes Detective Darnell. You are going to love how Rachel looks in her bridesmaid dress. Beautiful!"

Keith grinned. "I bet. I'm looking forward to wearing the tux."

Candace and Angel had shown concern for Lenora after Charmayne left yesterday. She hated that she was so visibly shaken to her clients and friends. Lenora asked Keith, "Did you and Rachel talk about anything else?"

Keith frowned. "No. Why?"

Lenora shook her head "Nothing. Look, I need to get your brother up so he won't be late. You know Grandma Eliza will be here if you need something. She will be glad to help, but don't get too used to this maid service, young man."

Keith grinned. "I don't know. I'm liking this."

Lenora laughed and swatted him.

She left and walked toward Michael's bedroom door. "Michael, are you up?" Lenora listened for a grunt. She opened the door and saw her youngest son still in the bed. She could barely see his head. "Michael, get up so I can get you dropped off on time. I have breakfast downstairs waiting on you."

Michael pulled the comforter all the way over his head.

"Don't let me come over there and have to pull you out of the bed. You are way too old for that. If you intend to drive more, you need to prove responsibility."

Lenora heard a muffled, "All right."

She headed back to the kitchen remembering she needed to check her phone. A Missed Call displayed on the phone alongside a notification that a voice mail had been left. Lenora looked at the number. It belonged to Charmayne. She had wanted to call Charmayne earlier. They needed to talk and figure out what to do together.

She pressed Play on the voice mail, but Charmayne didn't leave a message. *That figures!* She dialed Charmayne's number. The phone rang and rang.

After the voice mail greeting kicked in, Lenora said, "Charmayne, it's me, Lenora. I saw you just called, and I guess we're on the same page. I've been thinking you're right. We need to put our heads together and figure this out. To tell you the truth, and I know you don't want to hear this, but I think we need to let others know. This could have ramifications that we can't control. I'll swing by later this afternoon, so hopefully, you've pulled yourself together after yesterday. Bye."

As she ended the call, Michael entered the kitchen. His jeans were slung just a little too low for Lenora's taste.

"Do you have a belt for those pants? Let me fix you a bowl of oatmeal. You have some time to eat."

"Naw, Ma! I'm good. It would be nice to drive myself."

Lenora frowned. "We have two cars, and your dad is still thinking about getting you a car, but you have to show a little bit more responsibility. Like getting up without me having to practically push you out of the bed. Are you sure you aren't hungry?"

Michael shrugged his shoulders. "I'm good. Let's go."

She eyed him. "Okay. Why don't I let you drive to school, and we'll switch seats when I drop you off?"

Michael nodded and held out his hands for the car keys. Lenora placed her keys in his hands, and then they exited through the kitchen door leading to the garage.

As Michael drove, Lenora would have normally watched his every move, but was distracted with how her meeting with Charmayne would go later. It still felt like Charmayne wasn't telling her something. In fact, Lenora was pretty sure Bishop Hudson was a shrewd man and would have gotten all the details he needed from Charmayne. It was only a month before their high school graduation when the parties and celebrations were plentiful. The Charmayne who would sneak out of the house didn't attend not one party after the accident.

Her car being in the shop wasn't a reason, because Charmayne was known to get around and show up in places she had no business being at long before she had her own car. Lenora remembered Charmayne had the car back in time for graduation. She drove up in the parking lot not too long after Lenora and her mother arrived in time to line up for the graduation march.

Lenora blinked away the memories to focus on Michael as he turned on the right signal. North Valley High School came into view. Her son pulled into the drop-off lane and shifted the gears to park, but he didn't make a move to leave the car.

She touched her son's shoulder. "Mikey, what's wrong?" She knew he didn't really like being called by his nickname, but she glimpsed her little boy in her son's intense brown eyes.

"Mom, are you okay?"

Lenora removed her hand from Michael's shoulders and placed her hands in her lap. "Yes. I just have a lot going on, but you know I'm here for you. What's bothering you?"

"Are you and Dad good?"

Lenora waited a moment before responding. She certainly wasn't expecting that question. Tears appeared in her eyes as she watched her son's face droop. He was waiting for her to say something. Both of her sons had features from their father, but Michael really was the spitting image of Jonathan. She cleared her throat. "Your father and I are fine. Why would you ask that, honey?"

"Something is different, and it's been different for a while."

"It's been an adjustment with Dad taking over the church for Granddaddy, but we are going to be okay. Don't worry about us. Your father and I will be here for you and your brother. Now go inside before you're late for your first class."

Michael took another look at his mom, and then grabbed his bag before exiting the car. Lenora walked around the car and watched her son enter the building. She didn't think her heart could sink any deeper. Her sensitive young son knew something was off with his parents. She could only hope with Keith being away at college, that he hadn't noticed anything either.

Lenora got inside the car and wiped her tears away. She would talk to Michael later. Maybe it was time for her and Jonathan to have a family sit-down. Before she could work on her marriage or ease her son's fear, she had to deal with a situation that could change the way the men in her life viewed her forever.

Chapter Nineteen

Serena placed her bag on the floor by her desk. "It's about time." She reached for the envelope on her desk. It shouldn't have taken this long to get documents that were public record. She thought about returning to Charmayne Hudson's office yesterday to make demands. Serena had no problem stirring up trouble, if needed.

She looked around the newsroom before opening the envelope. If what she thought was in here, she was going to pitch the story to Alan James, her news producer. This was the kind of story Serena would enjoy for many months of investigation and right up to the finale. Would this story lead to someone's arrest, trial, and possible jail time?

The folder that Lance Ryan had given her on Monday was in a locked file drawer. She unlocked the drawer and placed his documents alongside the reports she pulled out of the envelope. With a pencil and ruler, Serena marked both pages to record matching donation amounts.

"Well, I'll be." Her eyes went back and forth from one document to the other. There were some considerable differences. Almost a three hundred fifty thousand-dollar difference on what was publicly reported. *Where did the money go?*

Serena grabbed the papers and stuffed them in a folder. She headed over to an office in the corner of the newsroom and knocked on the door.

"Come in," Alan said. Her news producer looked up from his monitor and leaned back in his chair. As he rubbed his eyes, Alan asked, "What's up with the Cheshire grin on your face, Serena? This better be good."

"Good enough to set a fire under my feet. Take a look at these." She handed him the documents. "Look at my markings and let me know what you see."

Alan picked up his reading glasses from the desk and placed them on the tip of his nose.

Serena sat and tried to keep from tapping her fingers on the side of the chair while Alan digested the figures.

After a few minutes, he eyed her over his narrow glasses. "Are these documents both supposed to represent the funds raised for the Hudson Housing Development Project?"

"Uh-huh." She raised her eyebrow. "Not quite adding up, huh?"

"Is your source to be trusted? Is he saying his report is the original? How did he get it?"

Good question! Serena pondered how to describe Lance Ryan to her news producer. She opened her mouth and snapped it shut. Should she admit that she had some reservations about the guy? If she did, Alan wouldn't let her run with this story. Serena was almost sure there was an underlying reason as to why Lance sought her out to take on this story.

Alan took his glasses off. "Serena, you're taking too long to answer my question. You don't know anything about him, do you?"

She closed her eyes. "He's a bit . . . weird. You have to admit he solidified some suspicions about this widely publicized project. I mean, you saw earlier this week, Mayor Carrington doesn't want to touch this project. He dodged my questions at the press conference like his life depended on it, but he was very supportive of this project until Bishop Hudson's death. I mean, come on, the mayor pulled back for some reason. Suppose something came up after the bishop's death, like some mishandling of funds?"

A thought jolted Serena as she talked. She expressed her thoughts out loud. "You know, the bishop had a sudden heart attack. He was working out deals to move the development forward up until the day he died."

Alan rocked back in his seat. "Whoa, Serena, let's slow down. You jumped to a whole other scenario. I agree about getting to the bottom of why the city council is battling over this hot-button topic right now. That's the real story. We need to be good journalists."

Serena snapped. "What? I pride myself on delivering the facts, Alan. We do have to ask the hard questions."

"Yes, but don't go into conspiracy mode. We have to alert the public to our findings. Do you know how wide and deep the love is for Bishop Hudson in this state, even outside of this state? We need to know more about your source. Not that you will reveal him. But we need to know how he obtained these documents. I mean, what if your source fudged this report, and we shared this with the public? Our heads will be on a platter for reporting erroneous information. You know better, Serena."

Serena did her best to keep her face looking natural, but she wasn't too happy with Alan calling her out as if she was some rookie. She smiled sweetly. "What do you suggest, Alan?"

"I suggest you either get with your source again or if you think you can do this without sparking a hailstorm, visit council member Charmayne Hudson. Ask her questions."

"I met with Ms. Hudson on Monday. She sent me this report four days later."

"So what do you think? She fudged the numbers?"

"I don't know. When I talked to her, she seemed convinced that taxpayer dollars were needed for this development to move forward. She could be oblivious to this report with the drastically higher number of donations."

Alan interjected. "You can't tell with politicians. They want to protect their image. It's an election year, and we know how fun those can be when stories like this become public. See what else you can dig up. If you have something more solid, let's prepare to hit the airwaves with our findings."

Serena stood. "No worries. I got this story."

Alan pointed to her, "Keep me posted and don't get in trouble on this one. You've had a few too many close calls in the past, Serena. By the way, the mayor sent in a complaint about you."

"A complaint?"

"Yes, we'll let Wes cover the mayor's press conferences for a while."

Serena opened her mouth to protest, but Alan held up his hand. "Get to your story, Serena. Bring us something we can actually put on the air."

She grimaced and closed Alan's door behind her. Did she really need him to remind her of her past transgressions? She was known to take a story a bit too far, but she had felt each of those times that it was necessary to push toward the edge. Wes was a really good reporter, but she wasn't too pleased about being pushed out of covering city hall. I guess she finally pushed the mayor over the edge.

Serena headed back to her desk. She was exhilarated by the possibilities of this story, but Alan did mirror the fears she already had. This Lance Ryan fellow could be a problem. Serena thought back to the other day. Lance was lingering around city hall and observed as she entered the elevator with Charmayne. Then there was the creepy elevator ride with him. What was the man's agenda?

She had two choices to move forward with this story. She could either contact Lance to get him to come clean or touch base with Charmayne again.

Charmayne was a big risk. She didn't want to go to the councilwoman with the discrepancies. It could backfire badly. Did Charmayne strike her as the kind of person who would be cocky enough to hide the real financial records? She was the daughter of a prominent bishop. Then again, that same prominent bishop was responsible for generating these fund-raisers. What role did the now-deceased Bishop Hudson play in this scenario?

Serena pulled out her phone and looked for Lance Ryan's number. She found it and dialed.

"What?" Serena pulled the phone away from her ear. She ended the call and dialed again. The same out of service message played. Serena stared at her phone. "Unbelievable."

It didn't take long to figure out which direction to pursue first. Her number-one priority was to locate her missing-in-action source, Mr. Lance Ryan.

Chapter Twenty

Lenora threw her head back and laughed. This was the best she had felt in the last twenty-four hours. She sat at a table in the back of Sweet Dreams Bakery enjoying the burst of lemon flavor in her mouth. The cake's light texture delighted her senses. Lenora smiled at her guests. "So which one do you like?"

Candace giggled and grabbed a napkin from the table to wipe the frosting from her mouth. "Definitely the lemon cake with the lemon filling. Oh my, that was so moist and refreshing."

"I could just eat the buttercream frosting," Angel added.

Lenora arched her eyebrow. Candace continued to slyly include their young friend in her wedding planning ventures. Lenora inquired, "So does this give you any ideas for your wedding, Angel?" She winked at Candace.

Candace returned her wink. "What? You and Wes chose a date and didn't tell me?"

Angel's eyes darted back and forth from Lenora to Candace. She placed her hand on her hip and pursed her lips. "What's going on with you two? Why do I feel like that was a trick question?"

"Trick? No trick." Lenora pointed her finger toward Angel. "More like a nudge."

Candace added, "You don't want to keep Wes waiting forever."

Angel rolled her eyes. "Ladies, I'm getting close to deciding on a date. Wes and I are best friends. I couldn't imagine being with anyone else for the rest of my life. That's a really important step, right?"

Candace piped up. "Definitely. Darnell and I are friends. Friendship is the solid basis for any relationship, don't you think, Lenora?"

Angel turned to her. "Yes, you and Reverend Freeman are an inspiration—the perfect couple."

Lenora's smile faltered. "Well, no one is perfect. We all have our issues, but I know I'm with my best friend."

She was still torn up after her conversation with Michael. Why did it never occur to her that her sons wouldn't notice the tension between her and Jonathan? They never spent quality time as a couple anymore. When the boys were younger, Jonathan and she would try to steal away as often as they could. Those were during the days when Lenora's mother was still alive.

Despite the distance between them, Lenora still felt as if Jonathan was the man for her, and she wouldn't change a thing about her life. Lenora knew she was as much to blame as he. They both needed to be reminded of the friendship that brought them together as a couple.

Candace touched her arm. "Are you okay?"

Lenora observed the concern in both Candace and Angel's eyes. Embarrassed for drifting off into her thoughts, she reached for her notepad on the table. She said, "Of course, I'm sorry. I'm a bit out of it today. This is your time, Candace. So, we have settled on the lemon cake, right?"

Candace ignored her question. "You've seemed troubled since yesterday. I didn't know you were friends with Charmayne Hudson."

"Oh." Lenora sat back in the seat. Memories from yesterday flooded her mind. She responded, "We've been friends on and off since we were little girls. I want to apologize again about the interruption yesterday. I know it didn't look or sound good, but I have always been available for when Charmayne is in crisis mode."

Candace shook her head. "No apologies. I just wondered if you needed to talk."

"Yes, it sounded like both of you were really upset," Angel added.

Lenora felt her cheeks grow warm. She spent her time keeping the men in her life satisfied or making sure her brides were happy. Since her mother died, she didn't share her troubles with anyone. Jonathan was not always available or understanding.

Angel walked around the table and placed her hand on Lenora's shoulder. "Both you and Candace were there for me last year when I found out what really happened to my mother. If I can help in any way, please let me know."

She was tempted to confide in both women about her fears, but instead, Lenora shook her head. "I appreciate you both, but I don't need to burden you with my problems."

Candace observed her for a moment. "Okay. Well, how about a prayer. You think the chef would mind if we use his room for a prayer session?"

Lenora bit her lip. How she needed prayer now more than ever. She stuttered, and then cleared her throat. "I don't think he would mind."

"Good." Candace stood and grabbed her hand.

Lenora reached for Angel's hand, and the trio stood in a circle.

Candace prayed, "Father God, we come to you in the sweetness of food and fellowship this morning. We have laughed and planned for an upcoming joyous occasion. We have a sister among us who is smiling on the outside, but, Lord, you know her pain and her fears. I want to ask for a special blessing of peace of mind, that peace that surpasses all understanding for Lenora Freeman. None of us are alone in our walk. Father, you are there waiting for us and encouraging us to lean on you. We ask that Lenora remember to lean and trust in you, no matter what struggles come her way. She is safe in your arms. Now, Father, we are about to depart, and I ask for traveling mercies for all of us. May your angels protect our coming and going. In Jesus' name."

All three women said, "Amen."

Lenora took a deep breath. Her face was wet from fresh tears that flowed. She wiped her face. "I'm so thankful for you taking the time to pray over me. We're supposed to be here for your wedding."

Candace held out her arms. "I consider you a friend. I do want you to know you can talk to me anytime."

Lenora returned Candace's hug. Then she pulled back. "Thank you."

She reached out to Angel. "You, young lady, I'm looking forward to setting up some cake tasting for you in the future and working with Chef Langston on your wedding cake." Lenora hugged the young woman too.

Angel stepped away. "I'm looking forward to doing this myself. I will be talking to Wes soon."

While Candace and Angel went up toward the front of the bakery to drool over the pastries at the counter, Lenora dropped off Candace's choices with Chef Langston. She smiled at him. "I'm looking forward to you delivering another exquisite cake in about two weeks. I do appreciate you fitting us in so close to the date."

Chef Langston tipped his hat to Lenora. "My pleasure. Always love working with you. You make it all work so easy."

Lenora laughed. She tried, but too bad she couldn't always plan for other areas of her life. She walked toward the front of the store.

Angel commented on the display of pastries in the front. "Mmm, you can hurt yourself in here."

Candace placed her hand on her hip. "Tempting, but I can forget about fitting in my dress if I mess with anything behind that glass."

Lenora, Candace, and Angel laughed as they walked out of the bakery. Lenora waved good-bye as the two women walked toward the parking lot. She watched them climb into Candace's car, and then headed to her own car. There was a rolled up paper sticking out from under her windshield.

Lenora rolled her eyes. She could not stand when people stuck their annoying fliers on her car.

She snatched the paper and looked around for a trash can. When she didn't see one, she unlocked the door and tossed her bag on the passenger seat. Normally, she didn't bother looking, but this time, she unrolled the paper.

Lenora gasped. It was a copy of the same article that Charmayne brought by her office yesterday. The only difference is someone wrote with a black marker across the paper, *"It's time."*

How did this person even know this was her car? Lenora crumpled the paper in her hands and jumped inside the car. She slammed the door shut and scanned the parking lot.

She had such a good time with Candace and Angel. The thought that someone had followed her to the bakery and purposely added this cryptic note to her car sent waves of panic. Lenora began to feel hot and suffocated and not just because she was sitting in her warm car.

She needed to get out of here.

Lenora stuck her keys in the ignition, but a buzzing sound startled her. She hesitated, reaching for her phone. Was her tormentor in the parking lot watching her every move?

She snatched the phone from her purse and checked the screen. Charmayne was calling. She'd tried to get Charmayne on the phone several times that morning.

She answered. "Hello, Charmayne!" Her voice sounded higher than usual in her own ears.

No one answered, but yet Lenora sensed someone was on the phone.

"Charmayne?"

The phone went dead. Lenora pulled the phone away from her ear and ended the call. The crumpled paper sat on the seat next to her. She stared at it like it was a large insect that had invaded her space.

It's time. What exactly did that mean?

She started the engine. An urgent need to go to Charmayne's home rose in her spirit.

Chapter Twenty-one

Lenora gripped the steering wheel as she zipped down I-77 in the left lane. Traffic was heavy as the lunchtime crowd traveled back to their workplaces. She concentrated on the cars around her and sought a way to pass into the next lane. As an opening came in front of a car to her right, she guided the car over until she reached the far right lane. She tapped the steering wheel as she slowed the car down. Her anxious thoughts were almost too much to handle.

God wouldn't give her more than she could bear. She took deep breaths and prayed for the terror in her mind to cease. Finally, she turned on the street leading to Charmayne's house.

Lenora slung the car into the driveway. Before jumping out of the car, she grabbed the crumpled paper and her purse. The loud roar of an approaching garbage truck drew her attention as she opened the car door. She turned away from the truck to focus on Charmayne's home. Charmayne's car wasn't visible, but Lenora assumed the Jaguar was parked in the garage. The silver Jag was a gift from Bishop and while Charmayne had a love/hate relationship with her dad, she gladly accepted the expensive gift. How the bishop could be so flamboyant was always questionable to Lenora.

No doubt, the Freemans had exquisite tastes, but they did linger on the side of sensibility and simplicity. At least Lenora tried. She was raised by a single mother who worked many night shifts at the hospital to support her family and eventually help pay for Lenora's college education. She was simply grateful.

Lenora scanned the neighborhood, noticing there wasn't much movement other than the garbage truck picking up trash bins along the way. As Lenora drew closer to the front door, she stopped before heading up the steps. There was a patch of no grass growing in Charmayne's yard. She stepped a little closer and noticed shoe prints in the dirt.

She shook her head and walked up the stairs. After she rang the doorbell, Lenora remembered Charmayne had a landscape person maintain the yard. The grass appeared to have been recently cut so Lenora wasn't sure why her eyes were drawn to the shoe prints. As she glanced back over her shoulder at the prints, she noted they faced Charmayne's living-room window. *Almost as if someone had been standing in that spot for a while.*

What was taking Charmayne so long to come to the door? Was she even home, and if she wasn't, where was she? It occurred to Lenora that she hadn't heard a single word from Charmayne since yesterday. It was Charmayne who came to her yesterday, upset and reaching out for help. Knowing Charmayne's tendency for soaking her sorrows in a bottle of wine, Lenora was wondering if her friend was passed out in the house. With the cryptic threats she had received and Charmayne revealing similar threats, this was no time for a pity party.

Lenora leaned on the doorbell again. Then she cupped her hands around her face and peeked through the windowpane next to the door. Through the white sheer curtains Lenora glimpsed the hallway. She narrowed her eyes in search of movement.

Movement from the side of her left eye startled Lenora. She stumbled backward from the window and spun around. Her heart was beating fast as she clutched her shirt. Her instincts told her she saw something, but no one was behind her. She glanced down at the shoe prints once more and frowned.

Lenora turned back to the front door and banged on the door. She shouted Charmayne's name. Now she was just making a fool of herself. She stepped back and clenched her hands. This wasn't helping her nerves at all. She turned around and folded her arms trying to figure out what to do next.

Her ears caught a sound. A low, steady rumbling sound. *How did I miss that before?* She turned and walked toward the garage. It sounded like . . .

Horrified, Lenora sprinted over to the garage and yelled. "Charmayne?" She stood on her toes to try to see through the garage-door window. She was tall, but she still couldn't see into the garage. Lenora began to bang on the garage door. How long had the car been running? It couldn't be safe for Charmayne to be running the car inside with the garage doors closed.

Lenora quickly calculated she'd been here at the most five minutes. She ran over to the garden area and searched for an object. Picking up a smooth stone, she threw it. After the glass shattered, Lenora covered her mouth as she clearly heard the Jaguar's engine hum louder.

She might be losing her mind, but she had to get inside that garage. With trembling fingers she reached for her phone from her bag and dialed 911. She prayed that this would all turn out fine. Charmayne would show up, give her a crazy look, and demand payment for breaking her garage window.

An operator interrupted her thoughts. "What's your emergency?"

She answered, "I think my friend is in trouble. She's not answering the door. It sounds like the . . ." Lenora choked. ". . . the car is running in the garage, but the doors are shut tight. That's not good, right? Can you send someone out here? Please?"

"Ma'am, can you tell us your location?"

Lenora had been to this house over the years so many times, but the house number failed to register. She stepped back and looked at the arch over the front door. "203 . . . 203 Quest Drive. Please hurry!"

Lenora ended the call and folded her arms around her body as waves of despair clutched her mind. She chided herself as she thought back to yesterday. What did Charmayne say before she left?

I'm sorry, Lenora. I will take care of it for both of us.

Lenora held her head. "Charmayne, what have you done?"

Or better yet, who did this to you?

Chapter Twenty-two

As Detective Darnell Jackson approached, Lenora was grateful for a familiar face. The handsome detective would be marrying Candace in a few short weeks. Too bad this meeting wasn't wedding related. Only a few hours before, she was enjoying cake samples with his fiancée.

Darnell's voice rolled out smooth and mellow. "I'm so sorry, Mrs. Freeman?"

She scolded. "After all this time, you know you can call me Lenora." She hated the way she addressed the detective, but it occurred to her how wrong the day had turned out to be. This man was a homicide detective. She shook her head. "I'm sorry, I know you're doing your job right now."

He bowed his head, his face was solemn. "It's okay, Lenora. Is there someone we can call for you?"

Lenora stared at him. "No, I'm fine. Is Charmayne all right?"

Darnell hesitated. "I understand Charmayne Hudson came by to visit you yesterday at the boutique."

Why won't he answer my question? "Yes, she came by during the fitting with Candace and the other members of the bridal party." Did Candace mention something to him? Lenora felt compelled to admit. "We did have a disagreement."

Darnell responded back, "Friends argue. It happens." He rubbed his goatee. "Would you care to share what the argument was about?"

Lenora twisted her fingers. "Why is that important, Detective Jackson?" Deep down she knew the answer to her question, but she asked again. "Is Charmayne okay?"

That's when she noticed an official-looking man walk up toward them. Darnell nodded, and the man returned his nod. As he walked by, Lenora saw CSI across the back of his shirt.

This was a crime scene. But it was Charmayne's house.

The neighborhood houses around her seemed to tilt. Or was that her body swaying? Lenora lurched forward.

Darnell caught her. "Why don't we go over here and sit down?"

She let the detective guide her away from the scene behind her over to a bench that sat in the middle of Charmayne's front yard. Lenora remembered this was Charmayne's mother's favorite spot. Rosebushes grew next to the bench.

Darnell cleared his throat. "I really hate to be the bearer of bad news."

Too late. He was only stating the obvious. Lenora held her hands up to her mouth and choked on the lump that had suddenly appeared in her throat. Tears sprang in her eyes as she rocked her body back and forth. "She's dead. I know."

"I'm so sorry, Mrs. Freeman. I mean, Lenora."

A memory of Charmayne's distraught face yesterday appeared in her mind. Lenora focused on Darnell's face. "She was in the car."

Darnell glanced over his shoulder before responding. "She apparently succumbed to the high levels of carbon monoxide."

"She would have never done something like this on purpose."

Darnell eyed her. "Maybe we should go down to the station to talk in private."

"Why do you need me to go to the station?"

"It's just an informal conversation. I would like to know Charmayne's frame of mind."

"You're homicide, but you think she killed herself?"

"Well, we need to determine the cause of death. I can say the manner in which she was found leans toward suicide."

Lenora shook her head vehemently. "Charmayne would never take her own life."

"You seem really sure of that, Lenora."

She held her hands up. "I've known her most of my life."

Darnell frowned. "Sometimes we don't always know people."

"I have been calling her and she . . ." Lenora thought of the phone call she received before she drove over to her house. Was that Charmayne reaching out for help? Lenora didn't know how severe the threats had become, but she knew her friend was scared. What the detective didn't know was there was danger lurking and Charmayne's death may not be so accidental.

"I need to show you something." Lenora pulled the crumpled piece of paper out of her pocketbook and stretched it out. "Someone put this on my car earlier."

Darnell's eyes furrowed as he tried to decipher the text on the paper. "What does this all mean? What's the article about?"

She shook her head. "I can tell you later. When my husband comes." She held out her phone. "She called me. That's why I came here."

Darnell peered at her phone. "You're saying she called you a few minutes before you found her?"

"Yes."

Lenora noticed Darnell kept looking behind her. She turned and saw the media starting to arrive on the scene.

Lenora closed her eyes. *This can't be happening,* she thought. She snapped her eyes open. "I really need to call Pastor Freeman."

Darnell looked at her with questions in his eyes, but he didn't say a word.

"I stand by what I know in my gut. Charmayne wouldn't have done this."

One of Darnell's eyebrows shot up. "Are saying there could be foul play with Charmayne's death? How do you know this wasn't a way for Charmayne to reach out to you?"

Lenora swallowed and folded her arms as though to protect herself. She looked back toward the garage and watched as two men carried out a black bag on a stretcher.

Her body shook as waves of tears flowed. This old secret lay solely with her now. Lenora wasn't sure who or what led to Charmayne's death. What she did know was that it was time to tell the truth.

Darnell touched her shoulder. "Why don't I call your husband and ask him to meet us at the station?"

Unable to answer, she nodded. Lenora realized she was about to test the limits of her marriage. What would Jonathan think of her? This was one of those times when she would have loved to hear her mother's no-nonsense advice. In the back of her mind, she could hear her mother stating her favorite Bible saying, "The effectual fervent prayer of a righteous man availeth much."

Chapter Twenty-three

So many thoughts passed through Jonathan's mind as he maneuvered his car into the Charlotte-Mecklenburg Police Department's parking lot. Something had been going on with Lenora that was more than grief for his father's passing or even Keith's accident. Underneath his wife's usual have-it-all-together exterior, he sensed her interior cracking. He just didn't know what caused it. She was an incredibly strong woman, solid in her faith.

His fear was he had finally pushed her over the edge by keeping his political considerations from her. They had grown increasingly distant since he took over his father's role at Victory Gospel Church.

Darnell's cryptic message on the phone didn't help matters. He said Lenora was all right, but it was important for him to come as soon as possible. Jonathan wondered if the detective had news to deliver about Keith's hit-and-run accident. It would be a relief to finally find justice. But why would Darnell have this information? The detective worked in the homicide division. They had been talking to a special detective in the CMPD Major Crash Investigation Unit.

Jonathan halted his speculation and parked the car. He shut the engine off, jumped out of his car, and walked briskly toward the building. Once inside, he asked for directions to Detective Jackson's desk. The detective walked toward him as he approached. He held out his hand to shake Darnell's hand. "Darnell, how are you, my brother? I'm looking forward to officiating your wedding to Candace in a couple of weeks. Time certainly does fly by."

Darnell shook hands with him and smiled. "Indeed it does, Pastor."

Jonathan noted Darnell's smile quickly disappeared.

The detective said, "Unfortunately, I have some bad news today. Will you join me over here in this room? Mrs. Freeman is waiting inside. She wanted you to be here, and I think it's a good idea for you to be here for support."

Support? Jonathan eyed Darnell. "Bad news?"

Darnell extended his arm toward the door. "Please, let's go inside."

Jonathan moved toward the door marked *Interrogation*. The sign on the door seemed so official, and thoughts whirled in his mind about what news he would find out on the other side of the door.

When Darnell opened the door, Jonathan focused on his wife. Lenora had her head cupped in her hands. She lifted her head, and Jonathan noticed her eyes were red and puffy. His heart plummeted, and he walked over to the chair next to her. He pulled out the metal chair and sat down. "Lenora, what's going on? Are you okay?"

"Charmayne is dead." Lenora's voice was flat, like she was numb of any emotion.

Jonathan touched her hands which were cold. He suspected his wife was deep in shock. That woman had always been trouble, but how was Lenora involved? He thought about Lenora's demeanor last night. What events had transpired between Lenora and Charmayne yesterday to result in his wife being so deeply troubled and her friend dead?

Jonathan turned his attention to Darnell for answers. "What happened?"

Darnell confirmed. "Ms. Hudson's body was discovered late this morning by your wife. She called 911."

"My God! Lenora, I'm so sorry." He gripped his wife's limp and clammy hand. Jonathan took a deep breath. His thick eyebrows were furrowed in deep thought. As he tried to grasp the news, a wave of alarm swept over him. He asked, "Why are we here? Detective, why do you have my wife in a police interrogation room?"

Darnell glanced at Lenora before speaking. "Lenora was possibly the last person to see or talk to Charmayne. We need her to help establish a timeline of events leading up to Ms. Hudson's death."

He directed his attention back to Lenora. "There is a voice mail on Charmayne's phone from you, Mrs. Freeman. It sounded like you had something urgent to discuss with her."

Lenora closed her eyes. "I needed to talk to her after yesterday. She was so upset, and I didn't know how to help her. We were supposed to talk and try to figure it out together."

Jonathan asked, "What was there to figure out?"

Lenora pulled her hand out of his grip. "I will try to explain, but it's not going to be easy."

Explain what? His wife has been acting strange enough to concern him, but Jonathan couldn't shake the deep sense of foreboding. "Why do you feel you need to explain anything, Lenora?" He turned to Darnell. "Do we need a lawyer or something?"

Darnell held up his hands. "No, this is just a visit to find out the frame of mind of Ms. Hudson. That's all."

With her eyes focused on the table, Lenora began to rock back and forth in the seat. She rubbed her hands up and down her arms as if she was trying to warm up. The room felt uncomfortably warm to Jonathan. He wanted to reach out to his wife again, but leaned as close as he could, waiting for her explanation.

Lenora had a commanding voice, but as she spoke, her voice sounded like the young girl he had met years ago in college. "Charmayne came by the boutique yesterday. Someone had been threatening her since her father passed away last December." Lenora lifted her head and looked directly at Darnell. "That's why I don't believe she would have taken her own life."

Suicide? Jonathan blew out a breath. "Wait a minute, are you saying Charmayne appeared to have committed suicide? She didn't strike me as being that troubled."

Darnell nodded. "We will investigate before making any definite conclusions about the cause of death. Lenora, what type of threats? Did Charmayne have any idea who may have been sending her the threats?"

Jonathan watched his wife twist her hands. He touched her arm and felt her arm twitch. He pulled away and dropped his hands in his lap.

Lenora grimaced as if she was experiencing pain. "This happened so long ago it really doesn't make sense now."

Darnell said, "Take your time. Anything you can offer will help us figure out what might have happened today. Ms. Hudson didn't leave a note behind that we have found yet, so there are a lot of questions."

Lenora nodded. "Well, the threats seem to focus on an event that took place when we were seniors in high school."

Jonathan frowned. He didn't know Lenora back then, but had run into Charmayne at youth church events on several occasions. He crossed his arms and leaned back in the chair to listen. Maybe he would finally get some understanding of his wife's complicated friendship with Charmayne.

Lenora cleared her throat. "We were on our way back from a party. I kind of knew we were going, but I had told my mother we were going to a study group at Charmayne's house. Charmayne picked me up, but we never went to her house. That in itself was the start of an evening that went very wrong."

"We stayed at this guy's house for hours. I finally told Charmayne I needed to get home. It was already after ten o'clock, and I knew my mom would question why I didn't come back by curfew. Charmayne had been flirting with some guy, and I saw her drink a few beers. I don't know how many she drank, but I have always regretted that I got into the car with her." Lenora's voice faded.

Jonathan peered at Darnell and noticed the detective was scribbling notes on a yellow pad. Jonathan took a deep breath, not sure he was prepared for what Lenora was about to reveal. In the entire time he'd been married to her, he'd never heard this story. Lenora was perfect in every way. She was the good girl your mother wanted you to marry. He never knew Lenora to attend a party when they were in college, so he knew Charmayne had to have been a questionable influence even back then.

Her eyes focused on memories of her past, Lenora continued to tell her story. "The music was loud in the car. I remember Charmayne almost ran into the back of a car. She slammed on the brakes, and it made this horrible screeching sound. After that, we went on as if the close call didn't happen. Then out of the blue something . . . someone crashed against the passenger side. The crash happened so fast, I couldn't tell what we hit. I yelled at Charmayne to stop the car. She did. We turned around and looked out the back window. I thought we had to have hit someone, but Charmayne hit the accelerator and took off."

Tears were running down Lenora's face. "I didn't sleep that night. The next morning I saw a hit-and-run accident on the news. The accident wasn't that far from where we took off. I called Charmayne. I asked what were we going to do and how did she explain the car damage to her dad."

"Bishop Hudson knew about the accident?" Jonathan asked.

"I don't know how much he knew, but I know Bishop Hudson got Charmayne's car fixed pretty quickly. I just couldn't get that night out of my mind for a while, but after I learned the man was released from the hospital, I asked God for forgiveness and thanked Him for saving the man." Lenora's voice choked. "I wish I had said something, but I didn't want to get Charmayne in trouble."

Jonathan's heart broke at seeing his wife's anguish. "I'm sure God has forgiven you. Thankfully, the man healed from his injuries. What I don't understand is what does this have to do with these threats Charmayne was receiving?"

Darnell leaned forward. "Was Ms. Hudson being blackmailed about this accident? It was a horrific thing to do and not confess to at the time, but why now?"

Lenora shook her head. "I don't know. Charmayne told me yesterday that this event didn't come up until a few days ago. For the last few months though, she has felt isolated, like everyone was working against her in some way. You know she had been having trouble with the city council too."

Jonathan remembered the conversation they had about him running for city council. Thanks to Charmayne, Lenora had found out before he had a chance to inform her. Now he wondered how much pressure Charmayne was experiencing and why had it seemed like his friend, Mayor Carrington, had turned against her. Bishop Hudson was very fond of Mayor Carrington. Jonathan tuned back into the conversation.

Darnell appeared deep in thought as he gazed down at his notes. He lifted his head and focused on Lenora. "Did Charmayne say how these threats were being delivered? Certainly we can locate this information if it exists."

Lenora nodded. "Yesterday someone sent her the article about the accident with a note attached. I'm not sure how she received it though. I don't remember seeing any postage on the envelope. We talked about receiving text messages and phone calls."

Darnell wrote rapidly. "Well, we might be able to obtain the numbers and trace them back to the source."

"I think whoever it was, he was using burner phones," Lenora said.

Darnell stared at her.

Lenora folded her arms. "I tried to call back the phone numbers."

Darnell asked, "Using Charmayne's phone?"

Lenora didn't reply immediately, as if she was thinking how to proceed with her response.

A bolt of fear shot through Jonathan as he observed Lenora. "What are you saying? Were you getting threats on your phone?"

His wife flinched. "I received a strange text after your father's funeral." She reached down to the floor and pulled out her phone. Lenora scrolled through a few text messages. She went to pass the phone to Darnell, but Jonathan grabbed it.

He read the message. For the wages of sin is death. Jonathan raised his voice. "Lenora, how long has this been going on and how many?"

Darnell stated, "Pastor Freeman, please lower your voice and hand over the phone."

Jonathan stared at the message once more before handing it over to Darnell. "Why would you not share this with me? This is serious."

"I thought the message was some prank at the time."

Jonathan pointed to her. "Charmayne is dead. I suppose she was getting messages like this too." He rubbed his hand across his head. Then it dawned on him. "Wait a minute. You were upset about Keith's accident. I kept wondering why you seemed overly cautious. You thought this message had to do with the accident."

He was fuming. How could Lenora walk around with this? It was his job to protect his family. Did she really think he was not competent enough to be the man of his house? What really infuriated him was someone out there was sending threats and possibly coming dangerously close to his family. Who was this person?

Jonathan tried to contain his anger. He spoke tightly. "What can we do, Detective?"

Darnell answered, "If you're saying that someone was threatening Charmayne, that definitely changes the direction of her case to a possible homicide. We have no evidence connecting anyone to a crime, though. I'm going to bring this information to my captain, and we will find this person delivering the threats. I guess we need to start by finding the victim of the hit-and-run accident that night long ago. It sounds to me like this person is reaching out to both of you. This is puzzling, though, because if neither of you ever came forward, who knows to send you these threats?"

Lenora shook her head. "I don't know. It could be the man who was hit in the accident, though I can't imagine why he wouldn't have stepped forward back then if he could identify us. After the man was released from the hospital, I never heard about him again."

Darnell rubbed his goatee. "You have any ideas of the date of the accident, Lenora? How about the victim's name?"

Lenora nodded. "I have never forgotten the date. May 3, 1989. I don't know much about the victim other than he was a white guy. I briefly saw him on the news when he was being rolled out of the hospital. His leg was injured because he had a cast on his lower leg. I heard his name briefly, but I can't think of it now. That's all I know."

"Okay, well, if you think of anything else, let me know. In the meantime, we can start there. If there is anyone else who knew, let me know as soon as possible. I will say that the timing is odd, and the fact that it started after Bishop Hudson's death indicates that we need to check into a few things."

Jonathan stood. He grabbed Lenora's elbow as she stood. This time she let him place his arm around her shoulder, but she remained distant. "Thank you, Detective. I will take my wife home now. We appreciate any information you can find."

As they exited the interrogation room, Jonathan pondered how easily Lenora remembered the date of the accident. Did that night still haunt her today? It appeared he wasn't the only one guilty of withholding information.

Lenora's confession was indeed more life-changing. Did the secret lead to Charmayne's death? He and Lenora had some serious talking to do.

Jonathan feared if someone did fatally harm Charmayne and Lenora was receiving threats, did that mean his wife was in danger now? Jonathan had felt useless and torn as he watched his father slowly wither away. How could he stand against an invisible threat that could snatch away the love of his life?

Chapter Twenty-four

Serena had been looking all over for Lance Ryan. She went back to the coffeehouse to find out more information. In her mind, there had to be a reason why this Lance fellow chose this coffee shop. Could have just been wishful thinking.

The tall, blond-haired male barista shrugged. "Sorry, people are in and out of here all the time. Anyone could fit that description."

Serena eyed him. "Really? So, you have a lot of tanned white guys come in here with buzz cuts and hazel eyes ordering espresso?"

"I just take orders."

"Fine. Please pass the description around to your colleagues. This guy dresses real sharp, and he is almost military-like in the way he carries himself." Serena grabbed the cup carrier and walked out. She jumped into the car with her cameraman, Bud Hillman.

Bud asked, "Did you get what you need, Serena?"

"I got coffee." She certainly wasn't having any luck finding her source.

"So, do you have enough footage for your story?"

"Yeah, let's head back to the station." She closed her eyes, realizing she needed to do a better job of getting more sleep.

By the time Bud reached the station, Serena felt like she could have gone home and slept for days. Better than having to face Alan. This story might just be dead before she made any real progress.

Serena left Bud to unload the station's car and entered the building. As she waited for the elevator, her phone buzzed. "Oh great!" Alan had texted her to meet in his office as soon as possible. As she rode the elevator, she guzzled down the rest of her coffee. When she exited the elevator, she crushed the cup, tossing it in the nearby trash container. No time to stop by her desk. She would only get caught up in her e-mail and social media feeds. Serena knocked on Alan's door.

"Come in."

"Hey, Alan. What's up?"

Alan looked up from touching his iPad's screen. "I should ask you that question. Have you heard the news?"

Serena arched her eyebrow. "News?"

"Your girl. Charmayne Hudson. Apparently she was found dead this morning." He frowned. "You okay, Serena?"

Serena had clutched her chest as though the wind was just knocked out of her. "What? When did this happen? She was on my list to go see today."

"Well, you're going to have to cross her off your list. You might want to see if you can make friends with someone at the police department. They are pretty tight-lipped over the details."

Questions scrambled Serena's mind. She was hesitant to tell Alan she had trouble finding her source. Did Lance Ryan have anything to do with this? She desperately needed to get some details. "You know what? I'm pretty sure I know who is working this case."

"Go get us some answers. You know this is going to be the top story tonight."

Serena headed straight to the elevator and entered it. Did Charmayne lose her life because someone was scared she was going to expose them? Why did this Lance guy give her those documents? There was a wall of mystery behind Lance Ryan. She'd been a reporter long enough to determine when a person had a secret agenda. How deadly was *that* agenda?

It took her about twenty minutes of maneuvering through traffic, but she found a parking spot and entered the Charlotte-Mecklenburg Police Department. For as long as she'd been a reporter, Serena always found herself doing crime investigations. If she could have skipped the police academy, who knows, she might have made a great detective.

Serena searched, hoping to catch a glimpse of Detective Darnell Jackson. She certainly didn't want to run into the captain who didn't take too kindly to her dropping by the station. Why did she have such a knack for getting under people's skin? She was just doing her job.

Just as she almost gave up, she spotted the tall, handsome detective. She started to walk toward him, but stopped. There was a couple leaving the room with him. Serena stepped over behind a group of officers to get a better look at the couple. Wait—she knew them. It was Pastor Jonathan Freeman and his wife. Why was Darnell questioning them? She imagined they knew Charmayne Hudson.

Serena waited until she saw the Freemans leave, and then drifted over to the detective. As she approached Darnell, she couldn't help but think, another one bites the dust. She had a very brief time to date the detective and like she always did, she destroyed a potential relationship because of her thirst for a story. Now Detective Jackson was getting married in a few short weeks. All the good ones were always taken.

"Detective Jackson, looks like you will officially be crossed off the bachelors' list in a couple of weeks. Congratulations." Serena smiled and held out her hand.

Darnell displayed his perfect set of white teeth and smirked at her extended arm. "Let me guess; you are here to pick my brain for information about . . ."

"Charmayne Hudson." She finished for him. "So, how does a woman who I just talked to a few days ago turn up dead in her own home?"

"Serena, you know it's too early in the investigation for us to reveal those details to you."

"So you suspect some foul play?"

"I didn't say that, Serena."

"But this is homicide?"

Darnell let out a sigh and sat down at his desk. "Serena, you know the Homicide Unit gets deaths that are not easily explained."

"Are you confident you can investigate what led to Charmayne Hudson's death?" Serena badgered.

Detective Jackson folded his arms. "Look, this woman was well-known and grew up in this community. We are going to look at all the facts."

"What about her city council disputes?"

Detective Jackson narrowed his eyes. He studied Serena for a moment. "Do you have something you should be sharing with me?"

"Why would you ask that?" Serena said innocently.

"I find it curious that you turned the focus of her death to her position as a city councilwoman."

"Well, you're aware she was at odds with Mayor Carrington and a few other city council members. I mean, you're going to talk to them about events leading up to her death."

"Of course. We will talk to everyone who talked and touched base with her recently."

"Did the Freemans help you? Are they friends?"

Darnell sat up in his seat. "That's enough, Serena. I've told you all that I can."

Serena gritted her teeth. "You're going to leave me hanging here with nothing. Come on."

"You know what?" Darnell stood. "You will get your information as soon as we are ready to share with the public. In the meantime, let this woman get a proper burial and memorial before you rake her name over the news with whatever you have been working on."

Serena smirked. "You know I have to get the truth."

"I know you, Serena. Just don't do anything stupid. See you around."

Serena narrowed her eyes as the detective walked away from her. This was not going her way. At the beginning of the week she had high hopes for a really good story. She knew in her gut there was so much going on under the surface. Now she was back to square one.

Or was she? Maybe all the pieces were right in front of her and she just needed to find the connections.

Chapter Twenty-five

Lenora stabbed the fork into the sweet and sour chicken. The sweet tangy taste usually would have excited her taste buds, but she just chewed the meat as if it was a least-favorite meal. She looked over at Keith who was wincing, but making an effort to enjoy his food. Michael held his head down, taking a long time between breaths to scoop more fried rice into his mouth. She noticed her youngest son would occasionally glance up, peering back and forth from her to Jonathan.

It struck Lenora when Jonathan arrived back with the bags of food that it was the first time in a while that the entire family sat together for a meal. Jonathan was at the other end of the table munching thoughtfully on an egg roll. He hadn't looked at her since he came back from the restaurant.

After leaving the police station, she and Jonathan decided to keep a lid on the threats Charmayne had been experiencing. Lenora sensed Jonathan was upset with her for not sharing she had received threats too.

Even Eliza was unusually quiet. She wondered how much he had shared with his mother. Regardless, Lenora was relieved Jonathan had apparently encouraged his mother to keep her sharp-witted statements to herself tonight. After all, what was there to say?

Charmayne was dead. Lenora could still picture the anxiety on Charmayne's face. Was it just yesterday? Why didn't Charmayne say something to her sooner? Instead of being uptight about the city council seat and the possibilities of Jonathan running against her, Lenora didn't understand why Charmayne hadn't confided the threats earlier.

Charmayne was known to take desperate measures, which was one of the reasons why she butted heads with her father. Still, Lenora couldn't believe that Charmayne would kill herself.

Eliza did what she did best: interrupted the silence. "I feel bad for that woman, I really do, but does everyone have to be so tight-lipped tonight?"

Lenora stared across the table at Jonathan. Maybe he hadn't said anything to Eliza.

Jonathan's eyes were tense as he returned her stare. He looked away. "Mother, Charmayne was near and dear to the community being Bishop Hudson's daughter." He wiped his mouth with the napkin and threw it on the table. "It's a bit of a shock and a tragic loss."

Keith sat up. "They're not saying on the news how she died. Does anyone know?"

Lenora noticed that earlier on the news. "They're still investigating."

"So it wasn't by natural causes?" Michael inquired.

Lenora rubbed her forehead. A dull ache had been throbbing in the center of her head since earlier that day. She hoped sleep would make the lingering headache disappear. She stood from her chair. "I'm sure we will find out soon enough." She turned to Keith. "You need to lie back down and get some rest, and Michael, don't stay up too late."

Michael grimaced. "It's Friday night, Mom."

"I know, I know. You don't want to mess your schedule up too much. Monday morning will be here before you know it."

Lenora squeezed her youngest son's shoulders as she left the kitchen. On the way out, she heard Eliza say, "She seems to be taking this death pretty hard, isn't she? I didn't think they were that close."

Lenora shook her head as she ascended the stairs. In a past lifetime, Charmayne and she were inseparable. She grew up beside Charmayne at Greater Heights Church, and they attended the same classes in high school. As adults, they were not the closest of friends. At least, they weren't the kind of friends who went shopping or attended a movie. Over the years, she had questioned if Charmayne was ever really a friend to her.

Lenora entered the bedroom and closed the door behind her. She reached for her nightgown behind the bathroom door. An early bedtime would do her some good although she wasn't sure her thoughts would settle and allow sleep to come. Lenora heard the door open behind her as she tried to snuggle under the covers.

Jonathan entered the room and closed the door. He sat down on the edge of the bed.

There may not be any sleep for either of them. She knew it would only be a matter of time before Jonathan stopped brooding and questioned her more. Lenora pulled the sheets up to her midsection. "Is there something you want to ask me?"

Jonathan snapped back, "Is there something else I should know?"

"Why, do you think I'm keeping secrets?"

"Well, it seems as if I was being accused of that a few nights ago. I just thought maybe we ought to put *everything* out on the table."

She had been worried about Jonathan's political ambitions destroying the fragile pieces of their relationship. What if she had destroyed their relationship all by herself by not coming clean earlier? "Jonathan, I don't have anything else to share."

"What if you get contacted again?"

"Obviously, I will let the police know this time."

He swiveled around and faced her. "I understand about putting the past behind you. I know what happened with you and Charmayne years ago was another lifetime. But—"

Lenora slapped the covers. "But *what?* Why do I feel like you are angry with me for what is not in my control? We don't know what happened to Charmayne. I don't know why I got these strange texts. If it was you, would you have showed them to me or would you have decided you didn't want to worry me?"

Jonathan closed his eyes. "I'm your husband. Your protector."

"You also inherited the pastorship of one of Charlotte's largest congregations and you lost your father. Our son was in a car accident with his girlfriend." Lenora threw her hands up, throwing the sheets back. "Okay, there were some strange texts, and it alarmed me, but I'm a sensible woman who, I admit, has a tendency to become anxious when things happen outside of my control."

Her eyes teared up. "Jonathan, it felt like something was wrong, but I wasn't sure. I have never run to you with every little thing. And I know I sound like a hypocrite now after going at you the other night. I just . . . I don't know what's going on."

She rarely cried in front of Jonathan. Something she learned from her mother. Her mother said never let a man see your tears. Why? Lenora didn't know, but she couldn't hold back being vulnerable right now, because frankly, she was scared to death.

Jonathan moved closer and wrapped his arms around her. "You were an independent woman when I met you. I expect that of you. I know you don't want me to feel burdened, but I don't like feeling shut out either."

She choked out, "You know as much as I know right now."

Jonathan rubbed her shoulders. "We're going to figure this out. Go ahead and get some rest. You're going to need your energy for what's to come."

She tried to catch her breath. "I don't want anyone else to know." Lenora looked at him. "It was a long time ago and the man survived, but I'm ashamed, even now."

"You were young. We all do things we are ashamed of when we're young. One day when you're comfortable, maybe it's a story you can tell that will help someone else get over whatever shame they feel. I'm going to do some work in my office now."

She nodded and watched as her husband stood and walked out of their bedroom. Suddenly, she felt all alone.

He was right. Jonathan was always right. She just didn't know what God's plans were in this case, especially with her friend dead.

Chapter Twenty-six

Jonathan shook himself away from the strange dream. Despite having a night's sleep, he felt fatigued, almost as if he had been physically fighting in his sleep. He lifted his head from the pillow to find his wife scrambling around in the darkly lit bedroom. The only light source was from the bathroom. He sat up and called out.

"Lenora, what are you doing?"

Lenora stood from where she had been bent over fixing her stockings around her feet. She stuck her feet into her heels. "I need to get to the boutique."

He frowned. "Why don't you just reschedule your appointments or ask Sarah to take over for you? I'm sure your clients would understand."

"I can't."

"Can't or you won't?" Lenora could be so stubborn. The crazy thing is she would call him out for doing the same thing.

She placed her hands on her hips and moved her head back and forth. "Okay, fine. I want to go in to the boutique. I need to be there. I need to work with my brides on their weddings. I need to soak myself into pretty fabrics, catered menus, table centerpieces, anything that I can do to not think about yesterday."

Jonathan observed Lenora as if he were seeing her for the first time. Her hair was swept up away from her face. Her dress fit perfectly, and despite the lack of lighting, he was sure her makeup was flawless. She was beautiful and in control of what she knew best. What could he say?

"Okay."

Before she turned the doorknob, he called out to his wife. "Lenora, please be careful. If there is anything strange, don't hesitate to call me."

"Of course." Lenora closed the door.

Jonathan fell backward against the pillows.

After he left Lenora alone last night, he went into his office and sat praying. Being helpless was something he'd fought the entire time he watched his father slip slowly away from him. He knew his marriage was slipping too, but someone sending threats to his wife Jonathan just couldn't tolerate.

He knew there was some fighting he could and should be doing.

Jonathan slipped out of bed to his knees. "God, I may never admit this to anyone, but, Father, I'm admitting my fear to you. Everything in me wants to fight to protect my wife and family. Lord, I can't wrestle with an invisible enemy, and right now, I don't know who or what we are up against. Father God, in your Word, it says no weapon formed against us shall prosper. Please send your mighty angels from heaven to protect us. We ask this in Jesus' name. Amen."

Saturday was the day he prepared his sermons. Like Lenora, he too needed to set aside yesterday for just a little while.

After taking a quick shower, Jonathan went downstairs to the kitchen. He went to open the refrigerator, but heard a slow rhythmic sound coming from outside the kitchen window. He walked to the window over the sink and peeked out. A figure was outside near the basketball net Jonathan had added many years before.

Certainly Keith wouldn't be out there this time of morning with his injuries.

Jonathan slid the patio door open. To his surprise, Michael was bouncing the basketball back and forth. Keith had shot up in height as a freshman in high school. It seemed like it took Michael a little longer to hit a growth spurt. Jonathan watched as his youngest son threw the basketball, making the net effortlessly.

An ex-basketball player himself, Jonathan beamed. "How did I not know we have another basketball player in the family?"

Michael grabbed the bouncing ball and looked at his father. "I'm just playing around, Dad."

"Just playing around?" Jonathan threw his hands out. "That was pretty good. I didn't think you were interested in playing."

Michael shook his head. "I'm not. Like I said, I just was looking for something to do." He threw the ball down. "This is Keith's thing."

Jonathan caught the ball. "Okay. So, Mikey, what is your thing? You're a junior now. Where is your head at about the future?" He tossed the ball back to his son.

"Not getting a basketball scholarship, that's for sure!" Michael rolled the ball up against the wall.

He frowned. Mikey could be sensitive like his mother. "I'm concerned. You are thinking about what you want to do, right?"

"Does it matter?" Michael entered back through the sliding doors.

Jonathan followed his son, then closed and locked the patio door behind him. "Of course, it matters. What kind of foolishness are you talking, boy? Your mother and I certainly will support you with whatever you decide, but having a plan or some goals would certainly help."

Michael sat down in the kitchen chair and looked up at his father. "Can I ask you something?"

Jonathan sat in the other seat. "Shoot!"

"Are you and Mom getting a divorce? Please be straight with me."

"What?" Jonathan was stunned. "Why would that thought even cross your mind?"

"You two are acting different, and you have been for a while. I asked Mom about it."

Jonathan cocked his head to the side. Mikey talked about this with Lenora? "What did she say?"

He shrugged. "She said something about you were both adjusting to you taking over for Granddad at the church and not to worry."

"Does it bother you that I'm so busy?"

"No biggie. You and Mom are always busy. It's just . . . I don't know . . . like last night you were both just tense, not even looking at each other. It's crazy to see you acting like you don't like each other or something."

Jonathan rubbed his hand over his head trying to process what his son was saying. "Son, I love your mother, and I know she loves me. All couples and families have difficult times, but the love is there. Don't worry about us. We are here for you and Keith."

"Yeah, Mom said something like that too." Michael got up from the table.

Jonathan stared at the door long after his youngest son's exit. *What could I say?* Last night he barely spoke to Lenora at the table, but that was because he didn't want to reveal too much information. His mom and the boys didn't need to know what Lenora revealed at the police station.

He was still processing the strange threats himself. It wasn't so much about the car accident from long ago involving Charmayne and Lenora, but the fact that his wife never shared the story or thought it important to share the threats with him. If anything, he received some more insight into why Lenora seemed to be so loyal to Charmayne.

A deep vibrating buzz interrupted his thoughts. He needed to turn his phone off. Jonathan shook his head as he recognized the name on his phone's caller ID. "Unbelievable. Carrington, couldn't you have waited until the woman was buried first to start hounding me?" The city council seat will definitely have to be filled now. Jonathan was unclear about moving in the political arena, especially after the way Charmayne died.

He turned the cell phone off and got up from the kitchen table to start work on his sermon in his office. There was nothing he could do about his circumstances right now, but he had a sermon to preach twice tomorrow, one for the eight o'clock service, and then again at eleven o'clock. The weekend would be busy outside of service too. He had already been called by Reverend Owen Wright, the recently appointed pastor at Greater Heights Church, to assist with the funeral ceremony for Charmayne.

He sat behind his desk and pulled open his leather Bible. The Bible was a gift from his dad when Jonathan decided to attend seminary. The Bible was the New International Version. Jonathan had been complaining about stumbling over reading the New King James Version Bible, which his father loved. He remembered jokingly sharing his surprise with his dad about purchasing a Bible without the "thee" and "thou."

That was his father. A man of a different generation, but quite open to change. It was no wonder the members of Victory Gospel loved Pastor Jeremiah.

Jonathan prayed for guidance before opening the Bible. The pages were wrinkled and creased from many sermon preparations. Oftentimes, he stuffed notes of paper inside the Bible as placeholders, so he didn't often use the burgundy ribbon. He grabbed the end of the ribbon at the bottom and let the Bible fall open to the marked passage.

The book of Hebrews, one of his favorites books of the Bible. Oddly enough, he hadn't studied or preached a sermon from Hebrews in some time. He had read these chapters many times, and even highlighted verses. For some reason, he had bookmarked Chapter Twelve. He read the yellow highlighted verses one and two.

Therefore, since we are surrounded by such a great cloud of witnesses, let us throw off everything that hinders and the sin that so easily entangles. And let us run with perseverance the race marked out for us, fixing our eyes on Jesus, the pioneer and perfecter of faith. For the joy set before him he endured the cross, scorning its shame, and sat down at the right hand of the throne of God. Consider him who endured such opposition from sinners, so that you will not grow weary and lose heart. (Hebrews 12:1–3, New International Version).

After he read and reread the passage, Jonathan jotted down at the top of the notepad *"Running Your Race."* They were all running a race. What did they need to throw off that may be hindering their steps?

He leaned back in his seat and meditated on the question. Sermons didn't become teachable until he felt the passages had ministered to him. He never wanted to come purely from a scholarly level in the pulpit, but wanted to reach people right where they need spiritual healing and encouragement.

Jonathan sighed deeply as his thoughts turned to his earlier conversation with Michael. Had he failed his sons? He was sure his father and mother had their share of problems, but Jonathan couldn't think of ever feeling as if his world would fall apart. His parents were ingrained in his foundation. Jonathan wanted the same for his boys.

Then his mind turned to his wife and their marriage. They'd been in this race together as a couple for twenty years. Jonathan was sure of one thing. He loved God, and he loved his wife, no matter what her past brought to light. They would endure together.

A sharp knock at the door broke his thoughts. He called out, "Yes."

The door swung open, and Lenora walked in.

Jonathan rose up from his chair. "What happened? Are you all right?"

She choked out a "No! They know, they all know."

"Who knows? What are you talking about?" Jonathan asked.

Before he could get any answers from Lenora, outside the office, his youngest son yelled, "Dad!"

Jonathan peered at Lenora. She sank down on the couch in his office. He left her to go find out what was going on near the front of the house. He saw both of his sons standing in the hallway. "What are you guys looking at out there?"

Keith pointed and said, "Look for yourself."

Jonathan went to the door and saw television station vans had parked outside their home. He rubbed the top of his head. What was the media doing at their home? The race had suddenly turned into an obstacle course.

Chapter Twenty-seven

Serena waited patiently at Starbucks. It was Monday, and she was still stuck about what to do with the story she once thought was a sure thing. Her source seemed to have disappeared into thin air and the woman she thought would be exposed had apparently committed suicide.

It was Charmayne's death that really bothered Serena. Charmayne Hudson was a woman of faith. She grew up the daughter of one the most well-known bishops in the area. Serena had her own gripes about church and chose not to go. It wasn't like she didn't believe in God. She knew He existed. It was the religion thing she despised. Her family lived and breathed church. None of that good ole time religion ever helped her. If anything, Serena deeply regretted her scars thanks to an over-the-top religious upbringing.

She grabbed her cup of coffee and drained it; then she went back to her iPad and typed another question in her growing list. What drove Charmayne Hudson to such despair? Was it the legacy of the Hudson Housing Development project left on her shoulders by her father?

Serena thought about Christians in general. The religion was based on forgiveness. She thought most Christians felt they were forgiven for anything they had done. What would make a person with this belief take their own life? Certainly not dipping your hands in a pot of money to use for one's own personal desires. How many people have done that, served their time, and kept on living?

No, there was something else going on here. That unknown factor was driving Serena crazy. With all the speculation around Charmayne's death, Serena had answers dropped in her lap. Or so it seemed. She looked at the time on her phone. Alan would be expecting her to stop by his office this afternoon to tell him how she was going to move forward with the story.

How could she tell her news producer for the first time in her career that she had an uneasiness about proceeding with a story? All weekend she scanned social media to catch a pulse of what people were saying about the events that unfolded at the Hudson home on Friday. The 911 call had been released, and everyone now knew Lenora Freeman had found Charmayne. That explained why Pastor Jonathan Freeman and the first lady were at the police station on Friday.

The Freemans were closed up shut, despite the media showing up on their front lawn Saturday. Serena intended to take a chance on contacting Lenora Freeman. She wanted desperately to get answers. With the beloved bishop and now his daughter deceased, what purpose would it be to expose the financial discrepancies at this time? Clearly, Mayor Carrington and the city council intended to place the development on the backburner. Who would take up the cause of the project that so many people donated their money and time to over the years?

Serena switched off her iPad. She only came in here today to catch a glimpse of Lance Ryan. The man dropped his bomb on her and disappeared. She stuffed her iPad, and then her phone, in the bag. Until Lance surfaced again, she decided she would tell Alan that the story would be on hold for a while. She needed time to investigate, and it wasn't like she didn't have other stories to pursue.

As Serena walked out, she was stopped by a group of women who recognized her. She smiled and listened to them compliment her about being on television. Serena thanked them for their kindness. She did enjoy these types of fans. There was the other type who seemed to have visions of knowing her personally or determined that she should tell a certain story. The crazy type she could do without.

She clicked the button to unlock her SUV and leaned in to place her bag on the passenger floor. As she moved backward, she heard a voice behind her.

"I understand you've been looking for me, Ms. Manchester."

Serena spun around in the seat and fell backward against the seat as Lance Ryan pushed his arm out and gripped her shoulder. Serena's eyes darted around the parking lot, not seeing a single soul. She didn't know if she should scream for help or not. She focused on the man whose pale green eyes were hidden behind dark shades.

She tried to remember to breathe and keep her cool. "Mr. Ryan, you're a hard man to track down. I needed a bit more information. You kind of left me hanging." Serena pointed to his hand on her shoulder. "Can we talk like two people having a civil conversation?"

Lance Ryan moved his hand, but he stared at her from behind the shades.

Serena swallowed. "Like I said, I only wanted to verify information with you. I'm not sure why we couldn't have met in the Starbucks like before and enjoyed another cup of coffee over conversation."

Lance smiled, and then removed his shades. His pale green eyes appeared to glint at her. She felt like he was peering into her soul. Her instinct was to look away, but she held his stare.

Serena asked again, "So, can I ask you some questions?"

"What is it you want to know? I gave you everything you needed to know."

Not everything. "You didn't tell me how you acquired your information. You were right about what Charmayne sent me. The numbers were very different."

Lance leaned forward. Serena shrunk in her seat away from his closeness. He asked, "So, you're having trouble with who to believe? I think it's quite obvious since Ms. Hudson disposed of herself."

It was midmorning, but the sun was sweltering hot. Serena felt her body perspire. "You're saying Ms. Hudson knew that money had been mishandled and that drove her to kill herself?"

Lance folded his arms. "You're disappointing me, Ms. Manchester. You are simply not getting the magnitude of this offense. Isn't it your job to tell the truth?"

"I . . ."

He placed his finger near her face. "I gave you what you needed."

Serena realized what she knew all along. This man was on the side of crazy. It angered her that he would have the nerve to seek her out. "What do you really want from me, Mr. Ryan? What do you get out of me running this story? Don't tell me it's just about justice."

He backed away. She observed how his hands were clenched against his sides. Serena flinched as if she fully expected him to hit her. She had a run-in years ago with a violent man, and this man showed similar signs of having deep-rooted anger. Whatever ate at him, Serena felt in her heart he was close to a breaking point.

Just as quickly as though he had a moment of clarity, Lance unclenched his hands and smiled as if he was having the best time ever. He answered. "I've known the

Hudsons for many years, and I know what they are truly like." He leaned forward. "Believe me, I know all the lies they've told. You need to deliver this story."

She frowned. "Need?"

His teeth were so perfect. Too bad the hate in his eyes didn't match the smile.

"Of course, you need this story and the people need to know the truth about the leaders they have placed on a pedestal. I will be in touch. I look forward to seeing your final report in the near future. Give my regards to Alan."

Serena's mouth dropped open. How did he know her news producer? She hopped out of the SUV and ran to the back, but Lance had slipped away as quickly as he appeared. She jumped back inside her car and locked the doors. Serena looked around the parking lot, still flabbergasted as to how the man could appear and disappear so fast.

She turned the engine on to get the air conditioning flowing in the car. The day had started off on the cool side, but the sun wasn't playing. As she placed her hands on the steering wheel, Serena noticed a tremor. She spread her hands out in front of her to be sure she wasn't seeing things, but she clearly had the shakes. She clasped her hands together.

So, what if she went through with developing this story of financial corruption and the possible connection to Charmayne's death? She knew the story would spark controversy, putting a prominent religious figure in the spotlight. Serena wasn't afraid to push a controversial story out to the public. Wasn't that her thing?

In the pit of her stomach, however, she knew there was something else going on. Lance Ryan had a clear agenda. Serena was more concerned with what Lance would do if she chose *not* to follow his wishes.

Chapter Twenty-eight

Someone had identified Lenora's frantic voice on the 911 call, which resulted in a weekend interrupted by calls from the media. Lenora still couldn't believe reporters had the nerve to show up on their lawn Saturday. She was on her way to the boutique, when she realized that what she needed to do was to turn back around. Her first thought was to go throw herself into work, but that wasn't stopping the thoughts that clutched at her mind.

Lenora wasn't convinced Charmayne had committed suicide and hoped Detective Jackson would find some clue to lead the investigation in a different direction. Knowing she'd reached Charmayne, but not in enough time to stop her friend's death, deeply bothered her. Reminded of the shoe prints she had seen, Lenora wondered if someone else was there before her. It was possible someone could have set up the scene to make it appear Charmayne decided to take her own life. But who?

Despite Jonathan's protests that morning, Lenora decided she would return to the sanctity of her boutique. She normally didn't open the boutique on Mondays, but she had convinced Candace to come in to wrap up her wedding dress fitting. She hung the closed sign and locked the front door after Candace arrived.

Lenora observed Candace as she stood on the small platform in the dressing room. Her seamstress, Dorothy Muller, smoothed out the bottom of the dress to ensure all of the alterations were perfect. Dorothy was one of

Lenora's mother's oldest friends. It was a comfort this morning to receive a hug from the short, heavyset woman who attended Greater Heights Church.

Dorothy had mirrored to Lenora what many other Greater Heights members were thinking. "Child, I'm so sorry about Charmayne. She was a special girl and grew up to be a special woman. I know being a PK and the daughter of Bishop Hudson was hard on her, but her death is such a surprise."

Lenora blinked back tears and focused on Candace. The crème-colored wedding dress hugged Candace's small figure in all the right places and even made her appear taller. Lenora wiped her eyes and walked in the room. "You look stunning. Are you still planning to wear your hair up?"

Like the professional hairstylist she was, Candace pulled her hair up into a quick do. "I think so. I did tell Beulah I was going to leave my hair in her hands. She's the only one I trust to do my hair right on my special day."

"Sounds like a plan because you don't need to be doing your own hair. It's your day to be pampered and dressed up. How does the dress feel?"

"Perfect. Now I just have to not eat for the next week or so."

Lenora waved her finger back and forth. "No, darling. No skipping meals for you. Plus, you're going to need your strength for the day." Lenora put her finger on her chin and looked thoughtful. "I believe you might want some energy left for that night too."

Candace clapped her hands and howled in laughter. "You need to stop. But you're right."

Lenora noticed her bride had teared up. "Honey, are you okay? Is that sadness I see?"

Candace shook her head. "I was thinking about my first wedding."

This wasn't the first time Lenora heard Candace mention her first husband who had been deceased over four years. "You do know Frank wanted you to be happy. Why else would God connect you and Darnell after such heartbreak in both of your lives?"

Candace nodded. "Well, it's certainly not rebound. Lord knows I mourned Frank for so long. It just never occurred to me that he would be replaced."

Lenora shook her head. "Not replaced. Honey, Frank, will never be replaced. What you are embarking on with Darnell is a new beginning."

"You're right. Look at me. I'm really blessed. Can you believe I get to do this marriage thing twice?"

"Honey, you got God's favor all over you."

They laughed.

Lenora said, "If everything is okay, let's let Dorothy get the dress packed and ready for you to take home." Lenora went to her office to finish up some business. About fifteen minutes later, there was a knock at her door. She looked up. "That was fast."

Candace walked in. "Well, I thought I would get out of Dorothy's way. Plus, I wanted to ask how you were doing. Charmayne's funeral is in two days."

Lenora had tried to block out her thoughts and focus on Candace's upcoming wedding details, but she had failed miserably. "I'm still in a bit of shock."

"I can imagine." Candace sat down in the chair opposite Lenora's desk. "When I lost my best friend I was feeling like you."

Lenora knew Candace was referring to her deceased best friend, Pamela Coleman. The defense attorney had been murdered two years before. While the tragedy could have brought more despair to Candace, Lenora and many others witnessed Candace's mission to find the truth. It was through this process Candace almost lost her own life, but here she was today, preparing to marry the detective from her friend's homicide case.

Candace continued, "Lenora, I'm not being nosy or anything. I just feel like you are probably trying to wrap your head around her death, and I want to help. Like today, I know we needed to get the dress fitting finalized, but you could've let Sarah help me. I would've understood."

Lenora sighed. "Work is the best thing for me. I mean, didn't you continue to work in your hair salon after Pamela's death? You and I are the owners of very service-oriented businesses. You know personally taking a day off isn't quite that easy anyway."

Candace nodded. "Believe me, I know. I did go back to work after Pamela's death. Frank's death paralyzed me. I really leaned on Beulah and the other girls in the salon for several months."

"Well, I still like to have my nose in everything. I know I probably drive Sarah crazy, but I just felt like I needed some normal today. My world was turned upside down on Friday."

"You know there's a lot of speculation about Charmayne's death. I'm sorry you had to be the one to find her."

Lenora bit her lip, but she couldn't stop the tears. "I wish I had arrived sooner."

"Oh, Lenora, don't go there. Guilt is so powerful. You have to know you did all you could've done. Thankfully, you went by her home. Who knew when someone would've found her?"

Lenora grabbed tissues from the box on her desk and wiped her eyes. "You're too kind, Candace, and I appreciate you coming to talk to me. I'm going to be fine, really."

"Are you? Who do you talk to, Lenora?"

Lenora stared at Candace thinking she certainly couldn't talk to Jonathan. The gap between them seemed to have widened even more in a few short days.

Lenora really liked Candace. She was more than a client or even the mother of her son's girlfriend. She confided, "You know what's strange is you mentioned Pamela was your best friend. Charmayne and I were not the closest of friends. We had this on-and-off friendship. When she needed me, I was there for her, but I can't always say my needs were reciprocated. Like the way you and I are talking, I never had these types of conversations with Charmayne."

Candace tilted her head. "It sounds like there was something that kept you loyal to her. I think she probably valued you as a true friend, but maybe she didn't know how to express it."

Lenora thought of the last twenty-four hours of Charmayne's life. She admitted, "She was so strong-willed, which is why I don't think she would've done what she did on purpose."

Candace leaned forward. "What do you mean?"

Lenora swallowed, not sure how much to tell Candace. Still, she needed a listening ear. "As you know, Charmayne reached out to me the day before she died. She had been agitated a few days earlier. When she came by the boutique she was the most stressed I had seen her in a long time. Since her father's death, she felt like everyone was against her."

"So, you don't think *that* would have made her consider taking her own life? I mean, it sounds so horrible because she grew up in a Christian home and was the daughter of a prominent bishop, but our minds are pretty powerful forces, especially when we focus on the negatives or the trial before us. It's easy to get overwhelmed versus praying and leaning on God for answers. Did Charmayne strike you as being strong in her faith?"

Lenora shook her head. "She had moments. We all do when we get into this superwoman role. We know God is

there, but life gets so busy and we are trying to be perfect."
Lenora weighed her next words carefully. "I'm finding it
hard to believe, but Charmayne grew up under pressure to
be perfect, and she rebelled. As she got older, she strived
harder to be the perfect daughter, the candidate, the public
servant . . . she liked to be in control."

Candace asked, "What if she reached a breaking point
mentally? There are so many questions."

Lenora twisted her hands. "Yes, there are a lot of questions, and maybe I'm just in denial." That's what she told
Candace, but Lenora felt strongly that another force was
at work behind Charmayne's death.

Darnell had called her earlier that morning to let
her know there was a considerable amount of alcohol
in Charmayne's system. That meant the investigation
would probably lean toward suicide via carbon monoxide
poisoning as the final cause of death. It wasn't looking
too good, and Lenora could only hope Darnell dug up
something from the past or followed the leads from the
threats.

There had to be evidence in Charmayne's home and
her phone. What about the shoe prints by Charmayne's
living-room window? Who did they belong to?

Lenora grabbed another tissue. "Candace, I appreciate
you listening to me."

Candace stood. "Please give me a call if you need to
talk—anytime."

Lenora also stood, and then walked around the desk.
"I really want you to concentrate on your upcoming
wedding, but I do ask that you keep us in your prayers."

The two women hugged.

Lenora broke away from the hug and said, "Now, let's
get your dress." She walked Candace back down the small
hallway to the dressing room. Dorothy grinned as they
walked in and went to the other side to pick up the long
white box. "Here you go."

Candace wrapped her arms around the box. "Thank you, Dorothy. I can't wait to wear this. I will feel like a queen that day."

Dorothy clapped her hands. "You certainly will."

Lenora reveled in the joy on her friend's face. For some reason, she was reminded of Charmayne standing in the boutique, also holding the box containing her wedding dress. The dress that her complicated friend never wore.

There were so many questions.

Lenora willed the swirling questions to disappear from her mind. "Let me walk you out, Candace."

As they approached the front of the store, Lenora heard the tiny bell on the boutique front door jingle. Dorothy must have taken the lock off the door because no one was supposed to be able to enter today. Lenora stopped in her tracks as she recognized the person who just entered her boutique.

Chapter Twenty-nine

Serena tore out of the parking lot, conscious that she had a potential madman watching her every move. She was no closer to figuring out what Lance Ryan hoped to gain by her pushing the story, but from what she interpreted, he'd spent some time around the Hudsons. In what capacity, she would dig into later.

To refocus her thoughts and gain a bit of the story's direction she found herself pulling up in front of Lenora's Bridal Boutique. Her gut told her to look more into Charmayne's death which was still very newsworthy. It appeared that Lenora came into work although there weren't many cars in the parking lot. Serena exited her SUV and looked around to make sure no one else had the same idea she had. It was public knowledge that Lenora had called in to 911 to report finding Charmayne. It was obvious the woman was in a garage with the car running.

When Serena arrived at the boutique's door, there was a closed sign, but the lights were on. She pushed the door, and to her surprise, it opened. As she entered the boutique, Serena felt a physical need to gag. A former romantic, the sight of all these wedding dresses only reminded her she had no happily ever after going on in her life.

Weddings were overrated. All that money people spent for one day. She was thankful that the two marriages she had were pretty much debt-free. Unfortunately, being battered by the first husband and cheated on by the second one had left her bitter. Serena only needed a man long enough to get what she wanted, and then she was done with him.

Still, like every other woman, she had wanted that fairy-tale wedding. She reached out to touch a form-fitting gown covered in lace, but quickly jerked her hand away when she heard voices. She watched as Lenora and Candace Johnson approached. Lenora laughed, not looking grief-stricken at all.

Serena bit her lip as she observed Candace. She folded her arms and watched the two women laugh. Candace was holding a large white rectangular box that Serena guessed held a wedding dress.

She was happy for Darnell, and like her coworker, Wes, she thought both men had met special women. Women that she was nothing like at all. Despite her looks, Serena had always been a bit too abrasive and aggressive. It didn't take long for her to spoil any good thing that came her way.

Both women stopped at the sight of her. Serena quickly unfolded her arms and let her arms fall to her sides. She looked directly at Candace, who returned a cool stare. For a brief moment, Serena forgot she was happy for Darnell and remembered her very brief interaction with the hot detective. Obviously, Candace wasn't too happy to see her.

"How did you get in here?" Lenora frowned.

"The door was open."

Lenora glared at her and walked over to the door to check the lock.

Serena took a deep breath and moved toward Candace. She pointed at the box. "Hello, Candace. I see you're about ready for the upcoming wedding. Congratulations."

Candace's mouth turned up slightly. "Thank you, Serena. I hope you're doing well."

"Always," Serena responded back.

Candace leaned in. "Don't upset, Lenora. Please!"

Serena stepped back and let Candace pass by.

Candace walked toward Lenora. "I will see you at the rehearsal dinner next Friday."

Lenora stopped fiddling with the lock and turned to her. "I'm so glad this dress worked out for you. You're going to be beautiful. I will check with the caterer about the rehearsal dinner."

"I appreciate you. I may try to make it to the funeral on Wednesday. Take care of yourself. Don't run yourself down." Candace glanced back at Serena, and then left.

Lenora locked the door, and then yanked on it. She turned around and walked back toward Serena.

Serena hadn't realized how tall the woman stood. She wasn't a shorty herself, but Lenora stood close to six feet in heels. It struck her how regal she appeared in the pants suit.

Lenora placed her hand on her hip. "This really isn't a good time, Ms. Manchester. I've been trying to dodge media all weekend. If I entertain at least one of your questions, can you leave a sister alone?"

Serena had never met or talked to Lenora Freeman before, but she had to admit she liked her no-nonsense attitude already. "I'm sorry to drop in on you like this, and I do appreciate your willingness to let me ask some questions. I really want to help the public get an under-standing of Charmayne Hudson's untimely death."

"Well, that may not be possible." Lenora walked away.

Serena frowned and followed behind her. "Why do you say that?"

Lenora kept walking until she reached what seemed to be the office area in the back. "Because it's looking pretty obvious that she may have killed herself. At least that is what the police seem to want to conclude."

Serena followed Lenora into an office. Lenora went behind the desk and glanced at her. Serena noticed a flicker of sadness appeared in Lenora's eyes. There was something else odd about the way Lenora looked away briefly.

Lenora continued to stand behind the desk, so Serena stood across from her. She noted Lenora didn't seem to know what to do with her hands as if she was calculating what to do or say. "Ms. Manchester, you know what? This really isn't a good time."

"Serena. You can call me, Serena. I'm so sorry for appearing insensitive. I understand Charmayne was a friend and you found her. I know that has to be very traumatizing. I'm surprised you're here at work."

"Yes, it has been, and it doesn't do me any good sitting around at home. I did that all weekend. What do you hope that I can help you with?"

"Well, I met Ms. Hudson last week, and she was very adamant about moving forward with the Hudson Housing Development. She wanted to honor her father's legacy. It has clearly been reported how she fought for this project only to run up against opposition at city hall."

Lenora frowned. "Yes, she was dedicated. I don't understand why you need to talk to me. I really don't deal with politics. I knew Charmayne was passionate about being a public servant."

"That's just it." Serena decided to sit down in the seat. "I have a difficult time believing that this woman killed herself."

Serena watched Lenora flinch. She watched as tears flooded her eyes. Lenora reached up to wipe the wetness away. She reached over for a tissue and sat down. "That's because she wouldn't have killed herself."

Stunned, Serena tilted her head. "Let me get this right. You don't believe she committed suicide."

Lenora continued to wipe the tears that escaped down her cheek. "The woman who I'd known most of my life didn't cave easily under difficulties. She was a fighter. Her dad was a fighter. I have unanswered questions that will haunt me forever. Now Ms. Manchester, this has been a difficult few days and I don't know if this conversation helped you, but I need some space. I will walk you out."

Serena couldn't argue with the woman. While she appeared strong minutes ago, her resolve had crumpled. When they reached the front of the boutique, Serena said, "I'm really sorry for your loss. I do have one more question, and I promise you I will then leave you alone."

Lenora eyed her like an irate schoolteacher.

Serena rushed forward with her next question. "Does your husband plan to take Charmayne Hudson's place on the city council? I heard that he planned to run."

The grief displayed by Lenora was replaced with a hardened look as the woman narrowed her eyes. "As I told you before, I don't deal with politics, and I certainly won't share my husband's plans. That's for him to share. If you want to do justice to Charmayne in your story, please remember to acknowledge her work and passion for the community she grew up in and loved. Now I have to deal with some mile long to-do lists for upcoming weddings."

Serena nodded and opened the front door. She heard the door lock after it closed. While their conversation was brief, she felt enough conviction in Lenora's voice to solidify her thoughts.

Before Serena could get to her car, she heard the patter of someone's shoes walking fast behind her. She spun around, fully expecting the madman from earlier to pounce on her, but instead, she was met by an older woman. The woman stopped and clutched her shirt.

"I'm sorry, child, I didn't mean to scare you. I just wanted to catch up with you before you left." The older woman glanced over her shoulder at the boutique.

Serena took a deep breath to get her bearings back. She looked down at her hands and realized she was shaking. "Who are you?"

"I'm Dorothy. I work in the boutique as a seamstress. I'm sorry; I overheard some of your conversation with Lenora."

Serena folded her arms and stepped forward. She towered over Dorothy, who was short and wide in girth. Serena couldn't tell the woman's age, but she eyed the jet-black hair. It wasn't a wig, so it seemed Dorothy spent a lot of time keeping the gray out of her hair. "Did you know Charmayne?"

Dorothy nodded. "I knew her most of her life. She and Lenora grew up together, and both attended Greater Heights Church."

Serena made note. She remembered Lenora mentioning she had known Charmayne most of their lives. "How would you describe their friendship, or better yet, what did you think of Charmayne?"

"I can answer both of those questions. Lenora has always been the stable one, Charmayne while she was the PK, or preacher's kid, she couldn't help but get into trouble. Anyhow, I just really came out here to tell you, I agree with Lenora."

"Agree?"

"That Charmayne wouldn't have killed herself. That girl loved life. Nothing fazed her." Dorothy looked around like she expected a boogeyman to show up. She moved closer to Serena. "I think she got caught up in something she shouldn't have. The day she came here, I overheard her say to Lenora that she had been receiving threats."

Serena widened her eyes and turned her attention back to the boutique. Now Lenora didn't mention that to her, although she could tell the woman was thinking carefully about her answers. "Do you know what kind of threats or who?"

Dorothy shook her head. "No, no, but I think someone needs to know. Lenora has always protected Charmayne. Growing up, Lenora's mother didn't care for her daughter being friends with Charmayne at all. I just feel bad for Lenora having to go through this. Anyway I need to go before she notices I'm out here talking to you."

"Thank you, Dorothy. Um, can I call you or talk with you again?"

Dorothy hesitated. "I guess. I don't really have anything else to add. I just want people to stop bothering Lenora. I also think it would help if someone found out the truth. Then maybe Lenora won't feel so burdened by Charmayne's death."

Serena watched the woman enter the boutique, and then headed to her vehicle. Once inside, she locked the doors and started the engine. So there was something suspicious about Charmayne Hudson's death. If the deceased city councilwoman was receiving threats, was blackmail involved? Lenora didn't share that information with her, but did she tell the police? Surely Detective Jackson was investigating.

Threats. A staged suicide. A possible murder.

Serena drove off thinking about the man who brought this story to her a few weeks ago. She could visualize Lance Ryan playing a role. How and why, she didn't know, but that was what she was determined to find out.

Chapter Thirty

Last night she woke up in a state of panic. Again. Lenora's body was wet with sweat and her damp nightgown clung to her. She felt like she hadn't slept at all even though the clock displayed five hours had passed since she climbed into bed. Her energy level was depleted from the running wheel of questions. As complex as her relationship with Charmayne could be sometimes, she grieved for her friend.

With much effort, Lenora had pulled herself from bed knowing today was the day she would officially say good-bye to a lifelong friend. She applied extra concealer under her eyes to hide the darkness. At one point she caught Jonathan staring at her in the mirror. She saw his concern, but she moved to applying her foundation without acknowledging his silent questions.

A few hours later, Lenora peeked out from under her hat. The funeral services had been held at Greater Heights Church. The turnout was not as great as for Bishop Hudson, but many came to pay their respects to his daughter. The entire service was a blur to Lenora, like how she felt after driving a familiar route and had arrived at her destination. She remembered feeling unsteady standing in her three-inch pumps.

Her mother-in-law had sat next to her while Jonathan sat in the pulpit with other clergy. Eliza stayed by her side as they sat in the Greater Heights fellowship hall. Lenora found her mother-in-law's presence strangely comforting.

Eliza inquired, "Dear, are you okay? You don't look well."

Lenora felt like her head was in a fog, and it seemed like every so often the room shifted. Or was she just that tired? She rubbed the back of her neck and moved her head from side to side. "I think I'm coming down with something."

"Honey, there's nothing wrong with taking it easy. You've been pushing yourself when you probably need to be sitting down. I know this has been rough on you."

She was touched by Eliza's motherly attention. "Don't worry. I'll be lying down soon." Lenora searched the crowd for Jonathan.

She finally spotted her husband. *What is he doing?* Lenora didn't know why Jonathan was talking publicly with Mayor Carrington. It could have been harmless banter since both men were friends, but she knew the mayor had an agenda. They had just buried Charmayne, but Lenora had no doubts a replacement for the district seat on the city council would be swift.

Who knows? Maybe that reporter was on to something. Maybe Charmayne's death was about political reasons. That might explain why someone would dig up an old crime to hold over Charmayne's head.

She couldn't think. Lenora placed the back of her hand against her forehead. Her skin felt warm and clammy. She was almost afraid to stand, but she needed to get out of the room which was full of people. Various conversations were going on around her and she tried to be polite when she could, but Lenora really wanted to leave.

"Eliza, I'm going to visit the sanctuary for a while."

Eliza frowned. "Do you want me to come with you?"

"No, I need some time alone. If Jonathan comes looking for me, let him know where to find me."

Lenora folded her arms and walked out of the fellowship center. Greater Heights Church was much older than Victory Gospel Church. It was a large church, but it had a historic structure to it compared to the contemporary architecture of Victory Gospel.

She pulled the walnut wood doors open. The sanctuary was quiet and lit only by the sunlight coming through the stained glass windows on each side. It was almost four o'clock and she could tell the sun would be descending in just a few hours. Lenora stopped for a few moments to revel in the deep silence. This was the church she grew up in, where she first met Charmayne in Sunday School. She stepped across the plush deep burgundy carpet, which she was sure had been changed over the years although it seemed to be the same.

After marrying Jonathan, Victory Gospel had become her church home. The last time she had been in the Greater Heights sanctuary was for Bishop Hudson's funeral. Who would have known a little over three months later his only child and daughter would be memorialized in a funeral.

Lenora kept walking until she came to a pew. Like others, at the end of this pew was a small gold plaque. A few years back she had purchased a plaque in memory of her mother and brother. Lenora leaned over and rubbed her hands across the gold plate. She sat down. There were some sweet memories. Her and Charmayne hanging out on the pews, giggling and poking each other while Bishop Hudson preached until his face was wet with sweat. When they were little girls, Charmayne had been sweet and gentle. As she grew older, Charmayne's tongue grew sharper. Lenora smiled and thought Charmayne was always sharp and smart.

You were too smart to do something like this.

Why would Charmayne come to see her the day before asking for help? Lenora thought again and again. There was nothing in Charmayne's demeanor that indicated a last good-bye. Usually when Charmayne said she would take care of something, that meant she was going into fight mode.

The sanctuary door behind Lenora swung open, startling her. She turned around to see who had entered the sanctuary. From a distance, Lenora could tell a male figure was standing at the doorway.

As the man approached, Lenora caught her breath. It was the same man she saw a few weeks ago at Pastor Jeremiah's funeral. He had crossed her mind on several occasions. She stood to leave, but had to grip the back of the pew in front of her as her head swam.

The man stood a few feet from her. "Are you okay?"

Lenora touched her right temple, which was throbbing. She spoke to the man, but her words seemed to sound slurred. "I'm sorry I'm in your way. I just needed some time away from the crowd."

The man came closer. "Of course not. This is the best place to draw comfort. Grief is a heavy load to bear."

Lenora shook her head. "You look so familiar to me. How do I know you?"

The man shrugged. "I knew the Hudsons well. I worked on a lot of projects with both father and daughter, in particular the Hudson Housing Development."

Lenora observed the man as best as she could. With her heels on, she stood eye to eye with him. He stood with his arms to his side and almost stood as if he had a superstraight spine. She didn't know what to think of him. Mainly she was trying to keep herself from falling apart in front of a stranger. "Okay. I thought I saw you a few weeks ago at Pastor Jeremiah's funeral too."

"Oh yes. He was a great man of God. I'm sure he's missed."

"Yes, he will be missed." A brief wave of nausea passed over her. She placed her hand over her stomach.

"Do you need some help?" he asked.

Lenora shook her head. She was startled with how close the man seemed to have come to her. Maybe he thought she was going to fall over. She certainly felt like the floor wasn't steady. Oh no, that was her legs.

"I'm fine. I don't think I caught your name."

"Lance."

"Lance, it was nice to meet you. It hasn't been a good day, plus I probably should be getting back before my husband comes looking for me."

"Pastor Jonathan Freeman. Another great man of God. It is so good to be around such genuine people."

Not sure what to think of the man's compliments, Lenora nodded. The sanctuary felt very stuffy all of a sudden. She walked down the aisle hoping she wouldn't stumble. By the time she pushed open the door, she realized she was feeling out of breath. Before she let go of the door, she turned around to take a quick look at the man named Lance.

He stood in the same spot where she had left him, watching her.

Not knowing what else to do she waved and let the door shut.

She really didn't feel good. Before heading back toward the fellowship center Lenora decided to veer off toward the restroom area. Thankfully, no one was in the restroom. She pressed her manicured fingernails into her hands but the pain didn't help her ignore the wave of nausea sweeping through her stomach. She stumbled toward the sink and grabbed a few sheets of paper towels. With a bit of effort, she twisted the cold water faucet on.

Once the paper towels were wet, Lenora squeezed the excess water and blotted her face.

The coolness briefly stopped the world from spinning. As she looked into the mirror, she thought about the man she'd just met. Lance. This Lance was a very strange guy. Why was it that the only time she saw him was at a funeral? And why did she have this feeling of familiarity about him, as if she had encountered him in her life before?

She was pretty sure he ran from her before when she spotted him at Pastor Jeremiah's funeral. Why did he come to her this time?

Suddenly, the mirror seemed to swirl in front of her. Lenora reached out to grab the sink, but she was unable to stop her descent to the tiled bathroom floor. She cried out as she hit the floor on her behind sending her legs sprawling. Lenora though she heard the bathroom door swing open as she slipped into a realm of unconsciousness. She didn't know who came in, but she sure needed help. She could see Lance's face as her eyes closed. Her last thought: *it's almost as if he's stalking me.*

Chapter Thirty-one

Serena sat in the television van with Bud reviewing interviews. They had covered Charmayne Hudson's funeral. Serena carefully questioned members of the Greater Heights Church congregation about their thoughts on the Hudson Housing Development project. With both the bishop and his daughter gone, she was curious to know if anyone was going to take up the reigns. The majority consensus from the people was the project may never see the light of day.

As Bud scrolled past footage on the editing monitor, Serena kept her eye on the clips she wanted to include in the evening lead story. She leaned forward. "Wait, go back. We definitely want this clip included." Serena couldn't help but feel smug about catching Mayor Carrington on camera with his deer-in-headlights look.

Earlier she had observed the mayor making his rounds, including talking for quite awhile with Pastor Freeman. She had questioned him as he was exiting the church. "Mayor, now that Charmayne is no longer on the city council, what's going to happen to the Hudson Housing Development project? You know many people in this church helped build up that funding for several years."

"I don't know the answer to that—"

Carrington had tried to take off down the sidewalk, but Serena walked beside him, keeping up with his pace. She knew the mayor was going to share the same rhetoric, so she spat out her next question and shoved the microphone in his face. "Mayor, I understand that there are some questions swirling around about the project. Is it possible that some of the funds are missing?"

The man stopped and whirled around, forgetting he was on camera. "Where did you hear that?"

Now as she watched Bud play back the footage, she observed the mayor's reaction. "Do me a favor; play that slowly forward for me."

Bud raised his eyebrow. "Are you serious? We got to get this piece edited if you plan to make the six o'clock broadcast."

"I know. Humor me; play the mayor's footage really slow."

Serena smirked as the mayor's eyes stretched wide in horror. It was only a split second when played in real time, but she got what she needed. The mayor was holding out on what he knew about the Hudson Housing Development. In her gut, she knew he'd pulled back from that project after Bishop Hudson's death for a reason. Now she just needed to dig a little deeper.

What if Charmayne Hudson wasn't the only one receiving threats?

"Okay, let's end the story with the mayor's interview. I'm going to freshen up my makeup before we go live."

Bud had already started making adjustments on the time. "Got it."

Serena stepped down from the back of the van. She was already dressed in a suit from attending the funeral. Her feet were about to kill her in those heels, especially the right foot which was sporting a nice-size blister by now. She opened the passenger door and pulled out her makeup bag. Before pulling the zipper on the bag, she paused. She was very aware of the hairs on her arm.

Serena spun around. No one was behind her.

Realizing her shoulders were practically up to her neck, she tried to relax, but the muscles around her back were tense. Ever since that Lance dude had snuck up on her, she had grown paranoid about watching her back. She doubted he would show up with her cameraman around. Up until now, she'd only met with Lance alone since the man seemed to be particular about keeping his identity a secret.

The thing was, she really wanted to know his identity. As much as she didn't want to run into him again, she knew there was a hidden story. Lance made a mistake showing his creepiness to her. Serena wanted to expose him and whatever plan he had brewing.

Serena popped open the powder and dusted her nose and forehead for any shine. She pulled out her lipstick and touched up her lips. By the time she brushed through her hair, Bud was out of the van getting the camera set up. She looked at the clock on her phone. It's about that time. Once she hit the airwaves at six o'clock, she fully expected to see social media heat up as others tried to clamor for her story.

Serena peeked inside the back of the van and saw the evening news opening. Tonight, Wes was sitting in the anchor seat. She smiled. That young man might as well say that position would be his as soon as the longtime anchorman retired in a year.

She had always been told she had the looks to be in the anchor chair, but Serena enjoyed hitting the streets, day or night, tracking down interviews and getting video footage. It was actually more exciting these days, because she was snapping photos on her phone and iPad, sending them to Twitter and Instagram.

Speaking of photos, she pulled out her phone and pressed the photos icon.

Bud yelled, "Hey, what are you doing? We need to check the sound."

"Okay, I'm coming." She pocketed the phone. Serena went over to Bud and placed the earpiece in her ear. She could hear Wes's smooth voice talking about a fire burning out in California. Serena stood in front of the camera and held the microphone to her mouth. "Sound check 1, 2, 3." She kept talking as Bud played with the camera. He finally gave her a thumbs-up.

Just in time she heard Wes say, "Now, tonight, we want to turn to a story that is affecting the local community, in particular, District 2. The daughter of the late Bishop William Hudson was laid to rest today after she was found unconscious in her home last Friday. Charmayne Hudson was pronounced dead on arrival at the Charlotte Memorial Hospital. Today, many came out to pay their respects. Tonight, Serena Manchester is live on the scene at Greater Heights Church."

Right on cue, Serena held the microphone up to her mouth. "Thank you, Wes. Behind me is the historic Greater Heights Church. Today was indeed a sad day as Charlotte lost one of its daughters, a woman who won the hearts of the community when she was elected as the youngest African American woman to Charlotte's City Council. Let's look and see what some people had to say about Ms. Hudson."

Serena listened as she heard the first of three interviews roll through. As far as she was concerned, these interviews were for fluff. The interview that would really hit home would be the man who insisted on isolating Charmayne on the council. In her ear, she heard the coolness of Mayor Carrington's voice turn to an odd strangle as he tried to respond to her question.

That wouldn't be the last time the mayor would hear from her. She knew next time he would probably be ready. Serena couldn't wait to hear the mayor's next response.

She composed herself as her turn came up again on camera. "There are many people in this community who will not forget the Hudson legacy here in Charlotte. We will keep you updated on what the city intends to do to keep this remarkable woman and her well-loved father's efforts alive."

Serena waited for Bud's cue. The story was done. She hoped wherever Lance was that he saw the story and he got what he wanted. People would be talking about and questioning the validity of the Hudson Housing Development. She placed her headset and microphone in the van.

It wasn't a cool spring night, but she was warm from the mad dash to get the story ready for airing. She removed her suit jacket, but before placing it on the seat, she remembered her phone.

A few hours back, she took and tweeted snapshots of an ambulance showing up at Greater Heights Church. It took her some maneuvering through the crowd, but apparently Lenora Freeman had collapsed. Remembering her meeting with the woman at her bridal boutique, Lenora was struck by the fact Lenora didn't think Charmayne had killed herself. The information shared by Dorothy meant that the first lady of Victory Gospel was still protecting her friend. Why? Was it worth it now that her Charmayne had been laid to rest?

What really concerned Serena was not Lenora's collapsing, but the person Serena had inadvertently caught in a photo. She flipped one photo forward and stared at Lance Ryan. Lance had been standing in the crowd watching Lenora being loaded into the ambulance.

Bud came up behind her. "Hey, you ready to head back to the station?"

Serena flinched, almost dropping her phone. She bounced the phone back and forth in her hand until she got a good grip. It's a good thing she didn't drop it. Serena had been known to break quite a few phones. "Bud, you scared the crap out of me."

Her cameraman shrugged. "Sorry! I just wanted to see if you were ready to go. Why are you so jumpy lately?"

"No reason, let's go." Serena looked back at the church. There was a storm cloud in the distance. They needed to make it back to the station before they got caught in a spring downpour.

She climbed into the van and shut the door. Serena peered down at the photo of Lance again. She remembered he was hanging around the day she was at city hall. Why was he there that day? Was he hanging around Charmayne? He couldn't have known that Serena was going to run into Charmayne and talk to her.

By the looks of the photo, she felt like Lance was more than just another spectator in the crowd. It could have been Serena's imagination, but the man seemed really focused on Lenora Freeman.

Whatever Lance Ryan's intentions, Serena was determined to find out now that she had his photo on her phone. Lance had slipped in and out like some phantom, but somebody out there had to know this man.

Chapter Thirty-two

Lenora rolled her head from side to side. Her eyes were still closed, but she could tell she was not in the king-size bed she shared with Jonathan. She slowly opened her eyes, but shut them tight as the bright lights caused tears to form. Her throat was dry and scratchy. She placed her hands over her parched lips and coughed over and over again.

"Lenora, take it easy. I'll get the nurse to come back in."

Nurse? Recognizing Jonathan's voice in the midst of her disorientation, she peeled her eyes open. Lenora focused on Jonathan's face. She opened her mouth to speak, but her vocal cords were unwilling to cooperate. Lenora struggled to sit up.

"No, stay put. You're very sick right now. I'm glad Mother found you. You had a very high fever."

She remembered being warm and lightheaded. They were at Charmayne's funeral. Lenora sank back against the pillows. Now she was starting to remember.

A nurse entered the room. "Mrs. Freeman, how are you? It's so good to see we got that fever down for you."

Her dry, parched throat allowed her voice to break through. "I'm thirsty."

The nurse nodded. "You were pretty dehydrated." She poured water from a plastic pitcher on the side table and handed the paper cup to Lenora.

Lenora began to gulp, but the nurse said, "Take sips. Easy, there you go. The doctor administered some heavy-duty antibiotics to help you clear up the rest of that nasty bacterial infection."

Lenora nodded and handed her cup back to the nurse. "Thank you."

When the nurse left, she looked over at Jonathan who sat quietly. He eyed her, and then stated, "I know you don't want to hear this, but you need to slow down for a while."

"I can't—," she began to argue.

He held up his hand. "Sometimes we don't have a choice when God wants us to sit still. I know it's a busy time for you, but you do have employees who can step in and help. Right now, you have a lot on your plate. I think you're taking Charmayne's death harder than you're willing to admit."

At the mention of her friend's name, Lenora's eyes watered. "That's because she shouldn't have left us so soon. Certainly not *that* way."

Jonathan leaned over and grabbed her hand. "I'm sorry. If I could change the events of these past few days I would. Right now, we can do something about making sure you get back to being 100 percent. Take care of you. You're not going to be good for anyone if you aren't well."

She knew Jonathan was right. Ever since Charmayne's death, Lenora had pushed herself so she didn't have to deal with the stark reality.

After getting the doctor's okay, Lenora was discharged from the hospital. As she walked into her home with Jonathan holding her elbow, she felt grateful. Grateful to see the photos of her family on the wall. She hadn't had time to jump into her annual spring cleaning, but their home was still welcoming and a safe haven.

"Let's get you upstairs. Straight to bed for rest." Jonathan guided her toward the stairs.

"Mom, you're home!"

Lenora turned around to see Michael and Keith both get up from the living room to walk toward her. She smiled, proud of her almost grown men. "I'm home. Need to get some rest, especially according to Dr. Jonathan Freeman here." She eyed Jonathan, who nodded.

After she entered her bedroom, she slipped into an old favorite, her light blue cotton nightgown. It wasn't the most attractive attire she had for sleepwear, but the long flowing fabric was what she needed to wrap up in under the covers.

"Do you need anything before I go?" Jonathan had come in the room. He placed her bag on the chair by her side of the bed.

The nightgown was not one of his favorites although she couldn't tell by his face. All she saw was concern. Lenora pulled the covers up underneath her neck. "Where are you going?"

"Tonight's Thursday. You know it's a busy night at Victory Gospel. Choir practice and other meetings. Members like to know I'm around."

Lenora nodded. "Sure. Just don't catch what I have."

He laughed. "I will keep that in mind. I don't think any of us want what you have. You're a real trooper, though." Before he walked out the door, he turned around. "Mother is still here. She will be happy to help, so don't hesitate to reach out."

Lenora sank down under the covers. She felt a bit ashamed knowing her illness was a long-awaited wake-up call for her. She hadn't been feeling well for a few days, but she was used to working through stress headaches. A superwoman she was not, and right now, her eyes were having a tug-of-war. Lenora finally let sleep win. Her dreams were fitful. She was standing inside the sanctuary of Greater Heights Church.

Charmayne was standing up front with her hands on her hips, waving her finger. Lenora tried to interpret what she was saying. All of a sudden, Lenora heard someone calling her name. She stared at Charmayne who now had her hands on the side of her face. Her mouth was opened in an "o" shape, and her eyes were wide. What was she trying to tell her? Lenora spun around and saw a dark figure coming toward her.

Before the person reached her, a persistent knocking snatched her away from the dream. Lenora sat up. Someone was knocking on the bedroom door. She peered over at the clock and realized she had fallen asleep for a few hours. She yelled, "Come in."

Eliza swung the door open. "Girl, you were starting to worry us. In a few minutes, I was just going to break the door down. We need to get some food in you. You've been sleeping too long."

Lenora sat up as Eliza shuffled in the room with Michael behind her. Her son brought her a tray. As he came closer, she saw a bowl of soup with crackers to the side. "Eliza, you didn't have to do this."

"Oh yes, I did. You need to keep your strength up. Girl, we can't have you go downhill like that again. I don't think I've ever seen you that sick before."

"Yeah, Mom. I hope you feel better soon." Michael set the tray over her lap. The steam from the soup rose up to her nostrils. She inhaled the chicken noodle soup.

Lenora caught her son's hand. "Thanks, honey. I'm doing exactly what I've been told. Rest."

"Good, well, I need to head out."

Lenora frowned. "You're going out on a school night."

"Study session. Don't worry, I'll be back on time."

"Okay." Lenora wasn't familiar with Michael having any friends in a study group, but she didn't always keep up with him like she used to do when he was younger. Back then, she knew every playmate and friend her sons had in their lives.

"You need to eat now." Eliza pointed to the soup.

"Yes, ma'am." Lenora wasn't used to Eliza being quite so motherly toward her either. She was sick and out of commission for twenty-four hours, and it seemed like everyone was acting out of character. Or maybe she just always took care of everything.

She took the soup spoon lying on the side and scooped up a few noodles and pieces of chicken. After she blew on the soup, she chewed and swallowed the hot, salty broth. Lenora looked up to see Eliza watching her closely.

"Eliza, I'm okay. I'm not going to fall completely apart."

"That's good to hear because I wasn't sure. No, I shouldn't say that. You're a strong woman and a woman of faith. Always have been."

Did her mother-in-law just compliment her? Lenora swallowed a few more spoonfuls of soup. "You sound like you're worried about me."

"You just lost a friend in a pretty horrible way."

Lenora let the spoon fall in the soup. She stared down at the soup in silence.

Eliza continued, "You know, Charmayne was strong-willed, very much her dad's daughter. Now her mother, Mrs. Valerie Hudson, was very meek. Poor thing."

Lenora eyed her mother-in-law, wondering where the story was going.

Eliza sat on the edge of the bed. "At least I used to think that. One day I saw Bishop Hudson raise his hand and strike Valerie across her face. The way he did it, I doubt it was the first time. I confronted her about it, and she said she could take him. She just didn't want him to ever take anything out on Charmayne."

Lenora responded. "She protected her daughter."

"Valerie was the referee, sometimes taking not just licks from him, but being the brunt of Charmayne's lashes too."

"Why are you telling me this, Eliza? Is this supposed to make me feel better?"

The old woman let out a deep sigh. "I don't know. I guess what I'm trying to say is when Valerie died, I regretted that I didn't stick up for her more. You know? You stuck by Charmayne through some thick and thin. I just don't want you to feel any guilt."

Lenora shook her head. "I don't. Guilt is not what I feel. I feel confused."

Eliza tilted her head. "Why? Because she took her own life?"

"It wasn't something she would ever do."

"Honey, we don't know what goes on inside of other people's minds."

"I'm tired. I appreciate you coming in here to help comfort me, but I've known Charmayne all my life. She could be a mental case sometimes. She would be quick to knock back a bottle of wine, but she didn't do this."

Eliza stared at her. "Well, if she didn't kill herself, what are you saying, Lenora? Are you sure this isn't just denial?"

Realizing she probably said too much, Lenora thrust the tray forward. She knew Jonathan hadn't shared with his mother anything she'd told him last Friday in front of Detective Jackson. She needed it to stay that way until she could figure out some things. "Maybe I am. I need time to process."

"It's okay. Anyone can understand, and you need to grieve." Eliza reached for the tray.

"No, you don't need to carry this back downstairs. Michael can come for it later."

"I'm sorry, Lenora. I really am. I hope God gives you some peace."

Lenora nodded and looked away. When the door had closed behind her mother-in-law, she grabbed the tray and set it on the floor beside the bed. She struggled until her foot hit the floor, and then she wobbled over to where she saw Jonathan place her bag.

Now that she had time on her hands, she was going to figure out exactly what was going on. She knew people wanted her to believe Charmayne took her life, but they simply didn't know what she knew. Lenora pulled out her phone and her daytimer. With a pen in hand she climbed back in bed.

She used to use her day-timer to jot down appointments. Now, since she was using the calendar on her smartphone more regularly, she had plenty of empty pages in the day-timer. She jotted down the first time she received a text, Keith's accident, the second time she received a text, Charmayne's visit to the salon, and finally, events leading up to Charmayne's death.

What about the man with the pale green eyes? She vaguely remembered talking to him, but Lenora couldn't recall any of the conversation.

Darnell had kept the copy of the crumpled article that had been left rolled up in her car windshield wipers. He did say he would process prints, but she knew enough from cop shows that there may not be viable prints. She'd touched the paper herself.

That didn't matter. What mattered is she needed to find out who else knew. She jotted down Charmayne and the bishop's name. Then her name.

So who else knew what happened that night? Lenora wrote down "The Victim" and circled the words. Detective Darnell told her he would look into what happened to the man who was struck that night. Was it really him doing this? Did he even see their faces in the dark that night so long ago? Did the injured man catch a glimpse of the license plate?

If he found out who had hit him, why didn't he come forward back then? For what purpose did it serve a person to sit on information for this many years?

Chapter Thirty-three

Jonathan welcomed Wes and Angel into his office. He had an early start. This couple's session was one of many appointments he had on his plate. Somehow, his Monday morning had been overbooked. Ironically, he had been scolding Lenora for not resting and being overly busy.

His wife seemed to be making a full recovery, but it was hard to tell what was going on in her mind. Lenora wasn't used to being still. He was pretty sure once the lingering effects of her illness vanished, she would be right back to her routine. But he knew deep down something had changed about Lenora since Charmayne's death.

Jonathan focused on the couple in front of him. "Have a seat. I'm so happy you were finally able to make it. I need to apologize to both of you, though. It seems like I have been overbooked a bit, so this session is not going to be as long as the others. I want to mainly meet and answer any questions you might have."

Angel held up her hand like she was in a classroom.

Jonathan said, "Yes, Angel."

"I hope it's okay before we start if I can ask how's Lenora doing."

He nodded. "Certainly. She's resting, or she should be resting."

As he sat down, Wes looked at Angel, and then back at Jonathan. "Well, we weren't sure if we should cancel the appointment or not. We were so worried about Mrs. Freeman."

Jonathan nodded. "She is out of the woods. Apparently she caught a bug and tried to work her way through the illness until her body gave out on her. Plus, losing a friend in the past few days hasn't been easy either."

Angel said, "I'm so sorry for her loss. I remember the day Ms. Hudson came in the boutique. She looked really upset and like she needed to talk to Lenora."

"It's a shame about Charmayne. Lenora is taking it pretty hard. We can only pray time will heal those wounds." Jonathan pointed his index fingers at both of them. "Right now, let's talk about you two lovebirds. How are the plans for the wedding date coming?"

Wes grinned. "We have a date now."

Jonathan raised his eyebrows. "This is good news."

Angel giggled. "I know, I know. Everyone was waiting for the big announcement. We've decided to have a New Year's Eve wedding."

"That is going to be very different. I know Lenora is going to be really excited to work with you on the details of your wedding," Jonathan responded.

"I know, I can't wait, but—" Angel stopped and looked over at Wes.

Wes finished by saying, "We know there are some issues we need to work on, which is why we are here with you for our first premarital counseling session."

"There are a lot of issues we will certainly discuss in the next few sessions. Some of the major ones that lead to the breakdown of a marriage are finances, starting a family, finding time to be intimate, and a real big one is communication. You two are off to a good start by understanding you need to begin this marriage by first getting an understanding of each other."

Wes nodded. "I know I have a tendency to move full speed ahead."

"And I like to take my time and be cautious," Angel added.

Jonathan smiled. "There is some truth that opposites do attract. In your case, it sounds like you two certainly complement each other. Now what you may need to learn, and this is a lifelong process, is the art of listening. It's real easy to want to get our point of view across, but we must have a listening ear to what the other partner needs."

He opened a folder on his desk. "Let's start this session off with this questionnaire. I want both of you to take a copy and fill it out individually. We will go over the answers with each other at our next session."

Wes and Angel both took the stapled documents from him.

Jonathan stood. "I look forward to the next four sessions with you so we can make sure to get you married by New Year's Eve."

"Thank you, Pastor," Wes and Angel said together.

Jonathan laughed. "I like the unity already."

As he walked the couple to the door, he added, "I do want you to keep something in the back of your mind. In this society, it's real easy to throw in the towel when life hits you hard. You are walking into a covenant relationship that includes God. Divorce is not an option."

As Jonathan closed the door behind the couple, he thought about some of the issues he brought up to them. Some of those were relevant to his marriage right now. How had the communication between him and Lenora gotten so far off? Of course, he knew the answer to that. In some ways, they almost led separate lives whenever they left the house. He had to admit he hadn't been there for Lenora like he should.

Jonathan picked up his cell phone from the desk. Lenora was doing well about staying away from the boutique, but he doubted she was truly resting. He dialed their home number. The phone kept ringing. He ended the call and looked at the time. It was 12:30 p.m. Keith had finally returned to UNC. He thought his mother mentioned she would be with some old friends that afternoon. Michael was still in school.

He dialed Lenora's cell phone this time. Still no answer. Where was Lenora? She was supposed to be resting at home. Jonathan sighed and said out loud, "Woman, please don't tell me you've decided to go to the boutique. It's Monday." He clicked over to his favorite contact list and dialed the bridal boutique's number.

"Hello, this is Lenora's Bridal Boutique."

Jonathan frowned. "Hello, Sarah, this is Reverend Freeman. You didn't open the boutique today? If so, I was wondering if you have seen or heard from Lenora today?"

"Hi, Pastor Freeman, I haven't seen her or talked to her on the phone today. I actually came in thinking she would be anxious about this weekend."

"Really? So she hasn't called to check in."

Sarah said, "I know, right? That's pretty unusual. Is Lenora okay? She sounded almost like herself last Friday. I hope she hasn't relapsed or anything."

"I certainly hope not. She has been slowly getting better. I hope she is just getting some rest. It's almost lunchtime so I'm going to go by the house to check on her."

"Okay, well, let her know everything is just fine. I have triple-checked."

"Will do. Thanks for holding down the fort for her, Sarah."

Jonathan ended the call. Something didn't feel right to him. He didn't know why, but Lenora's illness and collapse, plus the untimely way that Charmayne died, had shaken him more than he wanted to admit. He'd tried not to bother Lenora as she grieved in her own way for Charmayne, but the threats and the situation from years ago bothered him.

He looked at the clock and his calendar. Jonathan grabbed the calendar and headed out to the secretary's desk. He hated to make changes at the last minute, but he felt a strong urge to go home and check on his wife.

She was his priority at the moment.

Chapter Thirty-four

Lenora was officially sick of being sick and tired. It wasn't so bad over the weekend with Jonathan and the boys around her, but today everyone was gone. Even though she didn't work on Mondays, Lenora yearned to return to the bridal boutique after five days of being a prisoner in her bedroom. This morning for the first time in about a week, her eyes opened at her usual six o'clock wake-up time. She had promised Jonathan she would continue to rest. It was the least she could do. Everyone had rallied around her.

Jonathan had dressed and left to tend to church duties earlier. With no place to hurry to, she made a decision to not touch her phone. Like some addict, she found herself picking up the phone, staring at the dial button. There was so much to do and so much lost time.

Lenora knew that over the last few days, she had probably driven Sarah, the caterer, and other vendors crazy with her henpecking. She threw her phone and organizer across the bed. Then she nestled her head against her pillow and tried going back to sleep, but her thoughts seemed to heckle her more today. Lenora wrapped her arms around her head in frustration and yelled out, "God, I can't deal with this." She climbed out of the bed determined to tarry by the side of the bed on her knees. As she prayed, guilt pressed down on Lenora, almost suffocating her. Thoughts of failure tried to crush her desire to talk to God.

She wasn't on her A-game. Candace's rehearsal dinner was coming up on Friday. Was everything really in place for the wedding on Saturday? What really happened to Charmayne? Did Lenora miss the signs?

A voice whispered, *"Therefore do not be anxious about tomorrow, for tomorrow will be anxious for itself. Sufficient for the day is its own trouble."*

Lenora paused, hearing her own breath. The planning for Candace and Darnell's wedding was done, and it was all in God's hands. Why was she beating herself up with guilt? She had done the best she could despite obstacles over the last few weeks.

She started the prayer again, and this time, she thanked the Lord for healing her. She certainly felt close to death. Then she prayed in earnest for protection over her husband and her sons. Lenora lifted up Ms. Eliza's name and thanked God for her mother-in-law's kindness. She started to rise from her knees, but then she was overcome with a deep wave of warmth.

Cast all your anxieties on me, because I care for you.

She had cried tears for Charmayne, but the tears that she shed now were different. Like a faucet, the tears flowed. Her body heaved as she poured her heart out. The last time she cried like this was at her mom's funeral.

Lenora had been feeling sorry for herself as memories of Charmayne drifted in and out of her mind the past few days. With those thoughts came great confusion and anxiety. Lenora wasn't sure what to think of how Charmayne died, but she drew on a deep comfort in knowing her friend was safe in the arms of the Father.

"Oh, Father God, I do miss my friend. As complicated as our friendship could be, she was my sister. I loved and protected her always. I did, even when I didn't think she deserved it." Lenora rocked back and forth, humming. Eventually the tears dried, and she crawled back under the covers, her body emotionally spent.

She looked up at the ceiling. Keith had returned to UNC late Sunday afternoon. Michael was in school. Before going to the church, Jonathan had dropped Eliza off at the nursing home to do her monthly missionary work. The house was quiet and peaceful.

Almost too quiet.

Every day she'd been home, Lenora had managed to fall asleep during the daylight hours. Taking a nap was so rare for her, and the long periods of sleep were disconcerting. She felt lazy and unproductive, but she sensed her body needed to rest. Even now as her questions to the Lord and thoughts lingered, she could feel the soft persuasive fingers of sleep coaxing her body to relax.

The phone jolted Lenora from her overwhelming urge to fall back to sleep. She reached for her cell phone, but it wasn't where she thought she had put it. Lenora lifted her head and grunted. She forgot. The phone was at the other end of the bed. She shoved the covers off and scrambled toward the phone. She frowned at the caller ID. It read CMPD. Lenora answered the phone. As she said, "Hello," her mouth felt cottony.

At first she didn't recognize the man's voice. "Who's this?"

"Lenora, this is Detective Jackson. I hope I'm not disturbing you. I know you weren't feeling well earlier in the week."

She breathed a sigh of relief, not sure why her heart was pounding in her chest. "Darnell, I'm doing much better. Stress, I guess, from everything. Do you have something for me?" Lenora thought she heard a beep from call waiting. She tuned into the detective's news. Whoever was calling could leave a voice mail.

"Yes, if you don't mind, I thought it would be best if I came to your home. This information may be best shared in person."

"Oh. Do I need to ask the pastor to come home?"

She heard Darnell hesitate. "If you think you need the support, I encourage you to ask your husband to be there with you."

"Okay. I will see you soon, Darnell."

She ended the call. What did Darnell have to tell her? Lenora assumed it had to be about Charmayne. There was nothing she wanted more than to destroy the growing rumor mill surrounding Charmayne's death.

That reporter Serena Manchester didn't help matters. The WYNN reporter had managed to turn people's attention to the Hudson Housing Development project, giving the impression Charmayne had done something illegal. There was a wrong that occurred years ago, but it certainly wasn't what the public thought.

Lenora picked up the cell phone to call Jonathan, but stopped because she noticed the phone's battery was dangerously low. She smiled. She was proud of herself for choosing not to work this morning. What was the point of keeping the boutique closed on Mondays if she wasn't going to fully take advantage of the day off?

She crossed to the other side of the bedroom and plugged the phone in the charger. Then Lenora headed to the shower. Since she was home, she decided to dress in a comfortable pair of pajamas. Why did she have to get sick to appreciate the art of rest and lounging?

A crash from downstairs sent her clutching her pajama top. She stood very still, almost forgetting to breathe. *Was that the door downstairs?* No one else was home but her. She checked the clock. It wasn't quite lunchtime yet, and Eliza said she wouldn't be back until late afternoon.

She hurried over to the bed, shoved her feet into her slippers, and left the bedroom. Outside her bedroom, she leaned over the staircase railing. She listened for the noise, but after a few minutes she decided maybe she had just been hearing things. She shrugged and decided to head downstairs for lunch.

As Lenora descended the stairs, she hung on to the banister. She continued to try to convince herself that the quiet house and her sluggishness were encouraging her paranoia. Once she reached the bottom floor, she peeked into the living room. Somebody had left the television playing. The volume wasn't turned up loud, so whatever she heard before couldn't have been coming from the television. Lenora walked in and grabbed the remote off the coffee table. She switched off the television.

When she walked back into the foyer, she headed toward the front door. Lenora peered through the peep-hole. No one was there, but then again, it wasn't like anyone had knocked or rung the doorbell. She was not a squeamish person and didn't mind being alone, so why was she acting this way? Her stomach growled, remind-ing her she had more important matters, like getting some nourishment in her body.

Lenora turned from the front door and walked back toward the kitchen. As she entered the kitchen, she realized this was first time in a few days she was in her own kitchen, fixing food for herself. As she pulled items out of the fridge, she quickly assembled a ham and cheese sandwich, not sure when Detective Jackson would arrive. She chewed and gulped down a glass of orange juice. She sliced a bit more cheese and placed it in her mouth, enjoying the sharp, tangy taste.

A noise right outside the kitchen caused her to stop chewing. Someone was in the garage. That's when she noticed the door leading to the garage. The doorknob ap-peared to be turning. Sometimes after it rained, the door would stick. Someone was ramming against the door.

Lenora grabbed the butter knife from the counter. Charmayne's face flashed in her mind. She looked at the butter knife in her hand and thought, *What is this going to do?*

She glanced over at the cordless phone across the room. Should she grab the phone and make a run for it?

There was no time. The door burst open.

Lenora screamed and dropped the knife.

Chapter Thirty-five

Serena trailed closely behind Reverend Owen Wright as he walked through the sanctuary of Greater Heights Church. She recalled her conversation with Dorothy, the seamstress from Lenora's Bridal Boutique, and decided the church would be a great place to continue to dig into the Hudsons' history. Bishop William Hudson founded this church, and it was the place where he held very important meetings. While his daughter wasn't in the ministry, Charmayne was regarded as a symbol of pride for many people in the congregation and community.

Ever since the funeral, Serena had spent time reviewing interviews shot before and after the funeral. The people in the congregation really knew Charmayne since many had watched her grow up under her father's reign at Greater Heights, and then branch out to make her path in politics.

It was Monday, and Serena certainly wasn't getting any cooperation from Detective Jackson. He was just as closed lipped as he was over a week ago about Charmayne Hudson's murder.

She knew Lenora Freeman was still tucked away, recovering from the sudden illness that caused her to collapse after the funeral. When she could, Serena had every intention of making a beeline back toward the woman. In the meantime, the one person she didn't get on camera after the funeral was the current pastor of Greater Heights Church.

The tall, thin man seemed to not care for her presence. Serena had read as much as she could on Reverend Wright. He had been an associate pastor for many years under Bishop Hudson. Serena couldn't imagine how the man had coped filling the huge shoes of his predecessor. As Reverend Wright stopped to pull more programs out of the church pew, she tried to engage him again with her question. "Okay, if you don't want to share about the Hudson Housing Development, certainly you can share a few words about Charmayne. This was her church home, and you were her pastor, even if only for a short time."

Reverend Wright turned to her. The pastor had most of his wavy hair, which was graying around the temples. He was almost rail thin, as if she could touch him with her finger and he would tip over like a chess piece. She estimated he had to be in his late forties. While he was tall, Reverend Wright was in no way as commanding in size as the great Bishop Hudson. She hated to do comparisons, but she was really curious about this quiet man's perspective.

The man finally spoke as if in deep pain, "We will miss Charmayne dearly. To answer your other question, I don't know what's going to happen to the Hudson Housing Development project. It was really the bishop's dream. It wasn't Charmayne's dream."

Serena inquired, "So she was merely fighting for it because it was something her father wanted?"

The pastor sat down on the pew. Serena followed suit and waited for the pastor to compose himself. She recognized a deep sense of admiration and sorrow toward his recently deceased member. Serena inquired, "Were you close to Charmayne?"

Reverend Wright eyed her as if he resented the question. He looked down at his pants and picked a piece of lint from his leg. He responded with his head lowered.

"She was like a younger sister to me. We grew up here in this church. She always teased me and said she knew I would be in that pulpit one day. I would tease her back and say I always knew she would try to be the leader of something. Charmayne was the boss, even as a kid. She was similar to her father in that aspect."

Reverend Wright chuckled at a past memory that he didn't share with Serena. She waited for him to continue.

"You may find this hard to believe, but Charmayne, like quite a few of us, felt a sense of relief when her father passed away. He was a hard man to be around."

Serena quipped, "He was a man of God. A great civil rights leader. I can imagine he was intimidating."

The pastor lifted his head. "He was passionate about helping the people, but he wasn't always so kind to the people closest to him."

Serena looked away as her own memories came to mind. She didn't want to be disrespectful to the minister or the house of God. A long time ago, back as a girl in South Carolina, Serena had spent much time in a church built very much like this one except it was much smaller. Everyone knew one another. She had family members who were so religious and spirit-filled, they seemed to live at church. Those same persons often forgot that religion behind closed doors. That was another time, and Serena was no longer bound to that life.

It occurred to Serena that Bishop Hudson and Charmayne were used to getting their way. That meant they had to have created enemies along the way. She looked over at the pastor who had grown quiet, probably reflecting on his memories.

She hated to interrupt him, but she came to the church that morning for a very specific matter. "Reverend Wright, is it possible there are people who would've wanted the Hudson Housing Development not to succeed?" She observed the pastor turning from reflective to protective.

He straightened his back and folded his arms. "Why are you so interested in this subject matter? You know you have a lot of people upset. Your story made it sound like people who are well-respected in this community were doing illegal things."

Serena leaned forward. "Look, I just want to know why a sharp and ambitious woman like Charmayne Hudson would allegedly commit suicide. No one wants to say that because it's so shocking, but it's how she died. Don't you think it's odd that no one wants to touch this project, and the main people who kept it alive are gone now?"

The pastor slapped his hands on his legs and pointed his long finger near her face. "That project was doomed to fail from the very beginning."

Serena stood. "Why? This congregation worked hard for many years to raise money. Why would so many people be involved and it was a doomed project as you say?"

He threw up his hands. "I just told you or tried to tell you. Bishop Hudson got what he wanted. If he wanted this to be the main project for the church, it's what we did, no questions asked."

"So he threw his power around?"

"I don't want to speak ill of the dead, and even more important, I wouldn't be here without the man. I don't know what was going on in Charmayne's mind, but she did have a tendency to be impulsive."

"But you don't think she would have been *this* impulsive."

"I don't know what to believe. What I do know is the mind is a powerful force. Only Charmayne knew what was going on in her own mind."

Serena took a deep breath. "I have a few more questions, and then I will leave. Who else worked on this project? I would still like to talk to everyone involved."

Reverend Wright shook his head. "What do you hope to discover? Must you drag a good name in the mud, all for a story?"

Serena was taken aback by Reverend Wright's statement. Because she needed what she came for she took a moment to calm her angst. Of course she wanted to fully investigate the finances involved, but Reverend Wright didn't need to know that. She knew he would shut her down and not want to talk to her at all if he was aware of that.

After her broadcast the other night, Alan warned her to move forward carefully. Her news producer wasn't too pleased with her questioning the mayor the way she did, but Serena didn't regret the reaction she got from the mayor.

Now she just needed to have more concrete evidence before her next move.

Chapter Thirty-six

Jonathan rushed over to his wife. "Are you all right? What's going on? Are you hurt?" Lenora had her hands over her mouth and was visibly shaken. It was a good thing he'd decided to come home to check on her. Why his wife was borderline hysterical was a mystery to him. He prodded her. "Lenora, please calm down and let me know what happened."

She waved her hands in the air and began to pace the floor. "Give me a minute, okay?" Lenora tried to stand still, but started pacing again. She put her hands on her hips as if she was trying to catch her breath. She stuttered between gulping for air. "Why didn't you call and let me know you were coming home?"

He frowned. "I did call. I tried to call you on the home phone, on your cell, and I thought at some point you must have gone to the boutique. I called and Sarah was in the office. You need to teach that young lady to take Mondays totally off. What's the point in having the boutique closed?"

Relief slowly washed over Lenora's face. She doubled over and started laughing.

Jonathan stared at his wife, wondering if she was having a mental breakdown or something. "Lenora, you have me worried. Really worried."

She stood up straight and took a deep breath. There was wetness around her eyes. She hastily wiped her eyes, and then bent down to pick up the knife off the floor. Lenora tossed the knife in the sink and walked over to the counter as if all was normal. She finally said, "My cell phone is on the charger, and I guess you were the one who called when I was on the phone with Detective Jackson."

He was so confused, but he tuned into the conversation, hoping that whatever ailed Lenora wouldn't return. "Why did the detective call?"

The doorbell rang from the front of the house.

Lenora flinched from the sound. She gripped the countertop. "That's probably him. He wanted to come by the house to share some information. Looks like you're just in time. Can you get the door? I'll join you both in the living room."

Jonathan eyed her again. "All right, take your time." He walked toward the front door and opened it. "Detective?"

Darnell turned around. "Pastor." He held out his hand. "Good to see you. I'm so sorry we keep meeting under these crazy circumstances."

"It is what it is. Come in." Once the detective stepped inside, Jonathan closed the door. "Follow me this way." As they entered the living room, Jonathan looked for Lenora. "My wife should be with us soon. Have a seat."

Darnell sat down in the chair nearest the door, while Jonathan sat on the couch. He observed the detective pulling a notebook out of the inside of his jacket. "We appreciate you coming to our home. Going to the police station was a bit unpleasant last time."

"I do apologize. I really just wanted to get Mrs. Freeman out of the eye of the media. I hate that they managed to harass you last weekend."

Jonathan nodded. "Yes, that was an experience. I'm glad they have moved on to the next story."

Darnell glanced around the living room. "You have a nice home, Pastor."

"Thank you." Jonathan looked around for Lenora. *What is she doing?* He asked Darnell, "So, did you come by with news about Charmayne?"

"Yes, did you, Detective?" Lenora floated into the room and perched herself on the edge of the couch. Jonathan noticed she had changed from the pajamas she was wearing into a T-shirt and jeans. It wasn't often his wife dressed down so casual. It was a good look for her. Despite the worry lines around her eyes, she appeared young and fresh-faced without her usual made-up face.

Darnell confirmed. "There is still some investigation into Charmayne's death. I actually came by to follow-up on the story you shared last week. It did concern me that Charmayne and you were receiving threats, so I looked into some records."

"Oh." Lenora sounded small and quiet. "You found information about the man from the accident."

"Yes. As you already know, the man survived the accident. What was interesting about the hit-and-run was the victim didn't make much of a fuss about finding the car that hit him."

Jonathan inquired. "So back then, the man didn't appear to be upset enough to seek justice. Doesn't seem plausible over twenty-five years later."

Darnell nodded. "Exactly."

Lenora frowned. "Well, did you find out what happened to him?"

"He died."

Lenora sucked in a breath. "After the accident?"

Darnell held up his hand. "No, no. He died several years later. In fact . . ." He flipped through his notebook. "It was about eight years ago. According to his death certificate, he died from cardiac arrest. He was a heavy drinker. There were several DUIs. Around the time of the accident, he had no license. He also had been into quite a bit of trouble . . . robberies, auto theft, etc."

"Really? So Charmayne just happened to run down a criminal?" Lenora leaned back on the couch. "That doesn't make what happened comforting. He was still a human being."

"True, but I wanted to come tell you this because we needed to rule out anyone who may have influenced Charmayne's death. Right now, it's not the victim because he's been buried six feet under for almost a decade."

Jonathan said, "That's a bit of relief. Don't you think, Lenora?" His wife continued to look puzzled. "Lenora, are you okay?" He felt like he had been asking his wife this same question on a regular basis.

"I'm still confused. What about family? Did you check to see if this man has a family? Are you sure this man you're telling me about is the same man?"

Detective Jackson flipped a page in his notebook, "His name was Jack. Jack Sellars. I did look into the possibilities of whether he had some family. He had one sister who is also now deceased. He didn't have any children, but she had two boys and a girl."

Jonathan couldn't understand why Lenora couldn't let go of the fact that there was no one there from the past. He, in fact, was more concerned about the hit-and-run accident that occurred to his son a few weeks ago. "Detective, I know this isn't your territory, but it might be helpful to find out who was involved in our son's accident."

Darnell started flipping through his notebook. "You know what? That was something else I wanted to tell you. Since I was on my way here, I decided to check with the Crash Unit. Someone came forward."

Lenora leaned forward on the couch. "Who?"

Jonathan reached out and touched her arm. His wife appeared ready to take flight. He was still concerned by her earlier hysterics.

Darnell answered. "It was a young woman, a single mom. She turned herself in last night. Apparently, she had been drinking, and she knew something had happened. The damage on the front of her truck matched up to the accident."

Jonathan sighed out loud. "Well, I'm glad the young woman came forward. At least we know there was no malicious intent in our son's accident. That's good news, right, Lenora?"

Lenora stood and paced the room. "Yes, I feel better, but I still don't understand why I was getting those messages. Why did someone go out of their way to bring up the accident from years ago? It's like they knew it was a big secret. Someone called me from Charmayne's phone."

The room grew still. Jonathan studied how Lenora twisted her hands. He tilted his head to observe Detective Jackson's reaction. Darnell's eyes were locked on Lenora. Jonathan wasn't sure what was going on, but alarms went off in his head.

The detective narrowed his eyes. He stood and walked over to Lenora. "You know, we did acquire Charmayne's phone records, and you were the last person she called."

Lenora waved her arms. "I had been calling her and leaving messages all morning. Did you hear any of my voice mails?"

Jonathan stood. He was concerned about Lenora's behavior. "Look, Darnell, this is still a big shock to all of us, especially Lenora. I'm just happy that there doesn't seem to be any threat."

"What?" Lenora yelled. "I don't believe that one bit. There was someone out there threatening Charmayne. She was scared, and nothing rattled Charmayne." She walked up to Darnell and pointed her finger. "You can't just shut this case down and declare Charmayne's death was a suicide."

Darnell folded his notebook and placed it inside his jacket. "Nothing is closed yet, Lenora. I have to tell you we have searched the house. There are no letters or e-mails showing threats. We have looked for foreign fingerprints in the house. There were no fingerprints, other than Charmayne's and her housekeeper. In fact, her place was spotless. If she had a struggle with anyone before she died, there wasn't anything found under her fingernails."

Darnell took a breath. "What we did find was alcohol in Charmayne's body. Since she didn't leave a note, Charmayne reaching out to you is the closest we have that she had tried to send a message. I'm sorry, but right now, there is no evidence of foul play."

Lenora folded her arms again and rubbed her shoulders as if she had grown cold. "I think she said most of the threats were by phone. You just said you checked her phone records. Who else called her? She had to have made contact with someone else after she left the boutique that afternoon."

"We are making contact with everyone on that list. There wasn't a pattern of calls from one particular number. You mentioned whoever texted you was no longer accessible. There may be numbers that are dead ends, but we can certainly try to trace the serial numbers back to the stores where the phones were purchased. That's a long shot, though."

Lenora threw up her hands. "Well, someone is going to get away with murder. And why would someone send messages to me? Are you saying the warnings were about Charmayne's death?"

Jonathan looked over at Detective Jackson. The detective glanced at him and seemed to be pondering how to proceed. He finally spoke, "I will admit the fact that you received theses messages is bothersome. We can't be sure that it wasn't Charmayne."

"What? Are you kidding me? Charmayne was a drama queen, but why would she do something that elaborate? She came to me, clearly scared. Let me tell you, nothing or no one, with the exception of maybe her father, scared Charmayne. She didn't back down from anything."

Darnell nodded. "I'm aware of Charmayne and her work on the council. It's known she was a fighter."

"Then you make sure her death is investigated. I know you have done all you could, but someone is responsible." She walked out of the room.

Jonathan closed his eyes. *This wasn't good at all.* "Darnell, I'm sorry."

"It's fine, Reverend Freeman. I just feel bad. I was hoping I could bring your wife some closure from the past incident and about your son's hit-and-run accident. I just don't know how to answer what happened at Charmayne Hudson's home."

Jonathan nodded. "Keep looking. Lenora will be okay. It's going to take her some time to process Charmayne may have really committed suicide. We do appreciate you coming by."

He walked Darnell out. After Jonathan closed the door, he lifted his head to the stairs where Lenora had gone and then closed the door to their bedroom.

Lenora was more distraught than before Darnell arrived. The news brought no closure. Jonathan had always been at odds with Charmayne when she was living. While he didn't know what to think either, he knew for certain his wife needed to face the facts, no matter how painful.

Chapter Thirty-seven

Serena glanced at Reverend Wright and put on her best smile. "I don't want to make this difficult for you, I promise you. Look, I talked to Charmayne a few days before her death and she really wanted to fulfill her dad's legacy. It's just a shame that it's all crumbling now. Can you tell me who was on the committee? I know the meetings were held here once a month for several years. There has to be other people who believed in the project."

Reverend Wright sighed. "As long as you are not trying to smear people's names, especially those who are no longer here to defend themselves, I can ask the secretary to provide you with the committee records."

Serena clasped her hands together as though she'd won a prize. "Thank you. I really appreciate having access."

"You can follow me to the office."

She followed the pastor out of the sanctuary, trying to keep up with his long strides. If she didn't know any better, she had a feeling Reverend Wright wanted to get rid of her as soon as possible. Serena still couldn't understand why there was so much discomfort around the project and the Hudsons.

The pastor stopped inside the secretary's office which was next to his office. The office was jam-packed with a desk and a copier. Serena didn't know how the heavyset woman was sitting comfortably in the small room. A noisy fan kept the office relatively cool.

Reverend Wright extended his arm out to his secretary. "Linda, this is Ms. Manchester. Linda served as the secretary of the committee most of the time it existed. Linda, can you provide Ms. Manchester with copies of the last few meetings on the Hudson Housing Development project?"

Serena asked, "Are there any photos or videos with the record too?"

Reverend Wright and Linda both stared at her.

Serena explained, "I just wanted to know how the committee members looked for later reference. Plus, you know city council records their meetings. I understand it was Charmayne's idea. I thought maybe this committee did too."

Reverend Wright eyed her intensely. "Sorry, we aren't that high tech. We had a diverse group of people who had a common purpose to serve the community. You don't intend to harass these people, do you?"

"Of course not. Don't you like to be able to picture a face with a name, Reverend Wright?" Serena smiled and looked over at the secretary. Linda was looking down at her hands. Sensing that the room had grown quiet, Linda lifted her head and glanced at Serena briefly before looking back down.

"I will leave you two. Please don't cause any trouble."

Linda looked very familiar to Serena for some reason, but she wasn't sure where she saw the woman before. The woman glanced at the pastor, and then asked before he left, "Reverend Wright, the committee meetings started almost seven years ago. Exactly how far do you want us to go back?"

Serena raised her eyebrows. That was a good question. She didn't realize the project had been around that long. Serena suggested, "How about we start with last year?"

Linda looked for approval from Reverend Wright who was at the doorway looking ready to bolt. He threw up his hand. "Give her what she wants." He pointed to Serena, warning her again, "Just don't use anything to destroy a man and his daughter's good name. Remember, this church and community is mourning."

Serena watched Reverend Wright strut down the hall. He certainly was very protective of the Hudsons. Being the pastor of the church founded by Bishop Hudson, Serena could see the awkwardness for the man if a scandal occurred. She was thankful that their time together had ended. Something about Reverend Wright made her remember why she wasn't a fan of most ministers.

She turned her attention to Linda, who reminded her of most dedicated church women that Serena had known in her life. She wondered how much of a life Linda had outside of the church. Linda waddled her way from around the desk. Serena glanced down at the woman's ankles and noticed they appeared swollen above the orthopedic shoes she wore.

Linda tilted her head toward the door. "Come on this way. We keep the records in the other office. As you can see, there isn't much room in here for filing cabinets."

They entered a room down the hall from the offices which appeared to be a classroom. A table sat in the middle of the room. There were several metal chairs that didn't really fit neatly under the table. Sure enough, there were several filing cabinets lining the wall. As Linda pulled out drawers, Serena walked around the room. She turned and asked, "Have I met you somewhere? You look so familiar to me."

Linda nodded. "Well, I've seen you on TV, but I doubt we have met before. I have been the church secretary here for over twelve years, so who knows. It's been a transition not having the bishop around, but Reverend Wright, bless his heart, is a sweetheart."

Serena concentrated on a memory. "Do you have a sister or someone else here in Charlotte you're related to?"

"Just me and Dorothy."

Serena's ears perked up. "Dorothy? The seamstress at Lenora's Bridal Boutique?"

Linda had an armful of manila folders by now. "Yes, she's my older sister." She placed the stack of folders on the table. "How do you know Dorothy?"

"I met her the other day when I was at the boutique. She shared with me about Charmayne and Lenora's friendship."

"Oh yeah. Those girls were two peas in the pod growing up. They kind of grew apart when they left high school, basically meaning you didn't see them tied to each other any longer. Lenora married Reverend Freeman, and she has pretty much attended Victory Gospel. We occasionally see her back at her home church for various events. But, yeah, there was a time you never saw Charmayne without Lenora and vice versa. It was probably a good thing for Lenora."

"Is that so? Why do you say that? You know Lenora found her the other day."

Linda had pulled out several stapled papers. She stopped and placed her hands on her hips like she was tired. "That's not surprising. Lenora was loyal and dependable. I heard stories of her checking on Charmayne, even making sure the girl was sobered up."

"Sobered up?"

"Child, Charmayne had a drinking problem. It was more of an obvious thing when she was younger. Most people knew about it, but no one dared say anything to the bishop's face."

An alcoholic. Interesting. That changed some things in Serena's mind. She wondered if the police had made note of Charmayne's alcohol level. They certainly didn't make that information public. In fact, they still weren't saying anything about the official cause of death.

Linda grabbed an empty printer paper box from next to the cabinets. "I'm going to make copies of these for you. Here is the most recent list of committee members. You can have that copy. I will be right back with these minutes from the last year."

"Thanks." Serena quickly scanned the list and was immediately disappointed. There were a variety of names she recognized, most, of whom, were leaders of other churches and organizations in the district. The one name she was looking for didn't appear to be on the list. Then again, she shouldn't have been surprised since she had always felt Lance Ryan wasn't using his real name. So how did Lance get the financial records that he had?

Serena looked up and noticed Linda had left the drawer open to the filing cabinet. She tiptoed over to the door and peered around the door frame. She could hear the steady hum of the copier running. Serena glided over to the open filing cabinet drawer and quickly scanned the folder labels.

One folder was labeled Financial Records. As she kept looking she could see other financial records in the file drawer. Serena glanced at the door, and then reached for the first folder. She flipped open the folder thinking she should have asked Linda to make copies of these too. After all, the financial reports should be public record.

Serena noted the spreadsheet was a similar format to the ones she had obtained earlier. She scanned the numbers and from memory she realized the numbers were similar to the document Lance had given her. So he had the original document. Where did Charmayne get her numbers from? Charmayne's numbers were considerably lower than these.

Serena listened. The copier was no longer humming. She slapped the folder closed and placed the committee list on top just as Linda walked in with a pile of papers in her hand. As the secretary stuffed the papers in an envelope, Serena slid the folder lower so the secretary wouldn't notice.

Linda tucked and patted the papers to make them neater. Then she handed them to Serena. "All right, here you go."

Serena placed what she had in her hand on the table and reached for the papers. She waited until the woman turned to close the cabinet drawer and placed the folder she took from the drawer between the other papers. Serena held the contents against her chest. She said, "Thank you for your help, Linda."

Linda seemed to be trying to catch her breath. "Anything I can do to help, I will be glad to."

Serena got an idea. She carefully pulled the list of committee members off the top of the stack and placed it on the table. "There is one other thing you can help me with. I noticed the committee is not just members of Greater Heights."

"No, like Reverend Wright said, this was more of a committee of community leaders. Other churches as well as business leaders are on that list."

"So they all had a prominent place in the community."

"I would say."

"What other people would have been involved that weren't on the committee?"

Linda rubbed her chin, upon which Serena noticed tiny curls of hair sprouting. She recoiled. The woman needed to shave that atrocity. Serena tried to focus on what Linda was saying.

"I took the minutes at some of these meetings. I was the committee secretary for several years, although I stopped last year. I had to have some surgery on my feet. Anyhow, there were outside people that came to the meetings, mostly in real estate or construction. They did have a consultant who came in quite a bit in the beginning. He stopped coming one day. That was five years ago."

Serena perked up. "Really? Why did he stop coming?"

"I believe he had a disagreement with Bishop Hudson." Linda dropped her voice down low as though the deceased Bishop Hudson was about to walk into the room. "Nobody ever disagreed with the bishop. He might let you get away with it one time, but not more than once. He let that man go. I remember the man was really upset about it too. He marched out of the bishop's office, red in the face."

Serena asked, "Did he threaten the bishop or his family?"

Linda shook her head. "I don't know if it got that bad, but you never know. Bishop Hudson did have his enemies."

Serena didn't doubt that he did. She asked, "Do you have any information about this man or the company? What was his name?"

Linda looked up at the ceiling. "You know, I don't know. It's been so long ago. I want to say his name was Ryan something."

Ryan. This was the closest Serena thought she would be able to come. "Do you remember what he looked like?"

"He was a sharp dresser for his size." Linda chuckled. "Some of the ladies used to say we smelled his cologne before we saw him coming. Not bad looking for a white guy either."

Serena frowned. She wondered if Linda was talking about the mysterious Lance Ryan. No, he wasn't bad looking, but something evil lurked beneath that man. If he was involved with this project, it appeared the man had every intention of making sure the project never saw the light of day. Why, though?

Chapter Thirty-eight

Lenora sulked for the rest of the afternoon. She looked back at the list she had written last week and crossed off the victim. Jack Sellars. She vaguely remembered the name after Darnell stated it out loud. It was a bit ironic that she hadn't remembered his name. She recalled catching a glimpse of the man on the news when he was released. Now that she thought back, he hadn't revealed his face. Almost as if he didn't want the media attention.

At the time, Charmayne had laughed and stated, "See, he's fine. He's going on with his life, and we will do the same." That they did.

That's what bothered Lenora. There was someone else who knew. Someone who used a time in both of their lives when everything was going well. Charmayne was a media darling up until after her father died. Then she seemed to have become the black sheep of the council, unwilling to budget on a project her father had created. Why did this all happen after Bishop Hudson's death?

Lenora knew somewhere this had to do with him. The bishop covered and protected Charmayne. On many occasions, Lenora had been encouraged to keep quiet by the bishop whenever she found Charmayne in one of her drunken stupors. He would always look at Lenora and thank her for being such a good friend. Behind that statement, he was basically saying to her, "I'm glad you keep her secrets safe."

There was a knock on the bedroom door. Jonathan walked in. Lenora pushed herself up from where she had lay sprawled across their bed. Jonathan sat down and asked, "Are you all right?"

Lenora shifted her eyes upward, and then stared at him. "Of course not. Stop asking me that question like I'm about to have a nervous breakdown or something."

"I just need to know you're okay. We did just have a health scare."

"It's more than that. You think I need to get over Charmayne's death."

Jonathan rubbed his head. "I know you're having a hard time with what happened. I know there are a lot of questions left open, but you need to allow yourself time to mourn, and then move on with your life. You have a wedding coming up. That young man that was just in our house is the groom."

Lenora bit her lip. "I don't have anything against Darnell. I know he did the best he could in a short amount of time to find out some answers. I'm looking forward to going back to work. In fact, I plan to be there first thing in the morning."

"Good. I think it's time you get back to the things that are important to you. It's what Charmayne would have wanted, don't you think?"

She lashed out before she could stop herself. "Charmayne was important to me. I know we had an interesting friendship and you never really liked her, but I'm not just going to let this go. She would have wanted some type of justice."

Jonathan frowned. "You just heard from law enforcement. What type of justice do you hope can be found?"

She held her hands to her heart. "There has to be something I have missed that could help them."

"Are you talking about the accident when you were younger? You can't do anything about that night now. The man's dead. Goodness, it was what . . . almost twenty-five years ago."

Lenora fell back against the pillow. "I don't think anything going on now has to do with that accident. I believe this person involved went fishing for some skeletons to pull out of Charmayne's closet to use against her."

She sat up. "You know the development project that has been on the news. That reporter came by the boutique asking about the project. Charmayne said herself it felt like everyone was against her. Jonathan, suppose someone was trying to set Charmayne up for some fall. This could be someone with a political agenda."

Lenora placed her feet on the floor. With her hands on her hips, she started to pace. "In some ways, Bishop Hudson was untouchable, but people would strike out at Charmayne to get to her dad. Suppose this was the same thing going on here?"

Jonathan shrugged. "What you're saying is since the bishop was gone that someone saw an opportunity to pick apart Charmayne? Why? I mean, the woman could have her own enemies."

"Yes, you're right. Mayor Carrington certainly has been bent on thwarting her reelection. I bet he's still encouraging you to run for the district seat, is that true?"

"Lenora, stop." He stood. "This is crazy. Do you hear how you sound? You're trying to accuse people of being responsible for Charmayne's death. Look, we don't know what led her to sit in that car with the garage door closed, but you have to be careful here."

"I'm just asking questions, Jonathan."

He stood in front of her. "You're the first lady of Victory Gospel. You grew up at Greater Heights, and you are a well-known businesswoman in Charlotte. I'm begging you to let this go. Let the police continue their investigation and you concentrate on your upcoming responsibilities."

Jonathan walked out of the room and swung the door closed behind him. The loud thud against the door frame jolted her. She wanted to run after him and tell him not to tell her what to do, or, for that fact, even how to feel. But the steam that had built up over the last hour dissipated as her body went limp. Lenora plopped down on the bed. In the back of her mind, she knew that Jonathan was right. She had a wedding coming up that she had planned for over a year. It was time to press on.

Still, it upset her that it appeared the investigation was leaning toward the end of her friend's life as a suicide. Lenora thought back to when she heard the sounds of the car in the garage. She had picked up the rock and threw it at the garage window. What was her first thought? What did Charmayne say to her the last time she saw her?

I'm sorry, Lenora. I will take care of it for both of us.

Lenora pulled her feet closer to her body and tilted forward, then back. She rocked for a long time, trying to figure out what could have been Charmayne's game plan. In Lenora's mind, the truth had been overshadowed by a very big lie.

Chapter Thirty-nine

All morning Lenora had double-checked, and in some cases, triple-checked, the details for the upcoming weekend. She hung up the phone with the caterer a split second before she was sure the man on the other line would be ready to shoot a string of curse words her way.

Sarah sat across from her pretending to examine her nails. Lenora could feel the annoyance rising up from the woman's demeanor. "I appreciate you taking care of all this while I was sick. I know, I know. I'm anal. My apologies."

Her consultant stretched her eyes. Sarah opened her mouth, but no words came out.

Lenora burst out laughing. "What, you mean I made you speechless? Look, honey, I have been laid out on my back for about a week. At some point, I could have sworn death's door was about to open." Lenora leaned back. "I know that I strive for this false notion of perfection. I always have. It's a hard habit to break."

Sarah's eyes watered as she smiled. "That's what your clients appreciate about you. You do everything to make sure that day is one they will never forget. It's why I was determined to work for you. Your reputation is stellar, and I can see why."

Lenora waved her hand. "I know you still want to wring my neck. I do trust you. I just . . . I feel like I haven't been fully involved in the wedding planning for Candace, at least these last few critical weeks."

Sarah shook her head. Her hair swung back and forth. "That's the way it seems to you, but I know Candace is very pleased with everything. You really are too hard on yourself. Where does this come from?"

Lenora shrugged. "I honestly don't know. I've always had this good girl syndrome."

Sarah giggled. "Me too."

Lost in a memory, Lenora remained silent for a few minutes. She finally spoke, her eyes not focused on anything in particular. "You know, Charmayne used to get on me ever since we were little girls. She would tell me 'You're so boring, you have to have everything just right.'"

"Well, someone has to keep the order."

Lenora focused on Sarah, and then shook her head. "You're right, but we can't expect everything to be perfect. Sometimes I have been so caught up in having control and making sure everything was perfect that I have succumbed to feeling like a failure when things fall apart."

Sarah leaned forward. "You know, what you just said reminds me of something I read this morning in my devotions." She pulled out her phone and began touching the screen. "Here it is. Today's verse was from 2 Corinthians, Chapter Twelve, and Verse Ten. It says, 'Therefore I take pleasure in infirmities, in reproaches, in necessities, in persecutions, in distresses for Christ's sake: for when I am weak, then am I strong.'"

Sarah looked at Lenora. "I can forward this to you if you'd like."

"Sure! That's a good verse to meditate on today. Thank you again for everything, Sarah."

Sarah gave her a salute. "Not a problem, boss."

After the young woman left, Lenora couldn't seem to find the concentration she had earlier. She often played an online radio station in the background. Lenora reached over and flicked the screen to show the station. She saw Marvin Sapp's album cover. Lenora turned up the volume and listened to the chorus. "Be all glory and power, dominion and power, forever, and ever. Amen."

She thought about the verse that Sarah just read. Lenora hadn't been taking any pleasure in her trials and loss of control. She'd carried the weight on her shoulders, feeling more oppressed by her circumstances. During her illness, her prayers and time spent with God had grown on a deeper level. There was nothing hurried as she got up and went about her day. It was like God had been waiting for her to slow down and share her burdens. There was nothing cliché about let go and let God.

If anything, she needed to remember this simple concept.

She was still steamed at Jonathan. Well, not necessarily at him, but what he said to her. When she had received blows in her life, Lenora did have a habit of feeling sorry for herself over what she conceived to be a failure.

She had to really evaluate the root of where this came from. Always an overachiever, she certainly did her best to do everything with excellence, but even her mother had often told her, "Lenora, you have to live so you are not missing out on what God has for you. It's usually not about you working to get credit or the pat on the back, but for God's glory."

Lenora wondered what her momma would have said to her that night if she had known her daughter had become an accessory to what could have been someone's possible death. Lenora could have said something years ago, but she didn't. She had consciously made up for the terrible mishap by making sure she helped anyone in need. In a lot of ways, despite her complexities, Charmayne had done the same when she moved into the public service arena.

Lenora turned down the music and tapped on the keyboard to pull up some folders from an external hard drive. She kept meticulous records of all her weddings, mainly because she liked to go back and make sure she gave each bride the unique wedding they paid her to plan. It took her about fifteen minutes, but she found the folder she was searching for.

The photo was five years old and Charmayne's hair was long. Before she started chopping her hair off, Charmayne had worn weaves for years. In this photo, Charmayne had a jet-black, silky mane, a deep contrast to the princess wedding gown. Lenora still didn't know why Charmayne picked that dress. They went around and around. Charmayne wanted a fairy-tale wedding.

Her friend never walked down the aisle, which bothered Lenora more than it did Charmayne. Was her friend ever really happy?

The office phone halted her emotions and thoughts. Lenora cleared her throat and waited for the phone to ring again before she picked up the receiver.

"Lenora's Bridal Boutique."

"Lenora. Is this Lenora Freeman?"

She sat up straight in the seat. Lenora definitely didn't recognize the man's voice. She snapped, "Who's this?"

"Mrs. Freeman, this is Henry Bowman. I'm Charmayne Hudson's lawyer."

"Yes, what can I do for you?"

"I'm calling because I have been trying to contact you. Charmayne Hudson had some instructions upon her death. I have a package for you."

Lenora stuttered. Her brain was trying to catch up with her mouth. "A package."

"Yes, I felt like this wasn't something I could place in the mail. I was wondering if you could come by next week, possibly Monday, to pick up the package."

"Sure, what time?"

The man paused so long, Lenora was about to ask if anyone was still on the line.

"How about 1:00 p.m.? Will that work?"

Lenora jotted the time on her desk calendar. She would have to remember to add the meeting to her phone. She asked, "Where is your office located?"

"2200 Parklane Plaza."

"Thanks, I will see you on Monday." Lenora heard the dial tone and hung up the phone. She stared at the phone as if it were a snake about to strike out and bite her. Almost an entire week had passed since Charmayne's funeral. What was in the package?

She said out loud, "Really, Charmayne. Even from the grave, you're still causing drama."

Chapter Forty

It was Friday afternoon, and Serena had scoured over the Hudson Housing Development committee files until she was cross-eyed. She'd spent the last three days trying to cold-call committee members. It was like this project had the plague attached to it because no one wanted to cooperate and answer her questions. At least, it seemed that way to her.

The main players of the committee, Bishop Hudson and Charmayne Hudson, were obviously out of reach. That pained Serena because the two people who might have given her what she wanted were no longer here. Reverend Wright and Linda were the other members from Greater Heights. Linda, the secretary, had been kind and very helpful. Serena had come to the conclusion that either Reverend Wright's schedule was already filled or he was trying to avoid her.

Alex Carrington was appointed to the committee long before he was elected mayor of Charlotte. Other members were Reverend Donald Lawson of Springhill Baptist and Martha German, a longtime civil rights activist who had worked alongside Bishop Hudson in the 1960s. Over the past seven years, these seven people worked together on the proposal and the fund-raising circuit.

In a way there was no one to blame but herself if the mayor didn't want to speak to her. She had been a bit impulsive when she questioned Mayor Carrington on camera last Wednesday after Charmayne's funeral. Alan had sternly warned that her actions could backfire. She didn't really care. If anything, the shroud of secrecy around the once-popular project had convinced Serena something wasn't right.

She was going to find out. The money wasn't adding up, which meant they either had a bad financial secretary or someone had scooped some funds for themselves. Now the question was, did someone take the entire $350,000 or were there several individuals involved. From past stories of corruption, Serena knew there had to be several people involved, probably in areas she hadn't found yet.

The mayor seemed to be more of a guilty party based on his reactions to Serena's questions. Also, Mayor Carrington was the one who gave Charmayne the most grief about digging her heels in and fighting for the project. Serena moved the papers to the side and flipped open a folder she had personally assembled during election season. She had focused on Mayor Carrington, the womanizer, when he ran for mayor, but she had gathered quite a bit of information about the man's background.

Mayor Carrington was a self-made millionaire before he decided to run for office. The man owned one of the most reputable real estate firms in Charlotte. He was involved in the construction of several business developments over the past fifteen years. Alex was a shoo-in to have on the committee due to his keen business and real estate conquests.

Tapping the pen in her hand on the desk, Serena wondered out loud, "Exactly how did you make all of your money, Mr. Carrington?"

"Talking to yourself now, Serena? We don't want to have to commit you."

Serena lifted her eyes and grinned at Wes. "You got jokes, young man."

Wes shook his head. "Just concerned. You've been glued to this desk for a few days. That's not like you."

She leaned back in her seat. "Well, I've been forced to do my research on this one." Serena narrowed her eyes. "Is it me or are you looking exceptionally handsome tonight, kiddo?"

Wes was wearing dark slacks and a bright white Polo shirt. Serena blinked. She didn't know if it was Wes's smile or his shirt that was blinding her.

"I guess that's a compliment from you, Serena. I'm actually heading to Darnell and Candace's rehearsal dinner after I pick up Angel."

"Oh." Serena found herself speechless for a moment. She'd forgotten Darnell would officially get hitched this weekend. She realized Wes was watching her. Serena looked away and rubbed her eyes. "So, have you and Angel set a date yet?"

Wes turned up the power on his megawatt smile. "We are planning to announce to friends tonight since we know we'll be asked. New Year's Eve is the date."

"Wow! Biggest party day of the year. I like!"

Wes laughed out loud. "Yeah, I'm looking forward to it. We have a lot to do before then. We're hoping Lenora is cool with knowing she has about nine months of planning for us."

"I'm sure Lenora is a pro at wedding planning and will make your day superspecial. I'm really happy for you, Wes." Serena was surprised at her own sincerity. It was hopeful to see people could fall in love and still get married; something she'd pretty much thought was one of those fairy tales people got sucked into. Just because it wasn't in her cards didn't mean others couldn't keep the traditions going.

"Take care of yourself, Serena. It's Friday. You should be heading home."

"Ha-ha. Yeah, you're right." She watched as her young colleague strutted out of the newsroom. He was really happy.

Serena turned her attention back to the papers. He was right. It was Friday, and she was tired. She decided to check her e-mail, pack up some of the files, and head home. Maybe she would even soak in the tub. She was known to hit the club when she was younger, but lately, she was just another single woman enjoying the sanctity of her home.

There were tons of unread e-mail in her inbox due to the fact she hadn't checked since lunchtime. She did her usual quick scan. Only one e-mail stood out to her. The e-mail was from Linda. The Greater Heights secretary didn't strike her as the computer type, but in this age of smartphones, tablets, and social media, most folks of any age were glued to an electronic device. Serena clicked the e-mail.

She could tell Linda wasn't used to sending e-mails. In fact, the woman typed her message in the subject line instead of the body of the e-mail. Serena scrolled and read.

Ms. Manchester, I know you were looking for some photos or video from the meetings. I hope this helps.

Serena scrolled down to the message and saw the e-mail was a forward from Charmayne. The e-mail was dated April 4, 2008. The message was sent almost five years to the day.

There was a link to an online photo album. Serena clicked the link, not sure if it still worked or not. To her surprise the link opened to a group of albums. She peered closer and recognized some of the committee members like the bishop, Charmayne, and the not-yet-elected-at-the-time Mayor Carrington. Most of the photos were fund-raising events where the attendees dressed in black tie.

Forgetting that she was supposed to pack up and head home, Serena spent the next fifteen minutes scrolling through photos. She liked observing people. A photo, especially taken when a person wasn't aware, told a lot about that person's demeanor during that time.

Serena recognized Martha German, one of the committee members, who was dodging her calls. Martha was exactly as she pictured her: silver haired and stern looking. The woman reminded Serena of a former schoolteacher who had also worn her hair in a simple bun.

From her appearance, Serena couldn't imagine the woman doing anything wrong. Usually, the person you least suspected could be involved in the worst of crimes. Martha served as the main fund-raiser organizer/financial secretary for the committee. If anyone knew the real donation totals, Martha should know.

Serena glanced at the time in the lower right-hand corner of her computer. It was almost five o'clock. She wondered if anything was going on at Greater Heights. She had to chuckle at her own curiosity about church activities on a Friday night. Reverend Wright's secretary had been the most accessible person thus far. So, Serena called the church office.

She scrolled through her cell phone and dialed the Greater Heights phone number. The phone rang twice.

"Hello, Greater Heights Church. This is Linda, how may I help you?"

Serena smiled at her luck. Or maybe God was really looking after her. She tucked that thought away as she responded. "Linda, hello, it's Serena Manchester. I was hoping I could catch you."

The woman was silent on the other end.

"Do you remember me?"

Linda cleared her throat and spoke softly, as if she didn't want anyone to hear her. "Yes, I remember you.

I was getting ready to head home. I had to finish the programs for Sunday. Was there something else you needed? Did you get my e-mail?"

"Yes, I did. Thank you for the photos. I needed to see some more records. I was wondering if I could come by the church."

"Well, Reverend Wright did say to help you. I guess that's all right. When can you come?"

"I can be there in about thirty minutes."

Despite the five o'clock traffic on I-77, Serena arrived at Greater Heights in the time she'd estimated. There were certainly some activities going on at Greater Heights. She parked her car in the parking lot, clicked her alarm, and headed up the church steps. Once inside, instead of going straight to Linda's office, Serena made it to the office that held the records. Down the hall, she could hear what sounded like the choir rehearsing. She looked behind her and slowly turned the knob. *Dang!* It was locked. She would have to do this differently.

Serena rounded the corner and popped her head into Linda's office. The woman had her eyes closed, with headphones on her head. She wasn't sure what the woman was listening to, but she walked in and watched as Linda raised her arms to the sky and sang, "No weapon formed against me shall prosper, it won't work."

Then Linda shouted, "Thank you, Jesus."

Serena rapped her knuckles on the wood desk. "That must be a really good song."

Linda's eyes popped open in surprise. Then her face curved into a smile. "Ms. Manchester. Girl, I love this song and Fred Hammond. That man knows how to make a sister throw up her hands and praise the Lord for all that He has done. Even after a bad day."

For a brief second, Serena felt a slight hint of guilt. She hated to come by and disturb Linda after a bad day.

Before she lost her nerve, Serena reached for the folder in her purse. "I acquired these records and was wondering if there is some mistake." She laid the financial spreadsheets in front of Linda.

Linda looked at the spreadsheets and frowned. "Did I give these to you on Monday?"

Serena lied. "They were mixed up with the minutes. The minutes were very helpful, but I found these to be a bit confusing."

Linda lifted her eyes and cocked her head like a puppy waiting to see if his master would play. "How so?" she asked.

Serena pointed to the documents Lance had given her. "The numbers are just very different from what Charmayne's office sent me. I'm not sure which one is correct. Can you help?"

Linda sputtered. "I'm not sure why you have two different copies. And I don't know if I can help. I was mainly at the meetings to record minutes." She chuckled. "I've never been good at math, and I doubt anyone wanted to trust me with the finances."

"So who took care of documenting the finances?"

"In the beginning it was Charmayne."

Serena raised her eyebrows. "Charmayne was the financial secretary?"

"Yes, that's how it started. Of course, she eventually let it go, and Martha took over taking care of the finances. She still does. She's very smart and meticulous despite her age. Plus, the bishop trusted her."

"You know, I've been trying to get in touch with Martha. Do you have any idea when is the best time to contact her?"

"No, I'm afraid I don't know. I lost touch with most of the committee members after I stopped being the secretary. The bishop wanted to get representation from each of the major churches here in the district. Martha is the representative from Victory Gospel. So, she will probably be at the wedding tomorrow."

Serena cocked her head to the side. "Are you talking about Darnell and Candace?"

"Yes, have you been invited?" Linda asked.

Serena shook her head, though she was still looking for a way to crash the wedding.

"That's a shame. I'm looking forward to attending. Dorothy has been telling me how excited she was about the wedding. I get to come as her guest."

"Oh, lucky you." *They didn't have to leave me off the guest list.* Serena was sure a lot of guests were not connected to either the bride or groom.

Serena closed the folder and decided she would find a way to catch up with Martha German soon. "Thanks for your help, Linda. I know you want to get home."

Serena was about to leave, but Linda called out. "Oh wait, I wanted to show you a photo since you seemed interested in him."

Serena turned back around. "Photo?"

Linda shuffled back behind her desk. "Remember you said you wanted to know about the consultant. I just happened to find this photo when I was searching for the albums. I think I know why Bishop Hudson wanted to get rid of him."

Serena walked over to Linda's desk.

Linda was grinning as she turned the monitor around for Serena to view.

It took Serena a moment to comprehend, but when she did, her bottom lip could've hit the desk. If she hadn't seen the man's, face up close she wouldn't have recognized him. He looked like a totally different person.

The man she knew as Lance Ryan was standing next to Charmayne with a big grin on his face. Lance was tanned as usual, and his hair was a lot longer. He also wore thick glasses and had to be at least one hundred pounds heavier than he was currently. No wonder the bishop got rid of him. Lance was an intimidating man now. What kind of demeanor did he have as this heavyset guy? Since this photo was taken, the man had obviously taken great pains to transform his body. Why?

Serena leaned in closer. "Is it me or is his arm slung around Charmayne's waist?"

Linda raised her eyebrows. "Yes, ma'am. It appears that way. That's surprising."

Serena stood back. "It is surprising that Charmayne would be attracted to him." Of course, the Lance Ryan of today wasn't a bad-looking man at all. She recalled her initial impression of him. Some of the unease she sensed from Lance might have had something to do with the new body he was sporting.

Linda's voice drew Serena out of her thoughts. She tuned in.

"That girl could never keep a man around. The bishop didn't like anyone for his daughter. I don't care how old she was, he'd managed to butt into her love life. Anyway, despite all that, I agree with you, this guy can't be her type. Look at him. I wouldn't date him myself."

Linda's laugh came deep from her belly.

Serena couldn't help but chuckle too as thoughts raced through her mind faster than she could process. Was Charmayne really involved with this man? How was all of this related to right now? Serena was confident that she needed to find a way to contact Lenora Freeman.

Looks like I'm going to have to crash a wedding tomorrow.

Chapter Forty-one

Lenora walked briskly around Victory Gospel Center with Sarah in tow behind her. She stopped suddenly and turned. "Are you sure the caterer received all of the special dietary requests for tonight? I just remembered that Rachel mentioned she had started eating vegan food."

The clipboard in Sarah's hand flew in the air as she tried to keep from bumping into Lenora. She caught the clipboard right before it hit the floor. Sarah stood and stared at Lenora. "I promise you everything is taken care of for this evening. I even checked on the special dishes for the reception tomorrow."

"And what about—" Lenora interrupted.

Sarah held up her hand. "The cake is perfect. It will be delivered in the morning."

Lenora smiled. "I'm sorry. I know you took care of all this while I was sick."

The younger woman laughed. "I think we can agree that nothing stops you from aiming for perfection."

Lenora bent over the table and fiddled with the centerpiece. "Honey, I do believe God is dropping hints to remind me that everything can't be in my control." She turned to Sarah. "Please forgive your OCD boss. I do appreciate you."

Sarah shook her head. "You are too much! I'm going to go up front and gather everyone in to the sanctuary."

"That would be great, so we can get started on time." After Sarah left, Lenora crossed her arms. This wedding was really important to her. Not that all her brides weren't important, but she had bonded with Candace and her daughter, Rachel. They were like family.

"Everything looks good."

Lenora turned around to see her husband walking toward her. She sensed Jonathan studying her. She returned his stare. "What are you thinking?"

"Are you up for this tonight?"

She placed her hands on her hip. "Do I look fragile to you?"

He raised his eyebrows. "Not in the least. But I know you. You won't admit to me when something is wrong."

"Look, I'm still disappointed, confused, and hurt, but I'm happy to be here tonight. During the rehearsal and the wedding tomorrow, I hope these thoughts will get pushed to the side, at least for a while."

Jonathan placed his hands on both her shoulders. She let him pull her into his arms. Surprised at his public display of affection, Lenora melted into her husband's arms. Any tension she had dissipated for a few moments.

Jonathan stepped back. "I will be in my office. Call me when you're ready to run through the ceremony."

She nodded, unable to speak because of the lump that had formed in her throat. Lenora appreciated her husband's concerns. She was trying to move to a place of normalcy, but something wasn't right. She didn't know if she would ever make peace with Charmayne's death until she found out who was behind all of this.

Who hated Charmayne that much? Despite the police not finding any evidence, the threats were real. Lenora had been looking at her phone wondering about the strange text messages. What bothered her even more was why this person felt the need to pull Lenora into the situation. It was like this person knew Lenora was the perfect person to find Charmayne. It was no secret that they had been on-and-off friends since they were little girls.

Voices were making their way in the distance down the hallway. She took one last look at the setup for the reception. It was amazing how they were able to transform the Victory Gospel Center for either a basketball game or an elegant wedding reception. Lenora closed the door behind her and headed down the hallway that led to the sanctuary. She could see most of the members of the wedding party were sitting on the pews.

She walked up to Candace who was laughing with Angel.

"So what are we having so much fun talking about?" Lenora asked.

Candace looked at her wide-eyed and pointed her thumb toward Angel. "She didn't tell you yet?"

Lenora looked at Angel. "What didn't you tell me?"

Angel was grinning with tears in her eyes.

Lenora could tell they were tears of joy. "Did you do what I think?"

Angel nodded her head. "New Year's Eve is the date."

Lenora dropped her mouth open. "What? I have never done a New Year's Eve wedding. Ever." She smiled. "Come here." She hugged Angel, and then stepped back. "I'm so happy for you. You do know we have less than nine months to pull this off."

Angel waved, "If anyone can plan this wedding, you can."

"You're a mess."

The rehearsal took about an hour longer than planned, but Lenora felt good about all the participants. She took one last look at the sanctuary. It was all going down at one o'clock in the afternoon on Saturday.

Candace opted to go very simple with candles around the altar. Lenora thought the addition of baby's breath tied with lavender ribbon down the aisle was beautiful.

Lenora's body tingled all over. Without fail, for any wedding, she had that same feeling she had as a little girl getting ready for the first day of school. It was truly an honor to help a couple prepare for their first day as husband and wife.

"Lenora, you ready?"

Lenora smiled at her husband. "I'm ready." She hooked her arm inside his and let him lead the way to the car.

Lenora always planned the rehearsal dinners at a local restaurant. Tonight, Sammy's, one of her favorite restaurants, would serve as the setting for Candace and Darnell's rehearsal dinner. The restaurant had a large intimate room in the back. It was decorated like a dining room, with a very long mahogany table and burgundy-cushioned chairs. Lenora liked the fabric-covered walls because they blocked out the voices and noise from the other patrons in the restaurant.

Sammy's was a short fifteen minutes from Victory Gospel. When she and Jonathan entered, she looked around the table, happy to see all of the wedding party seated.

Keith had come down for the weekend. He and Rachel were sitting with their heads together.

Jonathan slid out her chair, and she sat down. Lenora nodded at Beulah Samuels, Candace's maid of honor, who winked back. Lenora grinned as she noticed Beulah was holding Mr. Harold's hand. Lenora was reminded of her brief, but very much welcomed hug from Jonathan earlier. Nothing like a wedding to bring out the romance for both the young and old.

She turned her attention to Jonathan who sat down across from her. After Jonathan said grace, salads and fresh hot rolls were placed on the table. Utensils clicked plates, and laughter floated around the table. Lenora kept an eye out for when everyone was finished with their salads, and then signaled the head waiter. Selections had been made earlier for those who wanted baked chicken breast or sirloin steak. Alongside the entrées were broccoli and a baked potato.

Lenora was enjoying brainstorming wedding ideas with Angel and Wes when her phone buzzed. "Excuse me while I check on this call." She normally didn't want to be rude, but with so many things done at the last minute for the wedding, she wanted to make sure not to miss a call.

Lenora walked to the other side of the room and frowned when she saw their home number. Michael usually couldn't be convinced to attend these types of events. He was a responsible sixteen-year-old, and Lenora felt comfortable with him hanging around the house on his own. Tonight, he wasn't alone since Eliza had decided to join the wedding festivities tomorrow.

Lenora wondered what would cause him or Eliza to call. "Hello, Michael?"

"Mom, you have to come home quick."

Lenora glanced over her shoulder at Jonathan. He was having a conversation with Darnell, but he must have sensed her stare because he turned his head.

Lenora swallowed. "Michael, what's going on?"

"Someone was trying to break into the house."

"What? Are you okay? Did you call 911?"

"The alarm went off, and the cops are here now."

Lenora whirled around and gestured to Jonathan.

Jonathan wiped his mouth and stood. As he approached, he mouthed, "What's going on?"

"Michael, we will be there soon." She clicked off the phone. The day had gone so well. She stepped closer to Jonathan, trying to keep the trembling and volume out of her voice. She didn't want to alert the wedding party to the chaos. "That was Michael. He said someone tried to break in to the house."

"Okay, let's tell everyone we have an emergency and head home."

She agreed. They said a hasty good-bye to everyone. Lenora did her best to dodge questions and assured Candace and Darnell that everything would be okay for their big day.

As Jonathan and she left the restaurant, Lenora's feelings of euphoria had been replaced with the underlying fear that had been by her side for the past few weeks.

When they arrived home, there wasn't only a police cruiser in the driveway, but an ambulance too.

Lenora sprinted behind Jonathan through the garage and up the steps to the kitchen. As soon as she entered the house, she called out, "Michael!"

"I'm in here, Mom."

Lenora rounded the corner into the hallway leading to the living room. She reached out to Michael, who was standing with his shoulders slouched. "Are you okay, honey?"

Her son turned his stricken face to her, looking ready to cry. "Grandma kept saying something didn't feel right. I should've listened."

Jonathan ran over to the paramedics who were talking to Eliza. Eliza was sitting in the seat with an oxygen mask on her face. She grabbed it and tried to remove it. "No, Mother. They gave you that for a reason. Leave the mask alone and let it do what it needs to do."

Jonathan turned to the paramedic kneeling in front of his mother. "What happened here?"

"Is this your mother, sir?"

Jonathan angrily asked, "Yes, tell me what's going on."

"Well, it looks like Mrs. Freeman here had an elevated blood pressure. Sounds like it was pretty stressful around here. When we arrived, she had passed out, and you can see, she's come around. We would like to take her to the hospital to get her thoroughly checked out."

Lenora walked over and stated, "I think that's a good idea." She patted Eliza's hand and observed her. Eliza's eyes were glazed, and she looked like she wanted to fall asleep. For a brief moment her eyes registered with Lenora's. Despite protests, she took the oxygen mask off her face. Her voice was raspy as she tried to speak.

She lifted her wrinkled finger toward Lenora. "You need to be careful."

Lenora exchanged a look with Jonathan, and then turned her attention back to Eliza. She couldn't ask the woman what she meant because the paramedics were ready to lift her on the stretcher.

As Lenora stepped out of the way and returned to her son's side, her heart was beating so fast, she didn't quite feel steady on her own feet. Why was she supposed to be being careful? Did tonight's break-in have anything to do with her personally?

Lenora's worst fear of bringing her own transgressions on her family seemed to be coming true. If only she knew which sin and the identity of the source.

Chapter Forty-two

After her conversation with the Greater Heights Church secretary, Serena decided to explore. She hated standing outside the woman's house like some stalker. Martha German was one of those people who didn't mind having her curtains open despite the fact the sun had long disappeared in the sky. At least she knew the woman was home. Serena had to figure out a way to talk to her.

Serena dialed her number and waited for Martha to pick up. Once Serena heard the gravelly voice, she hung up the phone. The woman must have been a smoker at one time. Maybe she still smoked. No concern to Serena. She had decided to rest her tired eyes and ambush the woman bright and early the next day. If Martha took over as financial secretary after Charmayne, then she seemed to be the only one who could give an accurate account of the finances.

It was morning as Serena approached the house she had scoped out the night before. She parked her SUV a few houses down from her destination. This must have been one of those neighborhoods that required homeowners to have well-manicured lawns. Martha German's two-story brick home appeared larger in the daylight. Serena had done her homework and knew the woman had her own healthy pension from being a schoolteacher. Digging a little deeper, Serena knew Martha was married to a well-known real estate lawyer who had acquired a significant amount of wealth before his death. So what reason would the woman have to comb money off the top of a budget designated to help a low-income population?

Serena walked up to the door, rang the doorbell, and waited.

The deep-throaty voice she recognized called out, "Who is it? No soliciting, please."

"I'm not here to sell you anything or to pitch a religion to you. I want to talk about Charmayne Hudson."

Serena heard locks, several locks, being unlatched. When the door opened, she could see that a gold chain kept the door attached to the door frame. The woman peered out at her.

"What do you want?" Martha narrowed her eyes. "You're some reporter, aren't you?"

Not just some reporter. Serena held out her hand. "I'm Serena Manchester. I understand you knew Charmayne Hudson fairly well."

Martha glared at her for a moment longer, and then decided to unlatch the chain. When she opened the door, Serena was surprised to see the elegant woman dressed in a T-shirt and jeans. She looked so ordinary.

Martha asked, "Why would you think that I knew that woman? I wasn't friends with her, but her father."

"That's good to know because I'm particularly interested in you inheriting her role as financial secretary on the Hudson Housing Development Committee. I understand you are the fund-raiser extraordinaire."

The slightest of smiles touched Martha's lips. "I wouldn't say all that, but it's a project my dear friend Bishop Hudson entrusted to me when Charmayne felt like being on the city council was enough for her."

"How much money would you say the committee raised over the years? I'm sure you know Charmayne had a hard time trying to get the council to see the benefits of supporting the project."

"I don't have financial records on me and it's all public record. From recollection, I believe we raised about $750,000. Which isn't bad, but we need a whole lot more to pursue some of the more ambitious elements of the housing development. In fact, before Bishop Hudson died, we were meeting with the Charlotte-Mecklenburg Planning Commission on zoning."

Serena asked, "How much money are we talking for the final budget?"

"This project was a dream that grew big in proportion. To really make it happen would involve millions of dollars."

Serena thought about Lance Ryan. Was he purposely trying to destroy the project? But why? What did he hope to gain by having her dig into finances that were minor in the evolution of the project?

Martha crossed her arms. "I thought you were here to talk about Charmayne."

Serena nodded. "I am. I'm sorry, but you did say you didn't know her that well, so I thought I would ask a topic that you may have some knowledge about. Would you mind if I ask another question?"

Martha's neck looked strained, like she really wanted Serena to move away from her front door. She finally answered. "I need to get ready for an event early this afternoon, so go ahead with your question, Ms. Manchester."

Serena looked over her shoulder. A next-door neighbor marched out toward the driveway. He appeared to be picking up a newspaper. The man looked over and waved. Serena smiled, and then looked at Martha. "Is it possible I can come in for just a few moments? I mean, you don't want all your neighbors to know you're talking to a reporter, do you?"

Martha stuck her head out the door. She sucked in a breath as though she was offended at the proposition. She opened the door wider and stepped to the side so Serena could enter.

Serena slipped inside the house, which, at a glance, was as immaculate as the outside. It wasn't like it was out of the pages of a magazine, but more or less very neat and orderly. The house smelled of lemon Pledge, like someone had just gone through the house on a cleaning spree.

Martha shut the door and folded her arms. "Well, what do you need to ask me, Ms. Manchester?"

Serena pulled out her phone from her bag. She scrolled to the photo she had downloaded and shared the picture of Charmayne standing next to the overweight Lance. "Do you know this man?"

Martha reached up as if to push her hair away from her face, but the woman's silver hair was wrapped tight in a bun. "Yes. I mean, I don't know him personally. He was invited, or rather, I should say he invited himself, to the committee meetings years ago."

Serena put her phone away and asked, "What do you mean he invited himself?"

"He was a friend of Charmayne's. She met him Lord knows where. Sometimes that woman wasn't too bright when it came to the company she kept. She convinced her father that her friend was a reputable housing consultant who dealt with housing development projects."

Serena narrowed her eyes. "Let me guess. He wasn't that qualified, which is why Bishop Hudson gave him the boot."

"The man actually was very knowledgeable. In fact, Alex Carrington, before he became our mayor, was familiar with him too. You know the mayor has his own real estate firm."

Serena nodded and stored that bit of information about the mayor in her head.

Martha continued, "He didn't strike me as a people person though. Bishop Hudson liked to be in charge. I had known the bishop for decades. He was always ambitious and a take-charge man. I think Bishop simply didn't like the man. He had only allowed him in as a consultant to pacify Charmayne. I guess she had a need to contribute."

"Interesting. Do you think Charmayne and this man were romantic?"

"I don't know. You know she never did marry, although a few years ago there was a rumor about her being engaged. No one ever met the fellow, but she was certainly seen trying on wedding gowns at her friend's boutique."

Really? Serena didn't think she had run across a woman who had more men issues than she did. She would have thought twice or more before pursuing a relationship with Lance in his heavier days. Funny though, he was all muscle now, and not bad looking. She thought the transformed Lance was the kind of man a girl should run away from. Maybe something changed in him after the weight loss. He could have been a really decent guy for all she knew.

Serena glanced at the clock. She needed to get home so she could dress presentably enough to crash a wedding. She looked at Martha. "I just have one more question. Do you remember the man's name?"

Martha placed her hand on the door. As she opened the door, she said. "I'm afraid not."

Serena stalled moving toward the door. "What about where he worked? Was he a one-man show? Did he have employees?"

Martha had opened the door wide. She looked at Serena. "I'm sorry, my memory isn't what it used to be. I used to be able to remember frivolous facts, but not anymore."

She could argue with the woman. Martha had to be in her seventies, though she was looking sharp in those jeans. At the rate she was going, Serena could only hope to look that good when she hit seventy. She walked out the door. "Thank you for your time."

Before closing the door, Martha stated, "Wait. I do remember there was a time we met him at his office, or I guess it was his office."

Serena spun around. "Where?"

"It was an office building out on Parklane Road. Different businesses could lease space. You know my husband was a lawyer. He knew everyone in Charlotte, but he wasn't familiar with the law firm in that building. Anyway, he may still be there."

With that, Martha German closed the door. Serena turned around and started walking to her car. The mention of the law firm seemed odd, but the woman was old and had been gracious. Serena finally had a place to start looking for the elusive Lance Ryan.

She had no doubts that Lance Ryan had an axe to grind with Charmayne Hudson from the very beginning. *You're not getting away with what you did.*

Chapter Forty-three

Eliza stayed in the hospital overnight for observations. Jonathan assured Lenora he still planned to officiate Darnell and Candace's wedding. He arose early so he could stop by the hospital before heading to Victory Gospel. Lenora was twitchy, unable to keep still for five minutes. The break-in piled on to a big wedding today was more than she could handle.

Jonathan stood in her path, to put a halt to her pacing. "Lenora, go take care of what you need to do at the church. Mother will probably be discharged this afternoon. No worries."

"Don't you think it's odd that this man tried to break in while we were out last night? Michael and/or Eliza could have really been hurt. Suppose he comes back?"

Jonathan didn't want to admit the break-in bothered him too. "It wasn't technically a break-in. He didn't get in here, and now that he knows we have a good alarm system, the man would be wise to not think about coming back. Besides, we had a lesson learned last night; we need to fix the motion detectors out in front, which will get done before tonight. The house was just too dark and inviting."

Lenora's eyes were weary. "You have an answer for everything, don't you?"

No, he didn't. In all of the years they had lived there, no one had bothered them before. In fact, he had grilled the police last night. There had been no reports of break-ins in the area. "Let's just be thankful that God was watching over our son and my mother. Mother will be fine, and we will all return to normal. Now, you go ahead to Victory Gospel. You have an important day ahead of you."

He followed Lenora downstairs and watched her grab her bag. She was dressed in a pale blue suit, looking very official as the wedding planner. Her hair was piled up high on her head in a mass of curls, showing off the curves of her neck. Despite the worry lines around his wife's face, she looked beautiful.

Jonathan walked Lenora out to her car and before she climbed in, he grabbed her by the elbow. She appeared puzzled. He pulled her close to him. For a few seconds her body was tense, but eventually, Lenora melted and wrapped her arms around him. They remained in the embrace, both aware of how much they needed to connect. He pulled away and kissed her softly on the lips. "Everything will be okay."

She smiled, though there was still a hint of uncertainty in her eyes. As the garage door opened, Jonathan stood to the side and observed as Lenora backed her Lexus out of the garage. After a slight wave, he returned to the house.

He had knocked on his youngest son's door earlier in the morning, insisting that he get up despite the fact it was Saturday. Jonathan didn't want his mother to be alone, and he knew Michael and Eliza were bosom buddies.

He called upstairs. "You ready, son?"

Michael's footsteps sounded like a puppy galloping down the steps. The boy was always sullen, but today, he looked weary and apprehensive.

"Did you get any sleep, Mikey?" Jonathan asked as he pulled on his suit jacket.

"Nope."

"Sorry to hear that, son. I appreciate your willingness to look after your grandmother today."

He shrugged. "No problem. She can come home today, right?"

"Yes, I'm going to check to see if they will let us bring her home today. I know she will be ready because there's nothing like sleeping in your own bed."

He and Michael walked out of the house and entered the garage. Jonathan started up the car. Before driving off, he waited for the garage door to close.

Jonathan knew Michael had made a statement to the police, but he didn't get the whole story. "Tell me again what happened last night."

Michael had been looking out the passenger window. He swung around and said, "They're not going to find anyone."

Jonathan frowned. "Why do you say that?"

"Because we didn't see anyone, Dad. How can they find the shadow of an unknown man?"

"Well, what alerted you to someone breaking into the house?"

Michael shook his head. "I was playing a video game in the living room. I heard a noise coming from the front door, but to be honest, I didn't pay attention at first. It wasn't until Grandma came into the room."

He swallowed. "I could tell she was scared. She said, 'Someone is outside the front door, Mikey. We need to check on it.'"

"So, I got up and we walked into the hallway. I started to turn the lights on, but Grandma said, 'No, not yet.' At first, I thought it was you and Mom coming back, but . . ."

Jonathan pulled up to a light and stopped. He had been so engrossed in his son's conversation, he hadn't realized he was about five minutes away from the hospital. "Then what? What did you see?"

Michael shrugged. "I thought I saw a man's shadow standing outside the window next to the door. At first,

I thought I was seeing things, but then Grandma had grabbed my arm. She squeezed really hard. Then, she started slipping. I could tell she was falling. I didn't know what to do.

"I was trying to concentrate on getting her to the living room. I got her on the couch. That's when the alarm sounded. I ran back out to the hallway, and whoever it was, they turned around and ran out. He was dressed in dark clothes and he had a hood on. I couldn't see his face. It happened so fast."

Jonathan had pulled into the hospital parking garage by then. He looked over at his son. "I'm proud of you. You were brave, and you took care of your grandmother."

"You sure she's going to be okay?"

"Yes, you know nothing knocks my mother down. Let's go inside to check on her. She will be tickled to have you with her."

They walked into the hospital together. Jonathan pressed the elevator button. It dawned on him that he had been inside this hospital a number of times in the past few months. He came to visit sick patients, but it was his own family that had him walking these corridors recently.

His father passed away just last month in this hospital. Then Keith's accident, Lenora's sickness, and now his mother. He wasn't a man who spent too much time worrying or complaining, but he had some discomfort that he was not accustomed to feeling.

He knew not to take his family for granted, but the number of wake-up calls was like sharp-edged reminders from God. There was a sense of uneasiness in the pit of his stomach as they approached his mother's room. Maybe he was letting Lenora's paranoia rub off on him.

Eliza seemed to be in good spirits and had just finished her breakfast. Jonathan leaned over and kissed his mother on the forehead. "Did you sleep okay, Mother?"

She patted his hand. "I slept as well as I could in this bed. I was tired though, so I closed my eyes for a bit. How you doing, baby?" Eliza had turned her attention to Michael.

Michael reached down and hugged his grandma.

She grinned, "Baby, you saved your grandma's life."

Michael shook his head. "I just wanted to make sure you got help, Grandma. I'm no hero."

"Well, you're my hero. Did you eat something yet?"

"No."

Eliza said, "Why don't you go grab something to eat? Jonathan, you give the boy some money."

Jonathan peered at his mother. She seemed a bit agitated this morning, though she was putting on a good show of being in good spirits. He handed his son a twenty-dollar bill. "Don't be gone too long. I will need to drive to the church in a bit."

"I'll be back soon, Dad."

When Michael had left the room, Jonathan turned toward his mother who had been watching him intently. "Something on your mind, Mother?"

"How's Lenora?"

"She's fine. I sent her up to the church so she can get what she needs in place before the wedding this afternoon."

"It's good that she stays busy." Eliza had folded her arms and looked around the room.

"There's something you aren't telling me. You sent Michael to get something to eat for some reason. Why?"

Eliza unfolded her arms and placed her hands in her lap. "I think someone is after Lenora."

Jonathan leaned forward. "What do you mean? I talked to Michael, and he couldn't see anything more than a shadow at the door. Did you see someone?"

"That's all I saw too. I knew the person was a man." Eliza twisted her hands. Not looking at Jonathan, she stated, "I wondered if he could've been the same person."

Jonathan sat very still, hoping he misinterpreted what his mother said. "Did you say 'same person'?"

"You know I was the one who found Lenora when she got sick after Charmayne's funeral. I didn't think anything of it until after we got her in the ambulance, but there was a man who I could've sworn was standing awfully close to the bathroom door. He might have even been coming out. He saw me and hightailed it in the other direction."

The sense of uneasiness that Jonathan had experienced previously bubbled like a pot of boiling water. "Why didn't you tell me this before?"

"Because it didn't make sense. Besides, Lenora was really sick that day. It was all about getting her fever down. Anyway, I overhead Lenora one day sounding really upset. Is it true that she doesn't think Charmayne killed herself?"

Jonathan rubbed his head as though he wanted to wipe away any mention of what his mother revealed. "Lenora needs to accept the truth, and you can't be leading her on." He closed his mouth shut as the door opened.

Michael had returned. The boy looked from his father to his grandmother, unspoken concern on his face.

Jonathan stood, shifting his eyes from his mother's intense gaze. "Michael will stay with you, and we will work on getting you discharged if the doctor says you're clear to come home. I need to get a couple married today."

Before Jonathan walked off, his mother reached for his hand. Her grip was quite firm, which indicated his mother was indeed on the mend. He eyed her.

Eliza said, "Don't be so quick to ignore her. A woman's intuition is a powerful thing. I can tell you something wasn't right about the man I saw."

Chapter Forty-four

For most of her drive to Victory Gospel, Lenora tried to keep her thoughts focused on the impending wedding ceremony instead of the previous night's events. She had drawn comfort from Jonathan's embrace. That man was her second rock. God being her first. It was those two thoughts that kept her from falling completely apart. She was clueless to what was going on in her life, but God knew, and today, she would trust His grace and mercy.

Lenora parked the car and headed into the side door of Victory Gospel. She stopped to check the sanctuary for a few minutes. None of the guests had arrived yet. She liked arriving early, not just to make sure all was in place, but during this time she walked and prayed.

Lenora walked down the church aisle, her feet cushioned by the deep, thick carpet. She prayed for Darnell and Candace who would exchange vows in a few hours. This was a second time around for both of them. Lenora prayed for them to walk into this marriage as a new beginning for both. She stopped and straightened one of the baby's breath arrangements at the end of the pew.

As she rounded the sanctuary, she prayed for the wedding party which included Wes and Angel. Those two had sprung a surprise on her, but she was delighted to plan a New Year's Eve wedding.

Lenora thought of her oldest son, Keith, and Candace's daughter, Rachel. Would they be like her and Jonathan, falling in love so young and remaining together for the next twenty years? Lenora prayed that both Keith and Rachel would be granted wisdom as they moved forward together.

Before she exited the sanctuary, Lenora looked back to where her husband would stand and marry the couple. She prayed for him and his role as shepherd of Victory Gospel. She prayed he was walking in his true calling.

"Lord, let this day be as perfect as it can be. I leave all of this in your hands."

Lenora let the doors of the sanctuary close behind her and headed back toward the classroom she had set up as the bride's room.

Soon, Candace arrived with most of her wedding party in tow.

Lenora squeezed Candace. "Your hair looks beautiful."

"Thank you. Beulah insisted on starting early this morning. Hopefully, the curls will last me until tonight."

Lenora grinned. "I'm sure your hair *and* you will hold up just fine. I'm so excited for you. It's been a long time for this day to come."

"You're not kidding. I hated not being able to talk to Darnell last night. You know we talk every night."

Lenora thought how sweet. She and Jonathan used to stay up for hours talking into the night when they were younger. She touched Candace's shoulders. "You will have a lifetime to talk to each other."

Tears had brimmed in Candace's eyes. "That's what I'm hoping for."

Lenora squeezed her bride's hands and went to check on the bridesmaids to be sure all of them had arrived. When she was satisfied that everyone was starting to dress, she walked to the other end of the hallway to check on the groom. She knocked on the door.

"Come in."

Lenora poked her head in to see Darnell and Wes standing and talking. Keith was in the corner on his phone. He looked up and walked over. "Hey, Mom, I've been texting Mikey. How's Grandma doing?"

"What happened?" Darnell asked.

Lenora noticed Darnell and Wes were focused on her. She took a deep breath. It was not her intention for last night to come up at all. She waved her hand. "We had a bit of a scare. Someone tried to break in when we were at the rehearsal dinner. The alarm system worked perfectly. The intruder was scared off."

Keith piped up, "What about Grandma?"

"Mother Eliza did faint from the excitement, but she will be home with us this afternoon." Lenora looked at Darnell. "No worries."

"Are you sure? Who took the report last night? I can certainly check on it for you," Darnell inquired.

"No no no! You're not going to have Candace wanting to kill me. Everything is fine. This is your day." Lenora checked her watch. "Remember, I want you and your best man to be at the altar ten minutes before we start the processional."

Darnell saluted her. "Yes, ma'am. I will be standing there waiting."

Lenora closed the door behind her and took a deep breath. She hoped the confidence she had displayed worked, because she had suddenly felt like she lost her peace. She quickly prayed as she headed back down the hallway.

I need you, Lord. I need that peace that surpasses all understanding right now.

Soon the time had arrived and everyone was in place. Lenora took a peek inside the sanctuary. She guessed that at least one hundred people were seated in the pews.

Lenora turned her attention to the front. Darnell fidgeted with his tuxedo tie. Behind him Wes stood with his hands in front of him. On the other side of Darnell, Jonathan stood in his robe. He looked back at her, and she waved to indicate it was time.

A few minutes later the wedding party began the processional down the aisle, one couple at a time, as Chrisette Michele's voice belted out the song "Golden."

Lenora's eyes watered as she watched Candace hook her arm into Mr. Harold's arm. Beulah's husband had insisted on walking Candace down the aisle. Lenora was touched to see Beulah and Harold stepping in as surrogate parents for Candace today.

Any troubles that had invaded her mind, her home, and her family were a distant memory as she watched Candace and Darnell exchange vows. She felt a weight lift off her shoulders as Darnell lowered his mouth to kiss his new wife. Mission accomplished.

Lenora looked over at her husband.

Jonathan returned her gaze.

Lenora began to ponder the vows as Candace and Darnell walked arm in arm down the aisle.

For better or worse.

Till death do us part.

In that moment, the dark cloud that seemed to linger over Lenora threatened to return. She knew the smile must have disappeared from her face because that concerned look that Jonathan seemed to always have lately flashed in his eyes.

This was one of those times when she would have loved to hear her mother's strict, but logical advice. Instead, in the back of her mind, a still, small, and quiet voice said:

The prayers of the righteous avail much.

So, Lenora talked to God.

Chapter Forty-five

Serena rarely felt guilty about anything. She hated to admit crashing Darnell and Candace's wedding had shifted her guilt meter to a new level. A level of shame. While Mr. and Mrs. Darnell Jackson were introduced, Serena ducked behind a group of men whom she assumed were Darnell's colleagues. For a brief second she contemplated what if she could have been Mrs. Darnell Jackson.

The thought left her as she refocused on her mission.

The woman she came to see was standing across the room hugging the wedding party. Serena thought hard about the best way to get near Lenora Freeman without causing any scenes. Serena just needed her for a few moments so they could talk in private.

Serena crossed her arms. Really, she could have waited to contact Serena on Monday. But something was driving the sense of urgency. For Serena, her interest in Charmayne Hudson's death had long turned from being just another story. *She* wanted to know. Even more important, Serena was concerned that someone else was in danger.

She turned her head and noticed that a young man stood slouched against the wall. Serena guessed he was maybe fifteen or sixteen. His face looked familiar, and then it dawned on Serena that this young man was probably Lenora's son. He looked just like his father. She slid closer to him.

"Hey, do you know where I could find Mrs. Freeman? I have a delivery outside she has been waiting on and I don't know where she wanted me to put it."

The young man pulled himself off the wall. "I'm her son. I could take it."

"Oh no, I need her to sign for it. Can you let her know that I'm outside the office?"

The boy pointed to where his mother was standing. "She's over there. I'll go get her."

"Thank you." Serena watched as the boy made his way over to his mother. She didn't want to be standing there when Lenora turned around so she sneaked out the door. Serena had been in the Victory Gospel Center for other events and headed down the hallway she thought led to the office.

She turned the knob and the office door opened. Serena walked inside and hoped Lenora wouldn't decide to throw her out.

Soon she heard the tapping of high-heeled shoes coming down the hallway. Lenora Freeman stood in the doorway and peered in. They made eye contact; Serena could tell Lenora was not pleased. "Were you the one who lied to my son?"

"Yes, I'm sorry. I needed a way to talk to you without disturbing the festivities."

Lenora put her hands on her hips. "And you couldn't do this on another day?"

Serena stepped forward. "Look, I have been research-ing information the past few days about your friend Charmayne and I really need your help on getting some answers. I know you want to see justice."

Lenora closed her eyes. When she opened them, Serena thought the woman would melt. Before Lenora walked away and completely dismissed her, she pulled her phone out and showed the photo. "Do you know this man?"

She watched as a lightbulb moment dawned in Lenora's eyes. Lenora looked at her. "Why are you asking?"

Serena didn't like that Lenora wouldn't just come out and say what she knew. "Mrs. Freeman, it's really important to know if you can identify this man." Serena shoved the photo of the heavier set Lance standing next to Charmayne.

"That man was engaged to Charmayne."

"What?" Serena thought she would choke on her own words. "You're kidding, right? Him?"

Lenora nodded. "I only met him a handful of times, actually, more like two times. She seemed to think he treated her well, and believe me, Charmayne had her run of men. Most weren't good for her or they became intimidated by her because of her father. I got the impression she liked him because he stood up to her father."

Serena looked back at the photo and felt a tremor in her hand. She flipped over to another photo and held it up for Lenora to see. "Do you recognize him?"

Lenora frowned. There was a glimmer of recognition in her eyes. Then Serena watched as another emotion appeared.

She nudged. "What's wrong? You look like you've seen a ghost or something."

"No. I'm confused. Is that the same man?"

"Yes. A lot thinner looking these days and without the chunky glasses."

Lenora stared off into space as if she was trying to re-member something. "I have seen him at least two times. He felt familiar to me, but I didn't know where I had seen him before. Why are you asking about him?"

"Why didn't Charmayne marry him?"

Lenora shook her head. "I have no idea. No, wait. I'm sure her father had something to do with it. She told me the bishop really didn't like him, but still Charmayne was a grown woman. She could have made her own decision, and it shouldn't have mattered."

Serena rubbed her chin. She was still stunned that Charmayne had been prepared to marry this man, not the muscular cut man she had run into, but this incredibly large man whose eyes appeared huge behind the thick glasses. She asked, "Where have you seen the new and improved version?"

Lenora sat down in the chair against the wall. "I saw him at Pastor Jeremiah's funeral. He looked familiar to me, but I am ashamed to say I couldn't recall where I had seen him before. In this business, I meet so many people. I felt an urge to try to talk to him because he was staring at me. Anyway, he moved so fast, I never saw where he went."

Serena watched as the woman paused as if she was recollecting the memory. Finally she continued, "The second time I saw him was at Charmayne's funeral. I wasn't feeling well, but he had walked up to me and we talked."

Serena leaned forward. "What did you talk about?"

"I honestly don't remember. I was so out of it with a fever that day. You still aren't telling me why you have questions about this man. Do you think he had something to do with Charmayne's death?"

"I don't really know how he's involved or what his intentions are, but I will say he was the one who brought me the story about Hudson Housing Development. He wanted me to look into the financial records. I have to say, I saw some discrepancies and I'm still not sure what to think."

Lenora began twisting her hands. "Charmayne had been receiving threats after her father died. She told me that it seemed like everyone was against her all of sudden."

Serena prodded, "The *they* Charmayne was referring to are the mayor and the other council members, right?"

"I guess. She wasn't very specific. We didn't have a lot of time to talk, and I wish I had asked her to let me see the threats. The police didn't find anything. What do you intend to do with this information? How do you think this man . . . you know, I don't even remember his name," Lenora admitted.

"He's been going by Lance Ryan whenever we talk."

"Ryan?" Lenora looked away.

"You know something else?"

Lenora shook her head. "No, I just—" The woman stood suddenly. "I can't do this right now. It's been nice of you to come share this information with me, but I need to be getting back to the reception where I belong."

Serena grabbed her arm. "Wait, you were about to say something else. What is it? I don't know what's going on here, but I believe this man, whoever he is, is a real threat. I think he wants to get to you."

Lenora wrenched her arm out of Serena's grip. "For what? I barely knew the man. I don't really know what Charmayne saw in him, but there is no reason for him to be bothering me. I planned their wedding up until Charmayne called me and said it was over. No explanation. I filed all that work away."

"Maybe something happened back then that you don't remember."

Lenora rubbed her temples. "I need to get back to the wedding reception."

"Okay, fine." Serena pushed her card into Lenora's hand. "If you can think of anything else, please call me. I have been up and close with this man and something isn't right about him."

There was a haunted look in Lenora's eyes that caused fear to slither up Serena's back. She watched Lenora return down the hallway. When the door opened to the Victory Gospel Center, laughter and good times poured out, and then went silent once Lenora entered and the door closed behind her.

Serena thought, *I don't doubt this man had something to do with Charmayne's death.* What was puzzling Serena was why Charmayne would want to marry this man.

Is Lenora really sure she isn't a target?

Chapter Forty-six

It took all of her strength not to go into the boutique on Sunday. Jonathan showed concern, but Lenora simply could not explain her thoughts to her husband. What she did know was she needed to look deeper into a man she barely knew. First, she had to know his name. She was having a difficult time connecting the two photos of the men that Serena had shown her. It appeared as if it was the same man.

She awoke Monday morning, trying to appear normal despite the anxiety that had been there for a few weeks, and had now increased. Lenora kissed Jonathan after handing him a steaming cup of black coffee with two tablespoons of sugar. She fixed some toast and a boiled egg for Eliza. Finally, she encouraged Michael to grab a bowl of cereal. She was thankful Keith had returned to UNC late Sunday afternoon. In her pursuit to appear normal, she noted odd looks from her family.

No time for that!

She knew the reporter was after a story, but Lenora was grateful that at least someone was digging in areas of Charmayne's life that the police probably wouldn't. Lenora's only real ally was now off on his honeymoon with Candace. When the couple returned in a week from the Bahamas, Lenora hoped to present convincing information to keep Charmayne's case alive.

Her drive to Michael's school was quiet. Her son was sullen as usual. Having to protect his grandmother over the weekend, and then have his mother drop him off at school as if all was normal had to be taking a toll. Jonathan and she had talked about getting Michael his own transportation but wanted to wait until he reached his senior year.

She waved good-bye to Michael and drove the Lexus with as much speed as she dared down the street and then off to I-77. Lenora fought to keep her patience in Monday morning traffic and within ten minutes, she pulled off at her exit. No one was parked at the strip mall where Lenora's Bridal Boutique was located. It was just a little after eight o'clock, and most of the other businesses opened around nine.

Lenora unlocked the door and closed it behind her. Despite her day off, she needed to do research. She opened her office and turned her computer on. While she waited, she started coffee because she was going to need it.

The office phone rang as the coffee started to drip in the carafe.

Lenora picked up the phone. "Hello."

"Mrs. Freeman?"

"Yes."

"How are you? I wanted to be sure that you could still come in this afternoon."

Lenora racked her mind. What appointment had she made?

The man on the other line reminded her. "Sorry, this is Charmayne's lawyer. I had some instructions for you from her will."

Lenora held her hands to her chest. "Oh. I'm so sorry. It's been such a busy weekend with the wedding and . . ." She stopped herself from babbling. "What time was the appointment again?" She looked at her desk calendar. "Oh wait, I see it. I wrote it down. It's one o'clock this afternoon, and your office is at Parklane."

"Yes, that is correct. I will see you then, Mrs. Freeman. Good-bye."

"Thank you, Mr.—" Before Lenora could finish her sentence, the man had hung up. She stared at the phone, not sure if the man had been rude or annoyed at her for forgetting the appointment. Lenora glanced down at her desk calendar. She didn't notice where she jotted down a name.

It was a personal policy of hers to always get the name and phone number of people who called. Apparently she'd been so distracted she didn't do either.

She'd worry about that later. Lenora turned to her computer and clicked to find the external hard drive she had attached last week. She went straight to Charmayne's wedding folder. After a few clicks through her organization of folders, Lenora found what she was looking for in the files.

The invitation stated, *The pleasure of your company is requested at the marriage of Charmayne Ann Hudson and Lance Ryan Matthews.*

Lenora held her hand over the mouth, staring at the invitation and the name.

Lance Ryan.

Lenora asked out loud. "Who are you, and why would you have a reason to come back to harm Charmayne?"

The invitation that Charmayne had asked her to create wasn't unusual, but it said a lot. Lenora remembered asking Charmayne why her parents weren't doing the invitation. In fact, Lenora pulled up the original invitation. It stated *Bishop William Hudson and Valerie Hudson request the honor of your presence at the marriage of Charmayne Ann Hudson and Lance Ryan Matthews.*

Lenora had assumed the wedding would take place at Greater Heights Church, but in the second invitation, Charmayne asked her to add the Ritz-Carlton. What surprised Lenora even more was Charmayne's off-hand comment.

"We don't have to get married in the church."

Lenora recalled responding. "No, but you're the daughter of Bishop Hudson. Why wouldn't you want the wedding ceremony at Greater Heights? I can see the reception being at the Ritz-Carlton."

"No, it will be easier for the guests with the ceremony and the reception at the same place."

At the time, Lenora didn't question the logic but thought Charmayne could have chosen a venue for the reception in the vicinity of Greater Heights Church. It was like Charmayne used the wedding as some stance to rebel against her father. Lenora was used to Charmayne's conflicts with her father, but she thought her friend would have moved forward with her wedding plans in an adult fashion.

"The wedding never happened. Why?" Lenora said out loud. Even though Lenora was furious at the months of work she had put into it, she never questioned or pushed Charmayne for an explanation. She had always assumed the bishop probably had managed to convince Charmayne to cancel the wedding.

Or did the decision come solely from Charmayne? The threats were directed at Charmayne after the bishop died, almost as if the man's presence was no longer a hindrance.

Lenora pulled up the bridal portrait Charmayne had taken. The photo was perfect. Not a strand of hair had strayed from Charmayne's updo. The makeup and Charmayne's skin were flawless, not a single blemish. Her friend smiled back at her from the computer screen with a bright white smile and joy in her eyes. There wasn't a hint of anything other than a woman delighted to be a bride.

Or was that what Lenora was seeing? The joy of finally being a bride, not so much a wife. How often had Lenora come across the woman whose sole focus was on the wedding day? Lenora could almost sense the crash of reality coming after, if not during, the honeymoon.

She had planned hundreds of weddings, with all races, nationalities, and religions. Like God was no respecter of people, love could come to a person in all forms, shapes, and sizes. Still, of all the men that had pursued Charmayne in her lifetime, why was this the man she chose to almost marry?

Who are you, Lance Ryan Matthews?

Chapter Forty-seven

Based on the information she had obtained from the records and her talk with Martha German, Serena tracked down the office building on Parklane Road. The building wasn't that far off the highway, but as she drove up, there didn't appear to be too many businesses that occupied the building. It was curious to her that this building was built by Mayor Carrington's real estate firm about a decade ago. She didn't know what that meant, but Serena had a feeling this scenario included the mayor in some way.

She parked her car a few spaces away from the few cars in the parking lot and turned off the engine. Not sure of what her plan was once she entered the building, she sat for a while. Her intentions for coming here was to see if Lance Ryan was still in business. The man had to be making a living doing something. The clothes that he wore were expensive. She suspected he was probably still in the real estate consulting business in some form or fashion.

What she wasn't sure about is what happens when she confronts him. He had made a point to be elusive about who he was and managed to control and manipulate the times they had met in person. How would he react to her just showing up and nailing his true identity?

She almost wished she had been more forthright with where her investigation had gone with Alan. He might have encouraged her to take Bud and the camera to get some more footage. Serena sensed now wasn't the time

to turn the information she had into a story. She clearly
didn't know what was going on and after talking to Lenora
over the weekend, she knew she had stunned the woman.

It sounded to Serena like the brief relationship between
Charmayne and Lance had gone badly and he may have an
agenda against her.

But why wait five years? Serena scratched out notes
after her visit with Lenora. Her one conclusion was that
Bishop Hudson's death served as a trigger.

She slapped the steering wheel, and then climbed out
of the car. This was about to drive her crazy. There were
so many bits and pieces not fitting together. At this point,
she was going to see if she could find where all the confusion had started.

Serena noticed a side door and walked up to it. She
pulled on the door, but it wouldn't budge. Then she
peered to the side and noticed there was an electronic
card reader. The building seemed to be pretty secure, and
this door must have been for employees to enter.

She walked around to the front of the building, noticing there must not have been many people who worked
inside because the parking lot was sparse with cars. *Why
even keep a building open if you don't have enough
tenants paying lease or rent?*

Serena reached the front which had a double glass door
entrance. She pulled on one of the doors, and it swung
open easily. Once inside, she felt the temperature drop.
While spring had arrived, it was starting to feel closer to
summer temperatures. The air condition felt good. She
looked over her shoulder and saw a security guard sitting
behind a large circular space.

He glanced at her, his eyes glassy. She waved to him,
but he continued to look at her as if he didn't care she had
just walked in. Serena shrugged and kept walking over to
the elevator area. The building was five stories, and there

appeared to be offices on each of the floors despite the nearly empty parking lot.

She scanned the listing next to the elevator. There were various businesses, but nothing jumped out at her. Her eyes stopped on Bowman and Watson Law Firm. Didn't Martha mention there was a lawyer in this building? The law firm was located on the fifth floor. There wasn't any other business located on that floor. Did that mean Lance Ryan had moved his business or was he in business at all?

It didn't hurt to check, so she pushed the elevator up button. Maybe the lawyer had information. Serena glanced over at the security guard. He was watching her. She turned around and rolled her eyes. Really, where did they get these folks from sometimes? She heard the hum of the elevator making its descent. The doors slid open, and she stepped in. She pressed the number five and waited for the elevator door to close.

The doors closed so slowly it made Serena nervous. Remembering the day Lance showed up at city hall, she almost expected his hands to appear stopping the doors from closing. She breathed a deep sigh of relief when the doors finally closed, only to have her stomach lurch when the elevator ascended. What would she find when the doors opened?

She watched the numbers light up at the top of the elevator until the number five was lit. Serena braced herself as the doors whirred open. She stepped out on the brightly patterned carpet and looked to her left. There was a window that showed the expansive skyline of Charlotte. She recognized some of the downtown buildings. Serena turned to her right and walked to the hallway. She looked down the hallway and noticed a few doors. The first door had Bowman and Watson Law Firm on the plaque outside the door.

She stepped up to the door and peered in through the glass beside the door. There was a receptionist area, but no one was sitting at the desk. Serena scanned what she could see and nothing looked out of the ordinary. Maybe she would stop back by after she explored a little more.

Serena continued down the hall. The next office space was dark. She grabbed the doorknob, but it was locked. Serena grimaced. This wasn't going to be easy. She continued down the hall until she came to another door. There wasn't anything on the plaque beside the door, but the office was lit. She looked behind her, and then walked up to the door. This time when she touched the knob it turned easily in her hand.

Should she do this? She could always say she was lost. With that little lie in place in her mind, Serena opened the door. As it opened, she glanced around. Like what she saw at the law firm, there was a receptionist area. Serena swung her eyes to the left to see a waiting room and a television set that wasn't on.

Was this a real office? Maybe someone was setting up an office?

She walked all the way in and closed the door slowly behind her, willing it not to click or make any noise. Once the door was shut, she listened for any movement or signs that someone was in the back area. Serena tiptoed across the office, grateful for the plush carpeting. She moved past the receptionist area. One office was closed, but two other doors were open. She peered inside the first open door. It seemed to be an office supply closet, but there were no supplies. A lone filing cabinet stood off to the side.

Her body was tense with anxiety, but she kept walking until she reached the second open door. From the light that came from the window, she could see the room had the usual office furnishings: a large desk, swivel chair, armchairs, and filing cabinets. The walls were bare. She did a 360 turn and noted the walls didn't have any artwork. Just plain white walls.

Then she heard a voice from outside the door. What should she do? Serena scrambled over to the utility closet and hid behind the door. Whoever was coming was either talking loud to someone or was on the phone. The door she had just entered swung open. Serena peeked through the crack in the door and saw the very man she was look-ing for stroll by her.

She pulled back as Lance turned around. His face was reddish under his tan, eyes flashing. "There's no one to blame here but you. You let that righteous bishop get into your business. He would have never discovered what you were into if you left this project alone in the first place."

Who was Lance talking to on the other end of that phone call? Serena tried to pull herself in the shadows as best she could and hoped Lance didn't need anything in this empty closet. He had grown quiet, and then started sputtering out a string of expletives that even made Serena's cheeks grow warm. The man was in a rage which put her in a real awkward, dangerous position, she thought.

Serena dared to glance through the door again and saw Lance had his back turned away from her. She listened as he continued. "You just make sure you have my money. You wanted the Hudson Development off the plate. It's gone. No one is going to try to resurrect that project. Even if they do, any missing funds would probably fall back on Charmayne. She's not exactly here to defend herself, is she?"

After a moment of silence, Lance threw his hand in the air. "What?

"I told you, I doubt the woman saw me at Charmayne's house. If she did, you better believe I'm going to take care of that."

"I *know* you're not threatening me, Mayor. I mean, would you really want it to get out that you were the last person to see Charmayne alive?"

Serena shrank back in horror; her heart was beating so fast she held her hand to her chest. *The mayor? Mayor Carrington?*

I knew it! So the bishop had found out the mayor had been making some money on the side. That had to be some federal money too. Did Charmayne know?

But what woman was Lance talking about? Was he talking about Lenora Freeman?

Serena listened again, but only heard the one-sided conversation from a distance. She looked through the door and saw Lance had moved inside the office that had the closed door. Okay, now she had a decision to make. She could either try to get closer and hear more of the conversation or she could get her behind out of this office before Lance discovered her.

Her mind told her she needed to do the latter. Now that she knew the mayor had probably seen Charmayne before she died, she could just confront him. It was coming up on an election year, and she could probably catch Mayor Carrington off guard.

Serena moved slowly out of the closet, her eyes glued to the door where Lance was still talking loudly on the phone. She could hear tidbits of the conversation as she tried to move toward the door. Serena was almost halfway across the room when she heard Lance clearly say, "I even cleaned her fingernails so no one would suspect that she fought for her life and connected the DNA to you. By the way, thanks for saving me the dirty job and giving me the insurance to make sure I get paid. Maybe I should up the amount you owe me."

Serena could have jumped out of her skin at that revelation. That made the mayor a murderer. Somehow,

Lance came in as the one to make it all look like a suicide. Charmayne was going to marry *this* man? No matter indirectly, he had played a role in her death and in some crazy way had probably achieved revenge.

She had to get out of there.

As thoughts raced through her mind, Serena didn't realize that Lance had stopped talking. She looked up at the office. Lance was walking back toward the door.

Serena turned and sprinted toward the door.

"Hey, what are you doing in here?"

She didn't bother to turn around to know the man had a murderous look of rage on his face.

Serena ran out of the office, thinking there was no way she was going to make it to the elevator. She ran past the lawyer's firm office, thinking, why didn't she just go in there? Instead, she headed to the door marked stairs and proceeded down the flights of stairs as fast as she could. Maybe she could get to one of the other floors, where there had to be more people.

As she started down the stairs, Serena made an error that she would soon regret. She turned just long enough to see Lance burst open the door to the stairway, his face was exactly as she pictured it.

Ready to kill.

She was thinking this man was some athlete as he moved swiftly down the stairs toward her. In a split second, she knew without a doubt he was going to catch her.

Whether he shoved her or she tripped, Serena didn't know, but for the first time in a very long time, she called out to God as she fell.

Chapter Forty-eight

"Are you sure you need to be going over there by yourself? Don't you think we should be looking more into this guy, Lance Ryan Matthews?" Jonathan had asked her as she relayed to him all the information she had learned. At this point, Lenora wanted to stick to the plan of hiding nothing. She asked Jonathan to meet her over near Parklane so they could have a late lunch. She wasn't sure what the lawyer had to tell her, but she knew she needed her husband's support.

Lenora assured her husband, "I should be fine. Let's just plan to meet at two o'clock. I can't imagine this taking more than thirty minutes, and certainly not an hour."

"Okay. I'll meet you there at two."

Lenora clicked the End call button and stared at the phone for a minute. She had already arrived at the Parklane Plaza. It wasn't until she drove into the parking lot that she thought to call Jonathan. She knew his favorite restaurant was down in this area, and she really wasn't sure what she was walking into right now. She got out of the car. Today, she had thrown on jeans and a blouse, with some Keds sneakers. The attire was something she would wear on the weekends for shopping.

She entered the office building and noticed the security guard. He glanced briefly at her and turned his attention back to whatever he was looking at behind the high desk. The man looked like he was in his late forties or early fifties; his thick, wiry hair was speckled with gray under his cap. He had a thick mustache that covered his top lip.

Lenora walked over to the elevators and looked for any signs of a law firm. The Bowman and Watson Law Firm was located on the fifth floor.

She pushed the elevator button, despite the increasing temptation to turn around and walk out of the building. She would check out what the lawyer had to say. It occurred to Lenora maybe the reason why the police hadn't found any evidence was because Charmayne kept the threatening information safe. What better place than to keep it with a lawyer or store it in some safety deposit box.

As Lenora entered the elevator, she imagined the lawyer's instructions consisted of a key or some type of package that Charmayne had delivered in the event of her death. Charmayne was so fearful the day she came by, it didn't occur to Lenora until now that maybe Charmayne saw her death coming. As impulsive and crazy as she was, Charmayne knew the art of covering her tracks.

The elevator doors opened on the fifth floor. Lenora stepped out. There was a great view of downtown Charlotte. It eased her mind a bit to know that she was in the heart of the city. As she walked closer to the first office door, she saw a gold-plated sign with Bowman and Watson Law Firm.

Just as Lenora placed her hands on the knob to open the office door, she stopped as she heard a scream. It was a woman screaming. Lenora whirled around to where the scream had come from. Was it coming from the stairs?

A memory from long ago grabbed at Lenora's mind. Someone needed her help. She wouldn't be guilty of not doing the right thing this time. Not sure what she was going to see or even if she really heard a scream, Lenora ran over to the door leading to the stairway and opened it.

She gasped. At the bottom of the stairs was a woman. Lenora immediately recognized her as Serena Manchester. Her body lay not moving.

"Oh my dear Lord," Lenora exclaimed. She ran down the steps, but stopped as she saw a man's face looking up at her.

It was Lance Ryan. His pale eyes focused on her.

Before she could stop herself, Lenora yelled. "You did this to her! What kind of monster are you?"

Lance bounded up the stairs toward her.

Lenora took two steps at a time with her long legs. She pulled the door open, thinking how in the world was she going to get away from him.

She prayed for God's protection as she ran toward the door marked Bowman and Watson Law Firm. Lenora yanked the door open and ran inside, closing it swiftly behind her. She stood leaning against the door, pushing her weight against it. She quickly glanced around the room wondering if she had done the right thing.

There was no one at the receptionist area.

"Hello!" she called out into the office. It was well past one o'clock. Suppose this was a setup the whole time. *You fool! You walked right into it.*

Lenora didn't have long to ponder the thought as someone threw their weight at the door. She screamed, almost losing her balance, but she bore her weight against the door, digging her sneakers into the carpet. She couldn't stand here all day trying to hold back a door against a maniac.

Tears sprang to her eyes. She hoped Serena was okay. The woman had done so much to find out what happened to Charmayne. Through her tears, Lenora looked at the doors in front of her. Maybe she could make a run for it to one of the offices. They had to have locks. Speaking of locks, in her haste she should have tried to lock the door she was desperately holding closed.

Lenora noticed Lance had stopped banging on the door. Probably because he intended to knock it down. She had to move fast. Lenora scrambled across the office. The first door she tried was locked. She banged on the door in frustration.

She ran over to the next door and tried the knob. Just as Lance stormed through the main entrance, she turned the knob. The door was open. Lenora rushed in and quickly turned the knob to lock the door behind her. She backed up into a chair. Lenora grabbed the chair and hauled it toward the office door. She tilted the chair so it was propped under the doorknob. She hoped that would hold Lance off for a while.

Lenora reached in her purse and dialed the last number she had called. She moved away from the door listening to Lance pounding and yelling.

She heard Jonathan's voice on the other end, but before she could respond, Lenora screamed instead. She could hear Jonathan frantically calling her name, but she was too much in shock.

A man lay on the floor behind the desk with his tie wrapped around his neck. His brown eyes stared up at the ceiling in disbelief and his mouth was open as if still gasping for air. He wasn't a tall man. A pair of glasses lay on the floor next to him. Lenora looked at the name on the desk.

Henry Bowman.

This was the lawyer who had set the appointment. She was so confused. Did Lance do this too?

Lenora stepped away from the dead man and stared at the door as the man outside continue to bang. Her desperate phone call to Jonathan was forgotten as she tried to process the plans of the man trying to get in and the one dead on the floor.

She didn't have long to think as Lance crashed through the door. Lenora screamed and grabbed the lamp on the desk. As Lance came toward her, she held the lamp in her hands. "Don't come near me. I've called the cops."

Lenora hoped Jonathan had called the cops after she lost the connection. She was sure her husband heard her scream.

"Cops? Really?" The man stopped and laughed. "You know I see why you and Charmayne were friends. You both are a handful. Just don't stop."

Lenora stepped back. She didn't want to take her eyes off this man's face, but she knew the dead man was behind her. "You're Lance Ryan Matthews. I don't understand why you're doing all of this. Charmayne loved you."

The man laughed again, and then abruptly stopped. His face turned hard and cold. "I thought she loved me too. She couldn't stand up to that father of hers . . . the great bishop. He didn't like me from the start. You know he had the nerve to call me white trash to my face. Not very godly of him, was it?"

She'd already seen Serena out there on the stairwell and the dead lawyer behind her. *What is he going to do to me?* She needed to keep him talking. Lenora asked, "So, you're mad with Charmayne for not fighting for your relationship? I remember her being really excited and hopeful. She would fight back against her dad."

"She didn't fight for me."

"Is that why you killed her?"

The man's eyes flashed as he came closer. "I thought about it. A long time ago. I finally decided I would just show her and her father what they missed." He moved closer toward her. "I have another friend to thank for ridding the world of Charmayne. Besides, I think he hated her more than I did. Believe it or not, I found great pleasure in just seeing her miserable."

Lenora held the lamp higher. She was ready to smash it across his head, face, back—wherever she could make it land. "If you are going to try to do me in, then you can at least tell the whole truth. So, you were the one sending her threats."

"Why would I admit that to you? Is the truth supposed to set me free?" he asked with a smirk on his face.

"It might help me understand what happened to my friend. I don't know you, and I don't know why you've involved me in this sick game of yours."

"Oh, I'm sorry. It occurred to me that I needed to step up my 'game,' as you call it. I knew Charmayne was a tough cookie. I had to get her where she was weak. I needed to expose her secret."

Lenora's arm was tired of holding the lamp. "She told you?"

Lance smiled. "She was full of her favorite wine. I must say when she first told me, I was shocked. Then she told me how the bishop cleaned it all up for her as if it never happened. I never knew that little secret would come in handy later."

Oh, Charmayne! You picked out the wrong man. Her arms were really straining now. She took a second and glanced at the door.

That was her mistake.

He leaped toward her.

Lenora yelped and sent the lamp smashing into his head. The impact didn't stop him as she fell backward under his weight. The lamp tumbled out of her hands.

Without a weapon, she slammed her fists into his head with as much ferociousness as she could muster. His head was already bleeding from where she smashed the lamp.

He grabbed one of her flailing arms and punched her in the jaw.

The pain was sharp, and Lenora saw flashes of bright light. As she struggled to gain her bearings, she kicked out with her leg and dug the nails of her free hand into his face.

Then Lenora felt something strong grip her neck. Her fight soon turned to a dire need to breathe.

Chapter Forty-nine

Jonathan was in the car on his way to Parklane when he received the call from Lenora. What he didn't tell her when they got off the phone the first time was he planned on telling someone at the police station about this man, Lance Ryan Matthews.

Darnell had insisted on working on the case right up to the wedding, but Jonathan had encouraged him to concentrate on his wedding, and then honeymoon. Darnell placed Jonathan in touch with his partner, Steven Brunson. Brunson would keep him abreast on any developments in Charmayne's case.

Jonathan called Detective Brunson and told him where his wife was heading.

Brunson answered back gruffly, "You need to get in touch with your wife as soon as possible. We need to be on the lookout for this Matthews fellow."

"That's what I thought, but Lenora tends to be a bit stubborn, especially when she is trying to get to the bottom of something."

"Well, I'll head over there now. I don't know if we have any just cause to try to get a judge to get us a search warrant. The best thing now is to make sure Lenora is safe."

After getting off the phone with Detective Brunson, Jonathan wasted no time continuing over to Parklane Road. As he swerved into the parking lot, he didn't like the number of empty spaces at all. He spotted Lenora's car and parked beside it. The case of paranoia may have been passed on to him, but he was not going to fail at protecting his wife.

Jonathan entered the building. He walked over to the guard who seemed to be staring at some small television. Jonathan hit the desk. "Hey, have you seen a woman come in here in the last thirty minutes?"

The man looked bothered by Jonathan's presence. "Which one?"

Jonathan snapped at the man. "What do you mean which one?"

"There were two ladies that came in here. They both went to the fifth floor."

"What's on the fifth floor?"

The guard shrugged. "Some lawyer."

Before the man could turn back to the television, Jonathan banged the desk again. "Look, you have something serious going down in your building. The cops are going to be here soon. If I was you, I would be ready for what's going down. You feel me, brotha?"

The security guard jumped up from the chair, his eyes looking bewildered.

Jonathan headed to the elevator. He noticed the elevator was still on the fifth floor, so he pushed the button. Jonathan yelled at the guard as the elevator doors open, "Be sure to send the cops to the fifth floor."

The security guard wobbled from behind the desk. As the doors closed, Jonathan heard the man shout, "I'll send them up."

Jonathan had loosened the knot in his tie earlier after hearing Lenora's scream. He snatched the tie off and stuffed it in his pocket. Not sure what to expect, he didn't need any hindrances.

The elevator door opened. Jonathan stepped out. He could see an office door was open. He ran over and confirmed from the gold plaque next to the door it was the lawyer's office.

Jonathan stepped inside. He heard a scuffle in the office to his left. He tore off for the door and ran inside the office. The first thing he noticed was the white Keds that Lenora wore when she was being really casual. A man was on top of her.

"Get off of her!" He leaped over a chair that had been overturned on the floor. Jonathan grabbed the man by his shirt and plowed his fist into the man's left jaw.

As the man fell to the side, Jonathan saw Lenora start coughing. He turned to hit the man again, but received a blow from the side in his gut. Jonathan staggered back. The man came at him again, but this time Jonathan was ready.

Both men threw blows. Jonathan landed a right punch in the man's face, while the man almost got his jaw. The man was staggering. Knowing he didn't have a bit of time to waste, Jonathan came back with an upper cut, knocking the man to the floor.

By this time, Lenora had managed to stand, propped against the wall. She was crying and holding her neck. He ran over to her, and she leaned in against him. Jonathan was surprised by the body behind the desk.

Lenora pointed and yelled. The man had gotten up off the floor and started to charge toward them.

Jonathan tried pushing Lenora to the side, but she wouldn't let go of him. He grabbed her by the arm, and they both moved to the right around the desk, making their way toward the door.

The man had grabbed an object from the desk and came after them. Jonathan thought it looked like a letter opener or a knife. As they entered the outer office area, Jonathan saw figures outside the door. He yelled at Lenora, "Get down." He grabbed her by the waist, and they both hit the floor. Jonathan covered Lenora with his body as gunshots rang out above their heads.

Chapter Fifty

Lenora leaned her head against Jonathan as they sat in the lobby of Parklane Plaza. They had waited for what seemed like hours. Interesting enough, there were people who worked in this building. Many had come out of their corners to find out what was going on in their building. Lenora's first thoughts were on Serena as they were ushered downstairs by a young cop.

Detective Brunson assured her, "Serena has been taken to the hospital. She took a nasty fall down those stairs, but at least she was conscious. I hear that's a good sign."

Lenora wondered if the reporter had any family in Charlotte. She called Wes who she knew worked with Serena. Wes promised to go check on his friend.

"Are you and the pastor okay?" Wes had asked.

Lenora sighed. "Yes, other than some bruises and sore body parts, we should be fine."

Almost an hour passed since she checked with Wes about Serena. Lenora had started to doze from exhaustion. Jonathan nudged her awake. "Here comes Detective Brunson. Maybe we can finally leave now."

"Wow, you two look like you went about eight rounds up there," the older detective commented. "Why didn't you go to the hospital?"

Jonathan shook his head. "We agreed that we both looked worse than we actually felt."

"Well, that's good after the ordeal you've been through earlier. Mrs. Freeman, I have something for you." Detective Brunson handed her a package with her name on it.

Lenora knew what it was before she opened it. She ripped open the tape with her fingernails. The first thing she saw when she opened the package was the document Charmayne had brought to the salon. She pulled it out. "This is what Charmayne brought me the day before she died."

Detective Brunson peered at the package. "Looks like that might be evidence. Why don't you let me have that box so we can keep it safe from too many fingerprints?"

"Sure." Lenora gladly handed the box to the detective, almost feeling a weight lifted off of her shoulders. Charmayne would at least not be remembered in her death the way she had been painted the past few weeks.

"Do you have any idea of what exactly went on upstairs?" Jonathan asked.

Lenora smiled, and then grimaced. Her jaw hurt like crazy. "I have some ideas. The one thing I do know is that the man who was killed was Charmayne's lawyer. She said she would 'take care of it,' so I guess she gathered everything to keep it safe.

"What I haven't figured out, and I'm hoping maybe Serena can once she is alert, is why Lance decided to start threatening Charmayne now."

"So he killed her?"

Lenora shook her head. "Lance said he didn't. Someone else did who hated her more than he did."

Jonathan's eyes grew wide. "Someone else was involved?"

"Yes, but I have a feeling whoever it was, they're going down."

The crazed man wasn't killed. Detective Brunson shot Matthews in the leg to stop him. As he was being handcuffed, Lenora and Jonathan stood to the side. The whole time his eyes were locked on them.

She would've been scared, but she was too exhausted, and she knew God had been good. All the scares and close calls that came to her family in the past few weeks, most people wouldn't have experienced in a lifetime. Lenora was just grateful.

Detective Brunson walked back over to them. "You two young people can head home. If I was you, I would still get checked out at the hospital."

"Thank you, Detective." Jonathan held out his hand and shook hands with Steven Brunson. "I think Darnell will be pleased this was taken care of while he was gone. He has some partner in you."

Detective Brunson winked. "Make sure you let him know that as soon as he gets back."

Both men laughed.

Lenora stood still as they laughed. She still had questions. What did Lance have against Charmayne? They were engaged five years ago. The man had transformed himself and could get any woman he wanted. He certainly couldn't have been bent on revenge against his ex-fiancée all this time.

Now she wished she had kept that package Charmayne had left her. She wondered what evidence had been gathered.

"Are you ready?" Jonathan asked, his eyes concerned.

She smiled. "Yes, I am. I'm so tired."

Jonathan responded back, "You and me both."

As they walked out together, for once, Lenora decided not to analyze or overthink anymore. She was just thankful to be alive. God would reveal all that was needed to be known in time.

Chapter Fifty-one

Lenora sat and waited patiently for Serena to open her eyes. She'd waited a few days to come see Serena, mainly because she needed time to recoup. Lenora hadn't slept well since Jonathan's and her ordeal on Monday. There was something, or rather someone, missing. She kept mulling over what the man said.

Besides, I think he hated her more than I did.

Lenora needed to know who else was involved or if Lance Ryan hadn't told the truth.

She was thankful to Detective Brunson for graciously answering her questions. Lenora had stopped by his office yesterday afternoon.

Detective Brunson explained, "Before Darnell left, he passed Ms. Hudson's phone records to me to tackle. It took me some time, but I did trace some serial numbers back to stores where the phones were purchased."

Lenora asked, "Can you tell who purchased the phones?"

"No, that's not quite possible, but we can see if our perp was in the vicinity of the store around the time a phone was purchased. We lucked up, not on a number on Charmayne's phone records, but on your phone."

Lenora sat stunned. "I don't understand. What are you saying?"

Detective Brunson explained, "We traced the serial number from the first text message you received back to a phone purchased at Walmart. You know these shopping centers have security cameras in the parking lot, right?"

She nodded. "Yes."

"Well, our guy in the cell, Lance Ryan, showed up on the camera." Brunson shrugged. "Could be coincidence and definitely circumstantial evidence, but I would say our guy purchased a phone and used it to send threatening messages."

"But what about Charmayne? Can you prove he was doing the same to her?"

Detective Brunson answered, "I believe we're close, but something interesting came up with her phone records that we are looking into now." The detective averted his eyes from Lenora.

She turned her head to see what had the detective's attention. Lenora frowned as she saw a man being guided in to one of the interrogation rooms. She whirled her head back around to Detective Brunson. "Why is Mayor Carrington here?"

"Well, all I can tell you is the mayor has some questions that need to be answered. We're really interested in his last conversation with Ms. Hudson."

Lenora inquired, "When was the last time he'd spoken to her?"

Brunson stood from his chair and buttoned his coat jacket. "He called Ms. Hudson on the morning of her death. When Darnell asked him about it earlier, the mayor claims it was council business. There were some papers in the package that Ms. Hudson left. Some of those papers indicated improper use of some funds."

Lenora left the police station after the detective went into the interrogation room. The police were trying to put the pieces together, but Lenora had a feeling that someone already knew the answers.

Serena stirred on the bed. From what Lenora had learned, the reporter suffered a moderate case of traumatic head injury. She didn't stay unconscious for long after she fell, but the doctors kept her in the hospital to make sure there was no swelling or bleeding on the brain.

Serena had also suffered a broken ankle. The bottom of her left foot was in a cast.

The reporter opened her eyes. She stared around the room, her eyes unfocused for a few minutes.

Lenora leaned in and grabbed the woman's hand. "How are you?"

Serena turned her head slightly toward her.

The doctor mentioned Serena could have repercussions from the head injury, like memory loss. Lenora hoped Serena would remember her and be able to recall what happened.

A slow, wry smile stretched across Serena's face. "I feel like I could sleep for days." She lifted her head. "What are you doing here? Did they get him?"

Lenora frowned, not sure how much Serena had experienced before her fall. "Lance is in jail."

"Good! That was one crazy man." Serena narrowed her eyes as if she was unsure of her next question. "What about the mayor?"

Lenora looked at her. "The mayor was being questioned yesterday by Detective Brunson. Why do you ask? What did you find out, Serena?"

The woman stared back at Lenora, her eyes were wide. "So, no one has gotten him to admit it yet?"

"Admit what, Serena?"

Her voice had dropped so low, Lenora had to lean in closer. "The mayor did something to Charmayne. I guess they fought, and he killed her. I overheard Lance talking to him on the phone. Lance basically came in and covered it up, making her death look like a suicide."

Lenora was stunned. "Why? I don't understand why Mayor Carrington would harm Charmayne. Was this about the Hudson Development?"

Serena nodded. "I bet you it had everything to do with it. From what I gathered before he became mayor, Carrington made his money swiping money that didn't belong to him. Like federal money meant to build low-income housing. Sounds like Lance was in on it too. They might have thought they could get away with something similar on the Hudson Development Project."

Lenora sat back in the chair. "You think Bishop Hudson got a whiff of their schemes. Maybe he pushed Charmayne to break it off with Lance because of his possible illegal activities."

"He had good reason. I'm thinking that Carrington was a little more complicated. If I can recall from the election a few years back, Bishop Hudson was really behind getting Carrington elected."

Lenora agreed. "It wouldn't have looked good for the bishop to out the man he helped put in the mayor's office. So, the mayor was trying to cover his activities after Bishop Hudson died?"

Serena said, "That's my theory. I think the bishop had something on Carrington. It also explains why Mayor Carrington wanted to back away from the Hudson Development Project. Martha German, one of the committee members, was telling me they were ready to move forward and work out the zoning. So the entire project was under more eyes, especially federal funders."

It suddenly dawned on Lenora. "I believe Charmayne left something for the police. I was supposed to pick up a package from her lawyer. I gave it to Detective Brunson. I believe there is probably a case being built against the mayor right now."

"The kind of stuff Mayor Carrington was into, he could have the FBI and IRS on his case." Serena grinned. "Good for her. I could tell she was a really smart lady. Just a couple of bad breaks."

Lenora smiled. Tears sprang to her eyes. "Charmayne Hudson was a good soul. Just like her dad. I'm very proud of her."

Chapter Fifty-two

Eight months later. New Year's Eve . . .
They had about thirty minutes before the clock counted down to the New Year. Lenora was exhausted but excited about the wedding ceremony earlier at eight o'clock. The reception in Victory Gospel Center seemed to almost whirl to life again as people crowded together buzzing about the upcoming countdown.

Lenora walked over to hug Angel, and then Wes. "I thought I would get my hug in now before the countdown began."

Wes grinned. "We really want to thank you for planning this for us."

"Yes, everything was so wonderful." Angel had her arm hooked in Wes's arm, looking radiant as Mrs. Wesley Cade.

"It was my pleasure."

"Oh, there's Candace, I need to talk to her. I'll be right back." Angel kissed Wes and took off toward the direction where Candace sat with Darnell.

Lenora turned to Wes. "Have you heard from Serena? I was expecting her to be here tonight."

Wes shook his head. "Angel and I had invited her. I think she's trying to hang low for a while. She's used to being on the other side of the media, not people questioning her."

Lenora nodded. "I don't blame her. I'm just really grateful to her. I know she was after a story, and it turned out bigger than she could imagine."

"Yeah, it looks like Mayor Carrington is going to do some real jail time. Apparently, he managed to swipe a good bit of money out of various projects over the years. He might have gotten away with it if Charmayne wasn't so determined to keep up her father's work."

"Charmayne had a complex relationship with her dad, but she respected him and his work. People misjudged the good heart that she had toward the community too." Lenora's eyes watered a bit. It still was hard to get over not being able to talk to Charmayne by phone or in person.

"How's everyone doing?" Jonathan had made his way in the crowd to stand next to her.

Wes answered, "Good. I will be even better as soon as I get to my bride. Don't want to miss our first countdown together."

Lenora and Jonathan laughed as they watched Wes sprint over to where Angel sat.

Jonathan placed his arm around Lenora's waist. They smiled at each other, probably looking like they were the couple married a few hours before.

They'd been doing a whole lot of laughing in the past few months, mainly to ease the tensions that had been built in their house for so long. Who knew they would physically be fighting an enemy together and have battle scars?

Mother Eliza moved back to her home after she started the soup kitchen at Victory Gospel. She seemed to be happy doing ministry work she enjoyed. Lenora decided to use her Mondays to come in and help Eliza and her staff.

Sometimes Jonathan joined them, helping with the servings. She was really proud of her husband. He took great care in being Victory Gospel's shepherd, as well as being a vital part of his community as the newly elected District Two City Council member.

If there was one thing Lenora took away from Charmayne's ambitions, her friend really did love her community. She could be overbearing like Bishop Hudson, but like father, like daughter, they both were dedicated to the people they served.

Both she and Jonathan promised to continue that legacy.

In the background, people were starting to count. "10, 9, 8 . . ."

Lenora turned to Jonathan. "Almost time for a new beginning. Are you ready?"

"Always. As long as I'm with you."

As the clock struck twelve o'clock midnight, Lenora kissed her best friend.

Discussion Questions

1. Lenora is a wife, a mother, first lady of a megachurch, and successful businesswoman. She seems to be handling all her many hats with perfection. When trouble comes, she begins to unravel as she loses control. Have you found yourself or do you know someone who is a "superwoman" like Lenora? What event(s) sent you (or them) over the edge?

2. Jonathan feels torn between his wife and mother. Lenora has a grudging respect for her mother-in-law. Have you had to deal with an unpleasant in-law? Have you had a parent or sibling who didn't get along with your spouse? How do you handle the conflicts?

3. Serena Manchester is twice-divorced and now single. She is bitter about love and religion. It's hard not to let your past experiences influence your future relationships. What advice can you give the "Serena" in your life who desires happiness, but hangs onto negative experiences?

4. Charmayne was a PK (Preacher's Kid). She not only grew up under a man who was the bishop of a megachurch, but her father was a civil rights and community activist. Charmayne had a rebellious spirit that started in her teens and seemed to continue into adulthood. Is there an intimidating figure in your life

(maybe a parent) who you still struggle to separate from your identity?

5. Lenora and Charmayne had been friends since they were young girls. The friendship wasn't balanced, and Lenora seemed to be the one always protecting or catching Charmayne when she fell. Do you consider this a real friendship? Are you loyal to a friend who hasn't had a habit of being there for you when you need her?

6. Michael is the sensitive younger son of Lenora and Jonathan. He sensed that something had drastically changed in his parents' relationship. In fact, it's his observations that alert both Lenora and Jonathan that they need to do something. Are you married? Are you aware of how your lack of communication or distance affects you, your spouse, and children?

7. What were your initial thoughts when you read the suicide scene? Do you know someone who has considered or succeeded at suicide? Not everyone can pick themselves up from despair. Are you aware of the signs and when to seek help for an individual?

8. This novel started off with a secret between two friends. Lenora and Jonathan had moments when they were secretive with information in their marriage. What have been the consequences to people keeping secrets in your life?

About The Author

Tyora Moody is an author and entrepreneur. Her debut novel, *When Rain Falls*, was released March 2012 (Urban Christian). This was the first book in the Victory Gospel series. The second book in the Victory Gospel Series, *When Memories Fade*, was released in April 2013 (Urban Christian).

Tyora has coined her books as Soul-Searching Suspense. She is the 2013 Urban Literary Awards Debut Author Winner and 2013 Urban Literary Awards Mystery/ Thriller/ Suspense Winner. Tyora is a member of Sisters in Crime and American Christian Fiction Writers.

As a literary-focused entrepreneur, she has assisted countless authors with developing an online presence via her company, TywebbinCreations.com. Popular services include virtual book tours, book trailers, and book covers.

When Tyora isn't working for a client or doing something literary, she enjoys spending time with family, catching a movie on the big screen, traveling, and when the mood hits her, baking cookies. Visit her online at TyoraMoody.com.

Are you a female entrepreneur? Visit VictoryGospel-Series.com. We would love to feature you.

UC HIS GLORY BOOK CLUB!

www.uchisglorybookclub.net

UC His Glory Book Club is the spirit-inspired brain-child of Joylynn Ross, Author and Acquisitions Editor of Urban Christian, and Kendra Norman-Bellamy, Author for Urban Christian. This is an online book club that hosts authors of Urban Christian. We welcome as members all men and women who have a passion for reading Christian-based fiction.

UC HIS GLORY BOOK CLUB pledges our commitment to provide support, positive feedback, encouragement, and a forum whereby members can openly discuss and review the literary works of Urban Christian authors.

There is no membership fee associated with UC His Glory Book Club; however, we do ask that you support the authors through purchasing, encouraging, providing book reviews, and of course, your prayers. We also ask that you respect our beliefs and follow the guidelines of the book club. We hope to receive your valuable input, opinions, and reviews that build up, rather than tear down our authors.

What We Believe:

—We believe that Jesus is the Christ, Son of the Living God.

—We believe the Bible is the true, living Word of God.

—We believe all Urban Christian authors should use their God-given writing abilities to honor God and share the message of the written word God has given to each of them uniquely.

—We believe in supporting Urban Christian authors in their literary endeavors by reading, purchasing and sharing their titles with our online community.

—We believe that in everything we do in our literary arena should be done in a manner that will lead to God being glorified and honored.

We look forward to the online fellowship with you. Please visit us often at *www.uchisglorybookclub.net*.

Many Blessing to You!

Shelia E. Lipsey,
President, UC His Glory Book Club